Second Chance Romance

HEARTS OF LOUISIANA, BOOK TWO

MAGGIE PRESTON

CYPRESS PRESS, LLC

About the Purchase of This Book

Contents

To Mindy, for too many reasons to put into words.

Chapter One

R iley Kenner pushed through the glass doors and into the crowded lobby of the bank, stumbling back as she was shoulder-checked by a harried Santa trying to escape a flash mob of kids with wish-list fever. The bearded fat man's eyes widened as they met with Riley's, but they clouded with fear and darted away as the kids zeroed in on their target. He gasped, a *huh-huh-huh* sound, and careened down Main Street's boardwalk.

She could relate.

She'd split from her construction crew, leaving them to find lunch with the rest of the after-holiday shoppers. Maybe she'd celebrate with a stop at the bookstore before grabbing a slice of pie from that little diner a few doors down. Her mouth watered at the prospect, both from the thought of the pie and from picking up the new Angelina Williams book she'd seen in The Book Nook's storefront window. She'd rejoin the crew as soon as she got the cashier's check. If she could remember how to sign her name.

It was finally happening. The not-very-jolly old Santa had nothing on her when it came to fear and uncertainty.

Reaching the bank counter, Riley scribbled the information on the withdrawal slip, pulling in big gulps of air, releasing slowly, then repeating. She walked toward the bank teller with to-the-gallows slowness, preparing herself to withdraw the money earned with her blood, sweat, and hard-earned calluses.

But it would buy her a house.

A home.

A place for her to find and to bring home the rest of the brothers whom she hadn't seen since she was ten. She'd found her oldest brother just last year. He'd helped her put the plan into action, and now it was all about to work out.

"Welcome to Bayou Savings and Loan." The teller's robotic greeting matched her plastic smile. "How can I help you?"

"I had some money transferred here on Wednesday from an investment account. I'd like to make a withdrawal." With shaky fingers, Riley slid the withdrawal slip across the counter before pulling out her driver's license from the pouch on her tool belt. "Cashier's check please, made out to Bergeron Estate and Auction."

Riley's nerves jangled like high-powered electrical wires. She fiddled with the tools hanging from the tool belt at her waist, wishing she'd left it in the truck, but its weight reminded her of what it had taken to put this money together.

Sixteen years.

She'd pulled out a hefty chunk of her life savings before Thanksgiving for the auction this past Saturday, knowing with the long holiday weekend the bank would be closed. The auction house had required ten percent earnest money to even bid on the property and that was a lot of zeroes. The unfinished house with thirty acres was appraised at almost a million dollars, but she'd gotten it for less. More people were interested in Black Friday deals than the property auction in Baton Rouge, so she'd been the only bidder.

And now the house was hers.

She'd sent her brother a message after the auction to transfer the rest of the money, so she could finalize the sale as soon as possible. She had until New Year's Eve but didn't want to wait that long. Her search for her missing brothers had been slow, but things were starting to fall into place thanks to those DNA testing and ancestor websites.

"Ummm, Mrs. Kenner?" The clerk worried her bottom lip between her capped teeth.

"*Ms*. Kenner." The correction automatic to Riley, like breathing. She really needed to go back to her maiden name, especially now that her ex was with someone new here in Belle Terre. But the memory of childhood taunts over the name's pronunciation, Fontenot, pricked her pride still.

Riley Fun-to-know...not!

"*Ms*. Kenner," the teller dutifully repeated. "That investment account was closed."

Riley's brain stumbled over the words. "Say that again."

The teller slid the withdrawal slip back toward Riley. "The investment account? It's empty. There was no transfer. You emptied out the account on Wednesday with your withdrawal, and the account closes automatically after seventy-two hours with a zero balance."

She'd tracked the withdrawal slip with the intensity of an eagle who'd spotted its dinner, but she didn't swoop in and snatch it. Riley's throat constricted, allowing only the tiniest slice of air to wend its way through. This was a simple misunderstanding. "The transfer was initiated *from* my investment firm on Friday. The money should be *here* today."

"It's not." The teller's expression tightened; the fine lines not quite hidden beneath too much make-up as her nails clicked against the keys. "The originating account was closed. The transfer never completed."

Riley's mouth went full-of-sawdust dry. Her chest tingled beneath the constricting of her ribs.

"That can't be right." Riley pulled out her phone, quickly logging into the mobile app for her investment account. Zero balance. That meant the money should be in her savings account.

Sixteen years of saving.

Sixteen years of waiting.

This could be easily fixed. Like a flat tire or a marriage where he still loved his high school sweetheart. "Can you look again? Maybe the transfer is still in process."

"I don't need to look again, *Ms.* Kenner." Ice crusted the words. "I can see it right here. The system would show a pending deposit if one existed. It shows the transfer cancelled due to insufficient funds."

Insufficient funds?

"No, no, no." The heartbeat in her chest hardened like quick set cement. "But—" Her hand landed on her waist to steady her. "I have a receipt from the ATM. I checked the balance on Friday." She blurted the words, and the teller took a step back.

Riley fumbled with the bag resting on her hip. She'd stuffed the receipt in her tool belt. "The receipt shows the investment account balance." She slapped a tape measure on the counter and reached in again. Panic nipped at Riley's nerves, her normal self-control tipping over the precipice. "It's here somewhere." *Breathe. Breathe.* "Just wait."

"Ms. Kenner..." The teller backed up again, and a slender man in a suit looked down his nose in her direction.

"There's some mistake." Her hammer came next, filling her palm with a comfortable familiarity that grounded her in the uncertain quicksand of the moment. Gasps ping-ponged behind her. Bodies shifted, shuffled, shushed.

"There was almost a million dollars in that account and that kind of money just does not disappear!" Riley leaned forward, reaching with her other hand for the withdrawal slip she'd written just seconds before her life fell apart.

That was when the teller's eyes saucered, her mouth opening in cartoonish-slow motion. Her scream, however, echoed in high definition.

The bank's alarm sounded a split second later.

Chapter Two

Technically, Riley comforted herself, she wasn't under arrest. The handcuffs were for her protection. At least, that's what the sheriff said.

"Are these the latest fashion trend in Belle Terre?" She clanked the handcuffs currently biting into her wrists against the chair where she'd been unceremoniously plopped. "What every innocent person under arrest is wearing for the holiday season."

Two dozen sets of eyes studied her in the bank's lobby—from a safe distance —their judgment washing over her like a bucket of nails dropped from the roof of a skyscraper.

"You're not under arrest." The sheriff's tone was clipped, but his ocean-blue eyes read like calm waters. His eyes dropped to the cuffs, while his body remained unmoving. "Those are for your protection." He paused. The crinkle of a smile he failed to hide lifted one corner of his mouth, and he added. "And ours."

"I didn't see anyone else getting tackled to the ground by a wannabe Saints defensive lineman." Frustration hissed from between her lips like steam from an overheated pressure cooker as she eyed the security guard standing over her shoulder. "I did *not* threaten that woman. You didn't have to handcuff me." Riley focused on the twinkling lights of the massive Christmas tree in the lobby, thinking calm thoughts. Very calm thoughts.

It didn't work.

She'd been in handcuffs before, deservedly so at the time, and swore it would never happen again. She'd kept that promise since her eighteenth birthday.

"And no one had to pull the alarm. There's a perfectly reasonable explanation for all of this."

But no one was listening, especially not Sheriff Sexy McDimple a.k.a. Jackson Guidry. They'd crossed paths before Thanksgiving, when her ex's girlfriend took over the construction site and chained herself to Riley's bulldozer. Thanks to a little *mishap*, it had gone up in flames. The bulldozer; not the girlfriend.

The sheriff leaned his impossibly long body against one of the lobby's columns, and Riley looked up to see if it would crumble under his weight. Not that the man was fat. Not a single ounce of fat would dare take up residence on that body. Though she wouldn't blame anything that wanted to stick close.

Based on the hungry looks of several women in the bank's lobby, she was sure he had more than ample opportunity to work off any extra calories.

He tipped his chin in her direction, fortunately oblivious to the wandering of her mind on his fat content. "I'm sure there *is* a reasonable explanation, Ms. Kenner. That's why I'm here."

Riley took a moment to watch the tall leanness of Jackson stand there and breathe; she could no more pull her eyes from him than she could fail to admire a Picasso or the perfect alignment of a platform frame when it came together on a building project.

"I thought maybe the bank needed an extra support column."

Another irritating twitch tugged at the corner of Jackson's mouth and broke the spell.

"Have you always been this annoying?" She didn't remember the smirk being so irritating, or so damned intriguing, when she'd first met the badge-wearing behemoth before Thanksgiving. And how had she missed that dimple in his left cheek?

"According to my sister, yes."

The drawl coated her like warm chocolate over toasted marshmallow.

His gaze slid to the bank doors, then to the star pinned to his chest, before finding Riley again. "But things were pretty hectic the last time we came face to face. Protesters, national TV coverage, and burning bulldozers tend to distract people from noticing the little things."

Judging by the myriad of faces staring at her from the bank lobby, so did bank alarms at the savings and loan.

Riley sighed, her eyes locking with JJ, her second in command on the construction site. He and another member of the crew, Noé Tam, had come running when the alarm sounded, pushing into the bank when others were rushing to escape. Noé stared daggers at the sheriff and Riley inclined her head toward JJ, who pulled Noé from the bank and back outside.

At least they wouldn't be witness to any more of her humiliation. This was not her life. She was used to being in charge. She was used to being the voice of calm. She was used to being able to ignore hunky men other women found irresistible. On a construction site, testosterone was as prevalent as two by fours.

"Sheriff Guidry." The bank manager's voice dragged Riley's attention back to her own unfolding drama as he joined them in the center ring of her life-circus. The fastidious man adjusted his tie with a little more care than it needed as his posture relaxed a notch below DEFCON 1. "I didn't think you'd need to save us a second time this year."

The good sheriff winced, an almost imperceptible tightening around the eyes. The comment confused Riley while the sheriff seemed content to ignore it. "I'm still just Officer Guidry, Mr. Michel. Now, about the alarm?" Jackson turned his attention to the teller.

"She had crazy eyes, sheriff," the woman cowering behind the bank manager offered, peering out as if Riley were taking aim with a sniper's rifle. "And she pulled that hammer like she wanted to *bash* something."

"I was just taking my hammer out of my tool belt to get to my receipt." Riley dropped her chin to her chest, the hopelessness of the situation a weighty thing. "It's all a misunderstanding."

"She withdrew all her money on Wednesday but doesn't remember doing it."

"I remember the withdrawal!" Riley jerked up her head and yanked against the restraints, grimacing as the steel scraped against her wrists.

The gawking crowd took a collective step back from their vantage point just ten feet away from her spot at center stage of the action. A small step, she noted, so they wouldn't miss anything. Entertainment must be scarce in the sleepy little town of Belle Terre, Louisiana. She'd liked that about the town when she first visited just six months ago on a survey trip for her employer, LCB Construction. It was part of the reason she decided to stay in the area.

Only she didn't want to be the entertainment.

She continued, trying for calm. "There was just supposed to be more money in there today. Another transfer."

The good sheriff just stared at her; his arms crossed as he stood guard over her chair in the middle of the lobby.

"And after March—" the twitchy-fingered teller continued, narrowing her gaze suspiciously on Riley.

"I wasn't even here in March." Riley hated that she needed to defend herself. Hated even more that no one seemed to be paying attention to her defense.

"We get it, Tabitha." Mr. Michel consoled the woman, patting her shoulder like one would a poodle that had done an old trick. "You were just being cautious."

Sheriff Guidry stepped toward the bank manager, his arms falling loosely to his sides. "I took a look at the closed circuit video you provided, and she didn't actually threaten anyone with the hammer. Just pulled it from her belt." He pulled a set of keys from a pocket on his utility belt. "Did she do anything else that could have been perceived as threatening? Verbal threats? Physical threats? Even a scowl like the one's she's wearing now?"

"Hey!" Riley chimed in, tired of being talked about like she wasn't sitting there handcuffed to the chair. "I don't scowl." She purposefully softened the scowl tightening her face when a nearby toddler cowered behind his mother's legs.

Guidry scrubbed a hand across his jaw, back over his ear, keeping his head down.

But she saw it. There was the damn smirk again. How could he find anything remotely smirkable in this situation?

It was disastrous to say the least. Her money was missing. Her life's savings. Was anyone interested in that?

The teller shrugged. "I guess not."

Her words answered Riley's silent question as well. Riley sighed, dropping chin to chest.

Sheriff Guidry bent to remove the handcuffs, a not unpleasing waft of musky cologne surrounding him if Riley wanted to notice that sort of thing.

Which she didn't.

She jumped to her feet the instant the cuffs were off, rubbing her wrists and her wounded pride.

The bank manager stiffened his spine and squared his shoulders. "Nonetheless, the account appears closed."

"A million dollars doesn't just disappear." The big fat zeroes on the new balance receipt they'd shown her shot bullet holes in her soul. "There's just no way both accounts can be empty." Maybe if she kept saying it, it would become true.

She'd set it all up with her brother before the holiday, knowing he'd be busy with family. A wife, house in the suburbs, two point two kids. They probably even had a dog. A family she'd not been ready to meet. She blamed it on her travel schedule with the construction crew, but in truth, Riley had trouble being a part of groups, always feeling the outsider.

The bank had been closed, but Ricky had assured her the transfer could be initiated over the holiday—it was all just an electronic movement of numbers the way Riley understood it. The balance was due to the auction house at closing on New Year's Eve or she forfeited her down payment. Not to mention losing her dream house.

And her dreams.

"I assure you, Ms. Kenner," Mr. Michel sing-songed the

words with the calming tone of a hostage negotiator. "The account is empty. Zero balance. Closed. As of Sunday at…" He consulted a piece of paper in his hand. "Four-fifty-eight p.m. when the wire transfer was cancelled. Your savings account was closed at start of business today."

She propped her hip against the bank kiosk, her knuckles a shade paler than the crinkled receipt laying at her fingertips. Panic swelled in her chest, lodged at the base of her throat like a sticky lump of quick set cement.

"There has to be an error with the transfer then. The money was all there last week. I made a successful transfer before Thanksgiving. The rest was due to show up today. I need that money." Her voice pitched high on the last few words. From the corner of her eye, she watched the bank patrons start to edge toward the door.

"You need to remain calm, Mrs. Kenner." The gravelly voice of the sheriff with its deep bass interrupted her meltdown.

"*Ms.* Kenner." Riley pivoted sharply in her steel-toed boots, raising one finger to jab in the direction of the sheriff's nose. Only she hit him mid-chest level. A very broad chest only a hairbreadth away as it turned out. "And no woman in the history of the world has ever calmed down when being told to calm down."

"I wasn't asking you to calm down," he said, calmly. Dammit. "Just reminding you to be calm."

She tilted her head back to meet his cool scrutinizing gaze. *Damn, he's hot*, her libido kicked in. Her frazzled nerves squashed the temporary insanity of attraction. She punched her fists into the curve of her waist. "I am calm! Do you think I yell like this all the time?"

"My gut tells me yes."

The barely contained smirk—that was the only word for

it, she concluded, and it warmed things inside of her she didn't want warmed right now—brought out the dimple in his left cheek again. Didn't he get what was going on? Maybe the air really was too thin when you topped out over six-and-a-half feet.

Plus, she didn't like being one-upped in the sarcasm department. She took a step back to reclaim some of her personal space. "What does your gut tell you about what I'm gonna do next?"

He smiled, but it wasn't for her. "Keep making a scene until you get the answers you want."

Riley followed the direction of his gaze to a woman off to the side helping the baby on her hip wave at Sheriff Guidry. He waved back, tugging at the knot of his tie. A jab of curiosity—nothing more than that, Riley assured herself—hit her center mass.

"Perhaps this instance is nothing more than a...misunderstanding," Mr. Michel conceded, and reluctantly at that if the tight moue of his mouth was any indication.

Riley's hands launched from the perch on her hips, palms up. "A mis—"

Officer Guidry held up his hand, and Riley, to her own surprise, stopped mid-sentence, letting his Yoda-like powers silence her protest.

"You disagree with that, we know." The officer turned his attention to the bank manager. "Ms. Kenner needs some help, however, resolving the issue with her account and the transfer."

"Certainly, *Officer* Guidry." Mr. Michel stiffened his spine yet again and swept a hand toward a high-walled cubicle in the right corner of the bank. As he passed Riley, he nodded his head toward the officer and shot her a look that said, *He's watching you.*

Pissed, Riley turned to follow Mr. Michel and felt the officer's hand fall casually to the center of her shoulders. The jolt of heat surprised her. She leaned back instinctually, letting the weight of his hand guide her when she didn't need it, which surprised her even more. Apparently, she'd lost all her money along with her ability to walk unaided.

"You two look like you expect me to blow up a bulldozer or something."

Mr. Michel paled, and Riley wondered if he was going to pass out. The officer's smirk deepened.

She groaned inwardly at the stupidity of the remark. Her brain could only handle one surprise at a time. Possibly losing her life's savings—her future, her security, her ability to protect her family when she got them back, everything she'd worked damn hard to build the past sixteen years—definitely counted as a surprise. Some would even call it a shock. That was it. She was in shock. She needed fluids. A warm blanket. Maybe a warm body would do. The officer could definitely fill that last role, her libido suggested, and her frazzled brain thought of telling it to shut up, but she didn't mind so much this time around.

Damn, she was screwed.

Chapter Three

Jackson Guidry recognized the desperate edge of panic when he saw it. He'd been up close to people with similar looks on their faces when they made really bad decisions, flashing back to the bank lobby only eight months ago. It was a day that had changed his life. He'd avoided responsibility for the past ten years. He still wasn't sure if taking the job as deputy had been the right thing to do.

However, when Riley had rolled into town right before Thanksgiving with her brash attitude and big bulldozer, Jackson was more than a little glad to be in Belle Terre. Not even the pre-Thanksgiving excitement at the construction site, all thanks to a group of protesters that resulted in the torching of Riley's favorite bulldozer, had changed his mind.

His attention drifted momentarily as he noticed the face of a young boy peeking around the corner of the cubicle wall. He recognized the kid as the newest addition to a local family who fostered kids in transition.

"Hey, Donavan." He nodded to the kid, keeping his voice relaxed and low key.

Donavan disappeared back around the corner, but Jackson could see the tips of his sneakers at the edge of the wall. He didn't take the kid's distrust personally. Cops were the enemy to kids like Donavan. Most of the bad stuff that put them in foster care came accompanied by men and women in uniforms like his.

A huff brought his gaze back to Riley. He watched her impossibly long legs bounce like they were on springs, unable to stop his gaze from traveling up her calf to a shapely thigh. It's not like she would notice his attention. They'd come in contact only a few times since her arrival in town. Her eyes— eyes like a bottomless tropical pool he recalled from when they'd stood nose-to-forehead back at the teller's station—barely left Mr. Michel as he pecked away on his computer.

They did wander occasionally to the generous piece of pecan pie stashed near the keyboard. Her stomach grumbled, but she shifted her body and coughed behind her hand.

"It seems," the bank manager started cautiously, eyes darting over the collection of poodle pictures lining his desk to Jackson and his gun. "That the transfer was initiated on Friday afternoon but was cancelled due to lack of funds from the originating account."

Lack of funds. Jackson had heard from witnesses that she'd claimed a million dollars was missing. What was a thirty-something year old construction forewoman doing with a million dollars? His mind see-sawed between the possibilities.

Mr. Michel *harrumphed* victoriously and re-arranged the perfectly straight line of mechanical pencils with the edge of the pristine blotter. "I knew this wasn't a bank error."

Riley jabbed her finger against the desk, grazing one of

the poodle pictures and knocking it from its perfect alignment with the other pictures. "But the money was in the originating account on Friday when I initiated the transfer. Weren't you listening?" More jabbing. "It showed on my receipt, and I didn't do anything with it, so it had to be transferred as planned. It has to be lost in cyberspace somewhere." *Finger jab. Finger jab.* "Find it. *Now*."

Mr. Michel readjusted the picture, squaring his already steely posture as well.

"Patience, Ms. Kenner," Jackson advised, though he didn't feel it himself. If her accounts had been accessed illegally, it would be a major investigation. Probably federal involvement. Cybercrime was the buzz in legal circles. Not that he minded. He just didn't have the experience for that kind of thing.

It wasn't what he bargained for when he came to the sleepy town at the start of the year. And he certainly didn't expect to end up as acting sheriff before Christmas.

"I suspect Mr. Michel has more to tell you." On instinct he reached out and brushed aside the dark rope of hair from her shoulder, laying his hand on her arm. She had all that blue-black hair stuffed into a ponytail, contained but just barely. Riley Kenner wasn't a woman to be contained. At least not for long. "Give him a chance."

The grim set of her mouth tightened even further, not that it lessened the appeal of those kissable lips. She didn't pull away from his touch either so he let his fingers linger.

"Then would you please ask him to *move it along*?" She grinded out the last three words, keeping her voice low.

Riley huffed and sat back against her chair, crossing her arms. He withdrew his hand, his fingers buzzing like a hive of excited bees where they'd touched her skin. Not that much of it showed. She'd pushed the long sleeves on her t-shirt above the elbow, but they fell back down anytime she moved her arms.

The t-shirt didn't even have a daring vee neck to show the cleavage he suspected lay hidden beneath the *My eyes are higher up* logo. Well-worn jeans hugged long legs he'd noticed earlier without being painted onto her athletic frame. Each pant leg was tucked snugly into the ankle of thick-soled worker's boots.

How could so little skin turn him on this much? But it did.

Without prompting, Mr. Michel continued. "As I was saying, the transfer failed on the *other* end. The bank is not at fault here, Mrs. Kenner."

"Ms." She corrected absently before closing her eyes. Jackson could swear he heard her counting to ten under her breath. When she finally refocused her attention on the banker, a level of false calm tinged her words. "And as I said, the money showed as available on Friday. The transfer was pending on Friday. Doesn't that mean the money was there when the transfer was initiated?"

"No." Mr. Michel said, his tone edged like a cliff diver milliseconds before the fall. "It just means the transfer was initiated while the banks 'talked'." He air-quoted the word. "But the transfer didn't clear. I even show the software reinitiated the transfer in case of error, as is protocol, but again, the transfer failed because the funds were not available in the originating account at the investment firm. Perhaps the investment firm transferred the money to another one of your accounts in error."

She scrubbed a shaking hand across her face, tucking a loose strand of midnight hair behind an ear. "I don't have any other accounts."

At least she was trying to maintain a sense of calm.

Jackson could admire the attempt. "Are you the only authorized user on the account?"

He watched the edge of desperation do a nose-dive into full-fledged panic, tracking the emotions flutter through her body. A hard swallow. The rapid blinking of her eyes. Then, finally, her body fell against the arm of the chair, away from him and Mr. Michel.

"He wouldn't do that," she said to herself, rubbing her arms unconsciously.

Curiosity pulled Jackson forward, trying to make eye contact. But her unfocused gaze didn't meet his. "Who, Riley?"

"My brother."

Damn, *she* was screwed.

Chapter Four

Riley paced the limited length of the bank manager's cubicle, her phone pressed hard to her ear. The cell reception sucked. Her brother's secretary's reluctance to answer questions sucked even more.

"When did you see him last, Marilee?" Her words rushed out, and she reined in the frustration.

Marilee sighed dramatically into Riley's ear. "Well, that's just it. I haven't *seen* him for weeks. He's been working from home. But he calls me every day." Tense pause. "Until Friday."

Friday. The day her money went missing.

The secretary continued on a huff of breath. "Your account was transferred, but I don't know to where. There are no new accounts in your name." A dramatic pause this time. "Which is unusual. Mr. Fontenot is very fastidious with his paperwork."

Riley hadn't seen her oldest brother, Ricky, since they were kids and being shuffled to different foster homes. She'd found him thanks to a private detective she'd hired. He'd married some rich chick from New Orleans and lived in the respectable part of the city now. Not like where they grew up. Even she knew this disappearing act to be unusual for the normally conservative, stable, ever-so-slightly boring Ricky. He wouldn't do this to her.

Would he?

"And that doesn't seem strange to you?"

"Of course." Another heavy sigh. "I can go talk to Mr. Guidry."

"Guidry?" Riley's curiosity spiked as red flags flapped in her brain. The name was pretty common in the area. It could be a coincidence.

"The firm's owner is out on a leave of absence. E.J. Guidry is our managing partner right now. I can go talk to him."

You've got believe in someone, Riley tried to convince herself. *He's your brother.*

Whom you haven't seen in twenty years, she argued back.

Trust was not something that came easily to Riley. But you were supposed to depend on family and Ricky was family. What if it were all a misunderstanding and he'd simply done what money managers do: managed her money. There could be a simple explanation for all of this.

"What do you want me to do?"

Marilee's voice broke into Riley's thoughts as the same question rattled around her head.

"Nothing just yet." Riley didn't want to cause her brother any trouble if this was nothing more than a matter of new accounts or a glitch with the transfer. She had a little over a month to figure it all out. "I need you to go to his house, Marilee. Find him. Talk to his wife." Surely the woman knew where her husband was at the moment. "Something isn't right."

"Duh," Marilee intoned under her breath.

Riley swallowed down the scathing words tickling at the tip of her tongue. She needed this woman. For now.

They disconnected. Riley wasn't worried about the immediate future. The job paid for her room and board. Her next paycheck would be direct deposited to her checking account in just a few days and would take care of anything else she needed, not that she needed much. She prided herself on being low maintenance, a skill she'd learned in juvenile detention. When you didn't need much you didn't have to bargain with what little you did have.

When she and LCB rolled into town a few weeks ago and she had seen Belle Terre, she'd decided this would be her last job. The last time she had to ramble across the country with thirty guys and her ex-husband. The town had welcomed her company and their design for the outdoor mall coming to town. Maybe in time they could welcome her as well. A place she could finally belong. Now everything she'd worked for and saved could be gone. Correction. Everything *was* gone.

Adding to the mystery of the missing money, her brother's actions counted as both weird and unexplainable.

Swiping her thumb across the phone's screen to disconnect, she pivoted sharply, once again coming up against the towering presence of Officer Guidry. Something spicy swirled around him, joining the sharp tang of the cinnamon gum he'd popped into his mouth just moments ago. She wanted to reach out and pluck the loose button from the pocket of his shirt, throw it to the ground and stomp it madly.

"Geez," she rasped, stumbling back.

His arm shot out to grasp her elbow so quickly she didn't have time to flinch or draw back. As soon as it became evident that she wasn't going to tumble into the garbage can or knock the poodle pictures askew again, the officer pulled back his hand.

"Do you have to keep doing that?"

The officer laughed, an aggravatingly pleasant sound that wrapped around her frayed nerves.

"Stand here? Yes." He shrugged casually. "I find people are less likely to do stupid stuff if the consequences are staring them in the face."

That infuriating smirk spread across his mouth and jawline like butter on hot toast. She didn't think a man with a chiseled jaw existed outside the pages of the romance novels she read whenever the guys in her crew weren't around. The women in those books always kept their cool. They didn't need to be rescued like their predecessors. They were their own knights in shining armor.

Riley was much the same. She didn't count on other people often and preferred to rescue herself.

"I haven't done anything stupid in years." She eyed the button again but didn't linger on it. No sense letting him know where her thoughts had strayed. Instead she pushed up the sleeves of her t-shirt before pulling them down again.

"That doesn't sound like any fun," he said, leaning his impossibly long frame against the wall of Mr. Michel's office. "Some of my best memories started with stupid decisions."

She waited for the wall to collapse beneath him, but it held. The bank manager had gone off to deal with another customer and Riley knew the fastidious man would be upset if they managed to demolish his office-in-a-box.

One of the officer's hands rested casually on the butt of the gun holstered at his side, but not as a threat or reminder, Riley realized. His casual manner and relaxed stance did not ooze one bit of intimidation.

How the man worked in law enforcement confounded

her. He had more of a beach boy vibe than a *you're-under-arrest* vibe. Short blonde hair, shaved close on the sides but spiky up top, helped shape the image of him strolling shirtless through the sand with a whistle between his lips.

"I'm sure your mother is proud of that fact."

The officer's eyes darkened and narrowed on her, a wave of emotions flickering behind the steely gaze in such quick flashes she would have missed most of them if she hadn't had a front row seat. Sullenness, wariness, pain, and beneath that a simmering anger which burned slow and steady in his soul. He snuffed it out in a single draw and release of his breath.

"About your money and your brother," he started. The switch in his demeanor was as sharp as the gaze he trained on her.

Now she saw it. The determined line of the mouth. The sharpened focus of his eyes. The long muscle that snaked up from beneath the collar to twitch impatiently beneath his jaw.

No one would dare mess with a man after he leveled that look on them.

"If he's authorized to move money from the account, it's not technically a crime. At least not yet. Doesn't mean we can't treat it as one."

She brushed the hair back from her face and tucked it back into her ponytail. She thought of asking Officer Guidry about the investment firm but decided against it. He'd moved here from out west according to the gossip she'd heard. No reason to think he was connected to the investment firm. "There has to be a good reason for this," she said, mostly to make herself feel better. "He'll call and explain it, and everything will be ok."

Officer Guidry didn't look convinced either. "Alright. We'll go with that for now. If you want, give me his name and basic info, and I'll make some calls. See if anything pops up."

The offer tempted her. Would it hurt to have someone make a welfare check? But if this had nothing to do with her brother, would he think she didn't trust him? She could give it some time. Her sister-in-law would have called if something were wrong. Or would she? She'd never met the woman, never even spoken to her. She wasn't even sure the wife knew Ricky had brothers and a sister, to tell the truth.

She shook her head. "Not yet. Let me get in touch with my sister-in-law and see if she knows anything. And I want to talk to his secretary again." Then, reluctantly, she added, "Thanks, though." Couldn't hurt to keep her options open.

He reached into the pocket with the loose button and pulled out a business card, leaning across Riley's personal space to swipe a pen from the desk. That spicy scent teased her nose again and beneath it, something earthy and sharp.

"This is me." He scribbled a number on the back. "Office on the front. Cell on the back. Call if you need anything."

The possibilities behind the word *anything* jumped to the front of her brain. So many possibilities. All of them quickly followed by the word *stupid*. She hadn't done anything stupid in years, she reminded herself. She wasn't about to start now.

"Thank you, Officer Guidry." She glanced at the white cardstock with block lettering. Simple. No nonsense. She tucked the card in the pocket with her ATM receipt.

"Jackson." The smirk and dimple returned in full force a moment before he added, "And I'm sorry you were put you in handcuffs."

Rather than ticking her off as they had before, the sight of that dimple and accompanying smirk sparked something to life deep inside her belly and apparently cut off the oxygen to her brain.

"It's not my first time," she answered, wanting to pull back the words as soon as she realized what she'd said. "The crew...construction crew...we've run up against the local law before. People get very passionate about endangering a spotted titmouse even if it isn't a spotted titmouse."

Even to her ears it sounded lame but he laughed at her joke, the deep rumble settling around her like a well-loved pair of jeans.

"I hear the protesters have moved on to bigger and better things." He tipped an imaginary hat to her with a slight incline of his head and turned, ambling toward the door.

She slumped against the cubicle wall he'd just vacated, watching his backside disappear out the front door. He elevated the dark brown slacks beyond their utilitarian style and filled out the shoulders of the matching brown shirt quite nicely. The color deepened the tan of his skin and brought out the chocolate undertones of the hair close to the scalp.

A quick shake of her libido brought her attention back to where it needed to be. Her brother and the missing money.

But Jackson Guidry's backside kept sneaking into her thoughts.

She pushed off the cubicle wall and stomped toward the exit, the other patrons smart enough to give her the right of way.

How could a man she'd only known for fifteen minutes

affect her like this? Hell, Riley corrected herself. She hadn't known him sixty seconds before she started wondering what those slate blue eyes would look like while she straddled his naked body.

Damn, she was *screwed*.

Chapter Five

Outside, the late autumn Louisiana air swirled around her body once she stepped out of the bank and onto the covered walkway running the length of Main Street. Christmas poinsettias filled flower boxes hanging from the hand-railing. White lights circled and draped every surface, support beam or post within sight. Posters taped haphazardly to storefront windows flapped in the breeze and announced a special election after the first of the year featuring none other than Officer Sexy McDimple.

Acting Sheriff Sexy McDimple, she amended. Whatever. He was the cop in charge at the moment.

She took a deep breath, the familiar scents of the Atchafalaya River basin, briny water, moist earth, air thick with the scent of sweet olive, comforting her. She'd grown up a few hours from here, just off the Mississippi below New Orleans. At times, she remembered that life. That was *before*. The *after* wasn't hard to remember. Forgetting was the problem there.

Her attention immediately jumped to high alert when she noticed the good sheriff surrounded by a gaggle of females a few storefronts down the walk. The women craned their necks upward like geese looking for a next meal, faces rapt with attention and longing, respective breasts jutting outward in perky invitation. One held out a pie that probably didn't come from a diner.

The sheriff, on the other hand, didn't seem all that impressed. His gaze stayed above their perfectly made up hairdos, while his hands were fisted at his sides. Even from a distance, the tight lines of tension sharpened the angles of his jaw and neck as he motioned the pie bearer down the boardwalk. Riley snapped her head to the left, not wanting to be caught staring. She barely wanted to be caught in the same town as Jackson Guidry after the last hour.

The downtown business district swirled with life this Monday after Thanksgiving, somewhat due to the pending build her company was starting at the end of the week. Her orange-vested construction crew mingled among the shoppers along the walkway, their lunch break long over. They'd stuck around for her, and the sense of belonging she felt with her crew tangled in a lumpy mess in her throat. Could she ever find that anywhere else?

The deafening roar of excited voices cut into her thoughts and she turned as a group of kids emerged from the bank, their tone no longer the inside quiet she'd observed in the lobby. The motley crew of kids – including one doing wheelies in a kid-sized wheelchair held together by duct tape – surrounded a man with a baby slung potato-sack style over his right arm while he wrestled a diaper bag and kid-sized backpack into submission.

One of the kids, a gangly collection of limbs poking out of shorts and an Iron Man t-shirt and stuffed into untied and worn sneakers, stopped dead center of the gaggle of kids on the walkway and stared at Riley. His mouth widened, making his high cheek bones almost too sharp on his boyish face.

She recognized the group dynamic: foster kids thrown together into a makeshift family. Emotion tugged at the frayed ends of memories, but they looked happy she told herself.

Riley smiled, unable to ignore the sweet face even as her life imploded on a nuclear scale, and gave him a nod and a wave. The family took off down the boardwalk and the young boy followed as soon as the dad called out for him. He side-stepped other shoppers on the walkway in rapid-fire succession and fell in line with the other kids like a row of ducklings.

A sigh escaped, and she sucked down a second one before shaking her head. Another life, she reminded herself.

She turned and spotted JJ on his perch along the Main St. seawall and waved at him. He rolled his stumpy barrel of a body off the bench and jay-walked through traffic to join her. Even in the mild temperatures, sweat glistened off his coffee-no-cream skin.

"I sent Noé to tell Will we'd be late and why. Noé says," JJ dropped his voice into a conspiratorial whisper, "the city jail is an easy camp full of ducks but that spring break was just around the corner because orange is definitely not the new black."

Riley rolled her eyes at the string of prison slang. LCB Construction hired people who'd had brushes with the law, many like Noé having served time for non-violent offenses. Her business partner, who also happened to be her ex-husband, believed in second chances. He'd found his second chance when they'd returned to Belle Terre and was now living the happily-ever-after ending favored in the romance novels she kept stashed in her motel room and office desk.

"He's not bribing anyone to get me out of jail because I'm not going to jail."

"Been there, done that, haven't you?" He swiped away a line of sweat trailing down his forehead as Riley shot him a withering glare. "Did your brother steal all your money?" JJ wasn't one to waste words. His keen eyes could spot insta-bility a mile away, whether on a build or with a crewman. Plus, he'd warned her.

She hated hearing the words she'd barely wanted to consider during the last hour. "I don't know, but my money's gone."

The single eyebrow connecting his temples shot up on one side. "Gone? As in 'there's been a negative turn in the stock market and the funds are temporarily unavailable while we reshuffle your portfolio?' Or 'gone' as in you're dead broke?"

Hearing it out loud twisted the knife in her gut. Stars danced behind her eyes, and she bent at the waist, propping her hands on her knees for stability.

JJ put a hand on her back, *whomping* her between the shoulder blades as she forgot how to breathe. "Definitely the second one." He took her arm and led her to the crew vehicle parked just a few feet away. Opening the door, he prompted her with a curt, "Sit. Talk."

So, she did.

Angling her hip onto the cracked leather seat, the words rushed out as she relayed the last sixty minutes of her life to her friend. She pushed herself farther into the cab of the truck with the toe of her dusty boots, feeling deflated and uncertain. Neither a feeling she relished. She prided herself on many things, her critical thinking skills being at the top of the list. Not a single, viable solution presented itself at the moment, and that more than anything took the wind from her sails.

Her right leg dangled over the running board, the nervous bounce picking up speed. "What the hell, JJ?"

JJ propped one foot on the running board, crossing his arms over his belly as much as he could. "I don't know, kiddo."

She sensed the *I told you so* behind his words. And he had. Warned her not to trust someone she just met, even if he was her brother. She toyed with a piece of torn leather on the seat, smoothing it repeatedly beneath her fingers. "Ricky was the oldest. He took care of us after mom died, even tried to take the blame when I..." The words trailed off beneath memories better left in the past. It defined her too much already.

"Is that why you handed over your money so quickly to him? You think you owe him?"

"Of course, I owe him." Riley bit back the self-incrimination. She'd failed her family as a kid. Bringing the family back together as adults would make up for that, at least in part.

"Did you tell him about the house? About the PI you hired?"

Her silence answered the question. Outside of JJ, she'd told no one about her trip to the auction house on Friday. Ricky helped put the money part of her plan together but didn't know the details. If she didn't get the house, there was nothing to tell. She'd only told Ricky this money was for a short-term investment.

"OK. Those are your secrets. You didn't even tell your ex-husband and you sit in an office with him all day."

JJ swayed his head from side to side, as if weighing what

to say next. He scratched at his perpetual five-o'clock shadow, a slow thoughtful motion she recognized.

"Go on," she said reluctantly, mimicking the gesture. It was their private signal to each other to be honest. Even if it would hurt. Even if it would be what the other didn't want to hear. "Say it."

"Have you let that nice sheriff do anything more than flirt with you?"

It was the last thing she expected, and the instant burn on her cheeks blossomed outward like nuclear winter. She didn't blush often, but when she did, it was a full body affair. "I am not flirting with the cop." Without meaning to, she searched the walkway for the tall blonde man who intrigued her more than she wanted to admit.

JJ laughed, a sound both familiar and comforting. She'd known the man for sixteen years, following him and her ex around from job to job. At first, they'd taken care of her, an eighteen-year-old know-it-all who didn't know anything. Then they taught her what she needed to survive and work on the crew without getting killed. At times, they protected her when the guys on the crew thought she was an easy piece of ass because she hung out with all guys. When she proved she could take care of herself, they stepped back and let her. It was why she loved them. Why she called them family.

"Kiddo, I never said *you* were flirting with him. I know you better than that. You spent all night rebuilding that garage by yourself after you backed the dump truck into the frame on your first build rather than ask for help. But he's been giving you puppy dog eyes since the night of the fire."

The night of the fire at the construction site, when her favorite bulldozer had gone up in flames, had been a little hectic. But Riley had noticed Jackson. She just didn't think anyone had noticed her noticing.

She smiled despite herself. Damn, she loved this man. "What should I do, JJ?"

"I think you should jump the nice policeman and—"

She punched his arm, and he had the good sense to flinch, rubbing the spot as he laughed at her.

"I hope it hurts, asshole," she said through her laughter, glad he'd made her laugh even when she didn't feel like it. As their laughter quieted, she got serious again. "Do you think Ricky would really steal the money?"

JJ shrugged in that non-committal way of his. He pushed off the running board and tucked his hands in worn jeans that barely contained his stomach. "A million bucks is a powerful motivator, even for someone you'd normally call honest."

The construction crew began milling around the truck, staying a respectful distance away while she and JJ finished their conversation.

"But that has to be chump change for him and his firm," she reasoned. Ricky's voice practically floated when he told her about the partnership last year at his father-in-law's investment firm. Would he risk all of that? Risk losing his family a second time?

"Talk to the cop." JJ finished, turning toward the men waiting as he pulled the truck's keys from his pocket. He twirled the key ring around his sausage-link fingers. "Can't hurt, can it?"

As she pulled in her legs and closed the door, she worked through the questions filling her head. Would her brother take the money? Why? What if it was gone for good? Her thoughts went briefly to the conversation she'd had just yesterday with the real estate agent. The property wouldn't last long. It was too perfect. She had until the end of the year to come up with the rest of the money.

She rubbed at her temples, pushing back the ache throbbing underneath.

As for the good sheriff...JJ was right. What could it hurt to talk to him? It's not like she would sleep with him. She groaned inwardly.

Even if she wanted to.

Chapter Six

Jackson's boots thumped against the pavement, the sound harsh against the quiet night as he walked Connie, the station's desk clerk, to her car. He tried letting go of the day in a single burst of breath. It didn't work.

"I sense a donation to the swear jar coming my way based on that hefty sigh."

Connie's sensible heels *click-clacked* as they walked, her no-nonsense, shoulder-length hair swinging to-and-fro like the metronome that used to sit on the piano during his lessons. He shuddered at the memory. "I think I *donated* half my paycheck today."

"You spent the last four days looking through the legal books in your office," she commented, referencing the small library inherited from the previous sheriff who'd announced his retirement on Friday to everyone's surprise.

Your office. The phrase stunned Jackson. He'd not actually moved into the office, nor did he plan to. What stunned Jackson, however, was that the town turned to him without hesitation to fill in the man's shoes. His name was on the election posters all over town. The responsibility over-whelmed him at times, galvanized him at others. Today he wasn't sure which set his nerves on edge the most.

"Reading up on internet banking. Cyber security," Jackson offered without saying too much, aware Connie probably already knew more than him. The woman was a walking encyclopedia of penal codes and criminal histories.

"There's a lot written on the topic," she rummaged in her purse for her keys. "Did you read that article by Dorothy Denning I sent you?"

He'd spent the better part of his week researching, barely scratching the surface of the information available. "I did, thank you. The only loophole I've found regarding the missing money has to do with the nature of the agreement between Riley, as account owner, and her brother, as an authorized user."

"It's a start."

They reached Connie's sensible sedan, and she beeped open the driver door, which Jackson opened and held as the clerk slid into the seat. "I appreciate your help, Connie. Good night."

"My pleasure, sheriff," Connie responded, and Jackson didn't bother to correct her. She seemed content to ignore him when he corrected her anyway. "I see the light is still on over at the construction site." She nodded her head in that direction, and Jackson followed her gaze. "Maybe you can give Ms. Kenner an update."

Jackson smiled at the woman's blatant matchmaking attempt. She'd been trying to marry him off since he stepped foot in the sheriff's office eight months ago. "Good night, Connie," he repeated, closing her door.

He watched her drive off but stood there thinking about Riley. Just as he clicked open the locks on the cruiser, his eye returned to the light coming from the construction trailer in the distance. Would she be at the construction site this time of night?

Only one way to find out, and before he could talk himself out of it, Jackson headed in that direction, eating up the pavement in long, determined strides.

Earlier, the high school principal called asking if he would serve as guest speaker for the graduation ceremony in May. It was the first time he could remember where his old man's name or money hadn't played a part in him being offered something: a place at a prestigious college, a job, and even a wife.

He shoved back memories of Natalie, his fiancé-turned-almost-wife, of the wedding that started as the happiest day of his life and ended as the worst. Not even his dad's threats could stop him from tearing up the marriage certificate before the wedding cake was served. Natalie never shed a tear. She'd been complacent with their fathers' plans, but she, apparently, didn't mind. Her integrity had a price. Jackson's didn't.

Ten years and you still haven't let that go, he berated himself.

He'd long ago stopped thinking of his family. They'd let him down that day. Except his sister. She'd just shaken her head and refilled his glass as he drowned his sorrows with the last of their dad's most expensive bottle of scotch.

He turned his attention outward, sick of what he saw looking inward. The sun set hours ago and took with it the warmth that made Louisiana bearable in the cooler months, and he stuffed his hands in the pockets of his jacket.

He'd had spent enough time in cities like Cleveland and Milwaukee to know true winter. Louisiana didn't even come close. Now summer was another story, he admitted, thinking of this past summer. It was his first here after being away ten years. He hadn't meant to stay when he arrived in town. He sure hadn't meant to end up running for the office of sheriff. Jackson huffed. He needed to end that little bout of insanity and soon.

The possibility of a real crime tested his resolve to escape the role thrust upon him by circumstance, which was how he ended up in uniform in the first place. He'd not been searching for it, certainly didn't want it. He'd rather leave town than screw it up, which was sort of his plan. You can't fail others if you're not around.

The decision ate a hole in his gut, a jagged and raw-edged wound he picked at. It wasn't who he wanted to be, but he'd grown tired of fighting it long ago. No one had ever expected anything more from him. Not his father. Not the woman his father paid to marry him.

He yanked himself back from the steep and narrow path his mind wandered, focusing instead on Riley and her problem. Maybe he could help, even if he didn't plan on staying around.

He turned the final corner, feeling more at ease. The lone streetlamp did little to break up the dark on this part of the block. The sky was moonless with only a thick blanket of stars to break up the black.

Riley Kenner wasn't his type of woman, he reminded himself, but he'd been unable to get her out of his thoughts after they'd parted ways at the bank Monday. He'd caught her staring at him from the corner of his eye while he tried to be polite but non-committal to what Connie called his posse. She actually called it something else, but he was working on his political correctness. Couldn't have the acting sheriff getting sued for sexual harassment. The station loved the buttermilk pie that had been donated that day regardless.

The six women constantly dropped off casseroles, cookies, cakes, dinner invitations, invitations of *other* kinds, and once a hand knitted sweater he wouldn't wear to an ugly sweater contest. The food he left in the break room. The dinner invitations he declined. The sweater he dropped in a donation box. The other invitations he just ignored. Try as he might, however, he'd been unable to ignore Riley.

He'd replayed their brief encounter at the bank enough to burn into his brain. The smooth silk of her hair, a color so dark it reminded him of space and how it would wrap around you, weightless and free, if you let yourself fall into it. Eyes the color of the Kentucky bluegrass on a horse farm he'd worked years ago. He wanted to look again, see if the silver flecks were reality or fantasy. The angled face that still looked soft and touchable. Skin the color of sunset he'd once watch sizzle over the ocean in Fiji while on spring break: gold, honey, amber. Eyes that watched beneath a veil of intelligence and wariness. And those lips...

No, she definitely didn't fit the type of woman he usually wanted. But man, did he want her.

The gravel crunched beneath his boots as he stepped off the sidewalk and into the construction yard, shaking loose a train of thought better derailed than traveled. Although with her short stay in their sleepy little town, only long enough to get the construction on the store completed, she would be perfect. No commitments expected and no hurt feelings when he didn't offer ever-lasting love or some other such nonsense. Besides, he didn't plan to stay in Belle Terre either. He wouldn't leave until after the election, however. Not until the town had someone to replace him. And not until Riley's future was secured.

His eyes adjusted to the darkness, and he weaved through the piles of lumber and equipment with ease, shaking his head at the burned-out remnants of the bulldozer. The meager light from the trailer's door and windows beckoned and he took the stairs in two quick steps. He raised his hand to knock but stopped to read a sign someone had posted on the door.

Dear Santa,
All we want for Christmas is a fire-proof bulldozer.
Sincerely,
LCB Construction Crew

He grinned and knocked on the door.

"Come in," a female voice inside said, and his smile widened, instant recognition zipping through his body like lightning.

He quashed the smile before he opened the door, not wanting to look like a fool or an eager pervert. Just checking on things, he reminded himself. Just doing his job.

"Hey," he said, ducking beneath the door frame before pulling it closed behind him.

She sat hunched over a desk piled high with neat stacks of paper and file folders, a paper cup of coffee, and the crumbs from what he guessed to be pecan pie from the local diner. Riley blinked her eyes a few times, as if to redirect her focus, before settling back in the chair and tucking a pencil behind her left ear. "Hey back."

He stepped farther into the trailer, spying a novel laying open on the desk. *Love's Lasting Promise*. He recognized it from a display in the window of the local bookstore. Riley swiped it into a desk drawer and slammed the drawer shut.

Jackson tried to contain the grin, knowing he failed.

"Saw the light and wanted to make sure everything was ok." He glanced around the interior of the Spartan office space, noting it was furnished for work and not much else, although a nice leather sofa filled the back wall. "No more excitement or protesters or book burnings."

He referenced the recent trouble before Thanksgiving, where a group of women protesting a display of erotic romance novels written by the author of the book now hidden in Riley's desk drawer had accidentally set the bulldozer on fire rather than the intended novels.

Riley swiveled the chair, turning her entire body to face him and bringing her legs out from under the desk. She propped a foot on an open drawer. "No flaming bulldozers. I've posted signs at the entrance that burning torches are not allowed on site."

"I'm sure the insurance company is relieved."

Riley grinned, and it tugged at something low and primitive in him to make her smile like that. "Not even a single protestor worried about a spotted titmouse."

It was his turn to grin. The environmental group had been the most persistent of the protestors, on site until last week when they were told the titmouse was not an actual mouse but a bird and shown that what they presumed to be the supposedly endangered titmouse was actually a family of escaped hamsters.

"It worked out for the town in the end. We're getting this great new outdoor mall versus the megastore originally planned thanks to LCB's owner."

Also the construction owner and his girlfriend-type person were currently living happily ever after, Jackson added mentally. Not that he wanted that. He'd worked hard to avoid it since his wedding day ended with no wife.

She leaned back in the creaky leather chair, pulling the pencil from behind her ear and tossing it on the desk. "And no one has put me in handcuffs in..." Riley glanced at her wrist though she wore no wristwatch. "Almost five full days."

"Good," he said and nodded, stopping when he realized he was nodding like a dashboard bobble head. "Like I said, I saw the light," and he pointed to the light in question. When did he become such a dork? he wondered and scrubbed a hand through his hair to hopefully corral the ping-ponging thoughts. "But if everything's ok I'll just ..." And he pointed to the door. Then out popped, "I was headed over to the diner for some dinner. I see you're familiar with their pie." He pointed to the crumbs dotting the plate on her desk. "Today's pecan. One of the best in town."

Riley patted her stomach and groaned. "I'm only slightly more partial to the Mississippi Mud on —"

"Tuesday," they finished in unison, the silence that followed neither awkward nor heavy as they each contemplated the other in the meager light trying to find purchase in the shadows of the trailer. Her blue-black hair sat high on the crown of her head corralled its usual ponytail, a few strands curling rebelliously over her ears. His gaze lasered in on her face, which was framed by impossibly long lashes that probably made women groan in envy if the commercials he'd seen on TV were any indication.

Only he doubted she was wearing a speck of makeup. The flawless skin, like honey filtered through amber, didn't need any. It was her mouth he was having trouble ignoring. Again. He'd noticed her lips in the bank. Tried to ignore them then as well. Failed just as miserably.

"Would you like to join me?"

Where the hell did that come from? He shoved his fists into the pockets of his work jacket and stood very still. Not that he didn't know where it came from. He'd been thinking of the woman for four-and-a-half days. Wondering. The smile on her face lessened, but other than that, she mimicked his statue-like stillness.

"I thought we could talk about the bank. I did some reading. I know a little about investment firms. And ... I ... could give you a few things to check on." At her continued silence, he added regretfully, "It's not like a date or anything. You can pay your own way."

The smile returned with force—or maybe she was laughing at him—and he wanted to sneak away and hide in the blackened ruins of the bulldozer outside. Definitely not a shining moment in his life. But he wasn't ready to say goodnight to this woman. They'd eventually say goodbye. He was always the one saying goodbye, leaving before there was time to form a connection. He preferred it that way. No commitments. No disappointments. But lately it left an ache he refused to name.

Riley pushed to her feet, gathering up the papers and adding them to the stacks around the desk. "Sounds good. I'm starved."

They narrowly avoided each other while she finished putting her things together. As she switched on the outside lights, they did a quick two-step, dancing around each other again as she moved to turn off the lamp on her desk. He tried to hang back, tried not to stare at her ass as she moved around the suddenly claustrophobic space of the trailer. She came around the corner of the desk at the same time he went for the door, and they collided. Instant recognition colored her face and sizzled in his veins like water on the July pavement.

Instead of pulling back, Riley's arms reached around his waist and held on while his own arms wrapped around her shoulders to balance them both. Enough outside light filtered in from between the window blinds that he could see the amused smile tilt one corner of her mouth.

That mouth. Pink. Full. Lush. Kissable. The last word played over and over in his head. She didn't look away or try and be coy. No lip-licking or false shyness. He bent toward her at the same time Riley raised up to meet him.

Jackson crushed her against his torso, rocking his hips into hers as their mouths met. Rather than go slack in his arms as he expected, she moved her hands up from his waist to tangle around his neck and pull him closer, demanding rather than conceding. Jackson had never been so turned on in his life, his body hardening in rapid, painful degrees.

A throaty moan rasped from between Riley's lips as her tongue slipped into his mouth, tormenting him with quick flicks and long swipes, deepening the kiss. He circled her waist with his hands, lifting to mold her even closer to his own body. Jackson wanted to grind against her, find some relief for the ache twisting in his gut. This was insane. Absolutely insane. And he didn't care one bit.

He broke from the kiss though it killed him to do so. "Tell me to stop." The words came out hungry and forced. "Tell me to stop, or so help me I'm going to—"

"What?" Riley interrupted, pulling them backwards to the desk, her own voice breathless. "What are you going to do, sheriff?" She palmed the length of his cock over the tight fabric of his slacks and slid her ass back onto the desk. "Put me in handcuffs. Again." She angled back even farther, and things he didn't care about clattered to the floor.

A slice of light cut across her face, her lips swollen, her eyes hooded. Strands of hair escaped her ponytail, and he reached behind her head to release the elastic band. The black silk cascaded over her shoulders, one swatch falling across her face. Riley peeked out from beneath the dark curtain, teasing, daring, promising. Then, like the elastic, he stopped holding back.

"I'm going to do this." He pinned her to the desk with the weight of his body, moving his lips from her mouth to the hollow beneath her left ear. Her skin tasted like honey, and the pulse in her neck jumped beneath his mouth. She opened her legs for him, and he slid into the vee of her body, fitting himself into the juncture of her thighs. With one hand he pushed up her shirt and bra and cupped her breast, tweaking the nipple between his thumb and fore-finger until she gasped. He liked the sound. He wedged the other hand beneath her ass and pulled her closer to the edge of the desk.

"I need to taste you," he rasped into her ear.

"Yes," she moaned, the sound husky and delightful to Jackson, and she moved his hands to the button of her jeans and lifted her hips as his fingers finally managed to work the confounded contraption. He didn't even bother to push the jeans and the slip of silk that passed for her panties off her body. Jackson just pushed them to her knees, then fell to his own.

She watched him move in for the first lick, lips parted, breath heavy. Their gazes locked. He parted her folds with his thumbs, then, with his eyes still trained on her, swiped his tongue across her clit. Her body arched, but her legs lay pinned beneath his arms.

"And I'm going to do this." Jackson went in for another taste, slower this time.

Her head fell back, and she slumped slightly to support her body on her elbows before raising her head to meet his eyes again.

The third lick tore a ragged curse from her throat at the same moment a wash of her juices coated his tongue, and he lapped at the musky warmth, sucking her clit farther into his mouth, biting it ever so gently with his teeth. Blood rushed to parts of his body already on fire. Each new maneuver on his part brought a fresh wave of curses from Riley, and he smiled against her body. She made sounds— oh, she made sounds, and each new sound pushed Jackson to elicit new pleasured gasps.

He'd never been driven to bring a woman to such heights like this. New and wicked things he wanted to do to her battled to be next on the list. He slid a finger into the heat of her body, careful at first because of her tightness, but as she relaxed, he added another finger and pumped into her with slow, deliberate thrusts.

Judging by the tremor in her voice, he'd found the right combination of pressure and speed, and within moments, her body arched backwards, and she cried out a release. Minutes later, another tremulous cry rocked through her body, muscles convulsing and contracting around his fingers and in his mouth.

The insanity of the moment again skittered across his brain as he kissed his way up her partially nude body, and again he failed to see reason to care. Jackson stopped at her breast, sucking the nipple into his mouth and rasping his teeth against the puckered flesh, before moving upward to the hollow of her throat. He paused, their faces barely a whisper apart, and she claimed that final space between them, hungrily devouring his mouth. Her scent and taste mingled on his tongue.

She pulled back, and he traced the starry pattern of freckles on her nose with his eyes, brushed the slope of her cheek with his chin. A flush darkened the contours of her face and heated her bronzed skin to a darker gold.

Riley pressed herself against his groin, and Jackson groaned at the exquisite pressure. If she did that again ... and then she did. The woman would kill him. *There are worse ways to die*, he reasoned.

"Do you have a condom?" Her words escaped on a hoarse breath.

He wanted to be a gentleman, he really did, but that twisty ache in his gut reminded him how long it had been since he'd had sex. "We don't have to," he said, unconvinced it was true.

"Like hell we don't," Riley's grin broadened with the words. "I'm not done yet."

Chapter Seven

Riley's body still pulsed where Jackson had caressed and licked her to senselessness, then licked her some more. *Too long*, her mind screamed when she first kissed him and dragged him closer. She'd thought her attraction to the acting sheriff was nothing more than the product of adrenaline and shock caused by the events at the bank. Not to mention her ignored libido.

Too much time had passed since she'd given in to those baser urges and found someone with whom she could let loose. She couldn't date the guys on the crew. She'd done that once, and even though they'd married, she wouldn't do it again. There was a fine line between *sister* and *slut* when you were the only woman at a testosterone showdown.

The smile widened as he pulled the condom from his wallet with shaky hands, dropping the leather wallet but not seeming to care. You'd think this meant more than a fast fuck the way he'd tried to be gentlemanly, even though every inch—and there were many inches—of his body obviously disagreed with him. As he tore open the cellophane with his teeth, she worked his belt buckle and zipper, slipping her hand inside. When she wrapped her hand around his cock, sliding from the base to the head, Jackson nearly dropped the condom as well.

She pushed back the flaps of the pants and slid the boxers and slacks down below his butt cheeks, her fist still pumping in slow, purposeful strokes.

It was Jackson's turn to curse. "Keep that up," he grinded out, "and we won't need the condom."

Riley admired the thickly corded muscles of his thighs, the light matting of dark blondish hair tracing a path from his chest to navel, the erection jutting outward from his body.

"I don't think you're that much of a newb but," she said as she splayed the flat of her palms against his chest and urged him backwards, sliding off the desk to follow. "I'll be good," she lied, certain the smile trembling on her lips gave her away. "For now."

Jackson grinned in return as he walked backwards. "I don't think you could be good if you were in front of a firing squad."

She kicked free of her boots, jeans, and panties along the way, letting him pull the sports bra over her head. He let loose a long, low whistle. Riley'd never been self-conscious about her body. It was pretty damn good. Not perfect. A few pounds extra but screw it. She carried it well with her height and the labor she put in at the site each day. She strutted toward Jackson in her naked glory as he bumped up against the couch, sitting down hard on the leather cushions.

"Damn, woman." A hoarse whisper, so very male.

The completeness of his attention on her—not just her body but on her, her eyes, her face, her hands when they reached for him—unnerved her for a split second. A fast fuck, she reminded herself.

"Yep," she agreed, shaking off the intrusive thoughts. Riley dipped her head to capture his mouth, sucking his lower lip between her teeth as she straddled his waist, nestling his hardness against her, dragging the length into intimate contact but not yet taking him inside. The heat of that touch wended its way through her, jagged and sharp like summer lightening, until it exploded everywhere at once.

She rode the edge of his erection, draped her arms over his shoulders, and leaned forward until her breasts were closer. He took the hint and sucked her nipples into his mouth, the dark stubble on his chin a rough contrast to the soft touch of his lips. When he caught her watching, he nipped her a little harder and the exotic zing went straight to where they were almost joined.

Riley watched his cheeks hollow and fill as he grazed her flesh with his tongue and mouth. The intimacy of their nearness, his focus on her body, gave her time to study him. The sharp slope of the cheeks into the jawline. The neck and shoulders thick and sturdy. Abs you wanted to lick. It all belied the surfer boy image she'd noted earlier. This was not a man soft from sitting around at a desk or watching bikini babes walk down the beach.

Jackson was different. She knew it as intuitively as she knew which new crew member would cause trouble and which one was truly looking for the second chance her company offered recently released convicts. But he was also trouble.

The sweet agony of the building orgasm diverted her attention.

"This needs to change," she said, and a moment's concern crinkled the corners of his mouth until she reached between them as he slid the condom in place. With a simple flex of her thighs, she lifted her body, positioned his cock, and slid downward, guiding his body into hers. They both sighed, their heads falling together. Jackson lifted a hand and cupped the back of her neck, the grip tight but not painful. But it turns out, necessary when he thrust upwards with his hips, pushing her thighs farther apart and pulling her closer against his body. Her gasp caught even her by surprise.

"Like that?" he teased, holding her still with the hand on her nape.

Riley resisted against the iron grip, taking back only a fraction of the space he claimed with his body. If she couldn't battle him that way, she knew of other ways.

She clenched her internal muscles against his cock and was rewarded by a deep, guttural groan and brief shuttering of his eyelids. "How about you? You like that?" She did it again.

And then they were done with talking. Jackson pulled back and pistoned into her with deep, hard thrusts. Riley met each, their bodies connecting the only sound in the universe. The fine sheen of sweat on his body transferred to her own, mingling with the dampness between her legs. She dug her nails into his shoulders to hold on, not wanting to lose the rhythm or fall ass-over-tea-kettle onto the floor. The edge hovered so close, a sharp ache on which she balanced between ecstasy and oblivion.

Oh, please, Jackson, she thought before crashing over the edge to ecstasy. Her body clenched once, twice, three times around him until he finally, with a final hard thrust, exploded inside of her. Each contraction and release of his muscle inside her body brought more tremors. She would have moved off him if she could figure out how to use her legs again.

They sat like that for an eternity of seconds until she couldn't tell where she ended and he began. The heat of their passion settled over her, a blanket of contentment, unsettling in its welcome. The crack in her own foundation of solitude widened, and she quickly sought to rebuild the boundary. Something safe. Something neutral.

"I hope there's some place around here to get a drink."

The laugh started slow, growing stronger as it rumbled from his chest. "How do you feel about craft beer?"

"I wouldn't want to hurt your ego, but if it's a choice between beer and sex ..." She let the statement trail off, but based on the growing smirk, she didn't think Jackson minded all that much.

Chapter Eight

J ackson nodded, impressed. Riley picked crabs with the expertise of a girl who'd grown up along the bayou. The final strains of Johnny Janot's *I'm Proud to be a Cajun* filled the back room at Gastenaux's de Louisiane Bar and drifted into the dining area. Patrons had pushed back chairs to join the dancing that would soon have the floors vibrating.

He loved this place but couldn't come as often as he liked. The reason for that—the owner—studied Jackson from behind the bar, a look of annoyance and curiosity tightening the deep furrows in the man's forehead. As a rule and as a matter of law, he wouldn't take gifts from the townspeople. Everyone came with motives and it was too easy to cross the lines if you didn't understand those motives. It didn't mean they were bad. He just preferred things clear.

Jackson also made it somewhat of a rule not to confuse a casual sexual encounter with commitment. Trouble was, he didn't know where Riley fit into that mix.

Jackson returned his attention to where he wanted it to

be. "You've picked crabs before." He wiped his chin around a mouthful of the butter-slathered meat, taking a final draw from the bottle of soda at his fingertips.

"You know what season it is in Louisiana by the seafood you can buy." She punctuated her words with the crab knife in her hands. "Fall means blue crab."

Riley stiffened and dropped her gaze as the entire wait staff shuffled by, candles blazing on an oversized cupcake. Ghosts swirled in a haunting dance behind her eyes. She stayed silent, and while he wanted to ask if she was ok, he knew she'd likely ignore the question. He let it go.

He and Riley had spent the last hour sharing their mutual love of craft beer and pouring over the extensive list the restaurant offered. The place had the best selection of brews Jackson had found outside of Milwaukee which is why he hated he couldn't come more often when he was off duty. Another side glance toward the owner sent up a few red flags. He wanted to get out tonight without confronting that one but doubted the man would let him.

She popped a length of claw meat into her mouth, her sour expression from moments before replaced with something close to bliss, whispering reverently, "Oh, yeah" as her eyes fluttered close in a gesture both familiar and erotic.

Riley looked the same way during sex. He didn't bother to get his pride rankled by the fact she had the same expression with blue crabs as sex with him. When it came to blue crabs from Gastineaux's, he expected the same look decorated his face.

He'd traded his uniform for a pair of jeans and a button down he kept in his cruiser, luckily realizing he'd dropped his wallet in the construction trailer. But the gun stayed at his side under the untucked shirt which was why he was sipping a soda. He was as off-duty as a cop in a small town got in his short experience. Not that he minded. It filled something inside him to have people look at him with expectation rather than disappointment.

The jukebox stopped, the void filled by a chorus of voices butchering the lyrics to Happy Birthday. Riley stiffened, dropping the half-eaten crab and snatching up her beer. Two long pulls later, she slapped the near-empty bottle to the table. Her eyes never lifted. Her attention keenly focused on the narrow slice of table in front of her. Flickers of emotion skirted across her face —remorse, wariness, loneliness—before a practiced mask fell into place.

He reached over the carcass-covered table to flick a piece of shell from her hair, wishing he could flick aside the pain as easily. "You want another beer?"

A subtle nod of her head brought her from the past to the present.

Jackson signaled to the waitress and another beer appeared. Riley, who flipped her hair casually over a shoulder, never lost a second as she finished off her Andygator and reached for the new bottle of Octoberfest he'd recommended. "No offense, but this is almost as good as sex."

The waitress slid another soda by his elbow, and he accepted it with a nod of thanks. "At least you said almost."

Jackson would never bring a date here. It wasn't a place the boardwalk posse would appreciate if he'd ever agree to date any of them. The main part of the dining room was under construction for Gastineaux's newest venture, a bed and breakfast, but not even the caution tape keeping patrons to the more rustic part of the business kept away the customers.

Gastineaux's didn't bother with plates, glasses, or salt and pepper on the table. Everything you needed came in a bottle or could be eaten with your hands. They even fried the coleslaw. And they seasoned the food so perfectly it would be a crime to add to it. The regulars would probably throw you in the bayou for trying.

They barely bothered with tables in this part of the dining room, rather using a massive cable spool with a garbage can in the center hole. The surface was covered with butcher paper when you sat down. You could be covered in butcher paper too if the waitress thought you'd make a mess.

Luckily, he reminded himself, it wasn't a date. Just a post-mind-blowing-sex meal.

"Sheriff Guidry!" a voice boomed moments before two hands grabbed Jackson's shoulders, shaking him in his chair like his hair was on fire. Jackson held tightly onto his soda and tried to relax into the movement to keep his teeth from rattling in his head. He recognized the voice instantly: the restaurant owner.

"Long time, no see, *cher*," Darren Gastineaux greeted a little too brightly, his thick Cajun accent carrying over the three-piece band picking up speed in the other room. He set down a mason jar Jackson suspected to be filled with home-made hooch and flipped a chair around, straddling the seat and crossing his arms over the back. "I done thought you not come back after the last time, but I'm glad to see ya in my place."

Riley's left eyebrow shot up in curiosity, and Jackson knew Darren's words caught her attention. She sucked the butter from her fingers, eased back in her chair and lifted the bottle of Octoberfest to her lips.

Jackson gestured to the pile of empty crab shells. "There's no place better for blue crab."

"We comin' to the end of the season, yeah." Darren

picked up the last remaining piece of corn and gnawed a line of kernels off the cob. "So eat 'em up good." He swiped the juice from his chin with the back of his hand, his attention going to Riley.

Something Jackson recognized and didn't like darkened in the man's eyes. He reluctantly held out his hand toward her. "Riley Kenner, let me introduce you to Darren Gastineaux, owner and Cajun chef extraordinaire." Jackson left out the part about being an all-around ass and skirt-chaser. No sense setting Riley against the man too soon. Darren could do that all on his own if history repeated itself. "Riley is with the construction crew working over on Main Street."

Darren dropped the half-eaten corn on the table, wiping his hands on his pants. He slumped down in his seat, dragging his eyes up and down Riley's body. And the man had the nerve to look under the table to see what wasn't visible.

Riley stiffened beneath the not-subtle-in-the-least perusal, and Jackson tamped down the instant flash of jealousy spiking behind his eyes. So much for giving the man a chance.

"Lawd a mercy, girl." Darren drew out the words until Jackson thought the man would have to take another breath to continue. "You could make an atheist call for the Almighty."

"Call me a girl again and you'll need some divine intervention yourself." Riley said without blinking an eye, and Jackson's estimation of her went up a notch. She tipped the beer into her mouth but never let her gaze waver from Darren's surprised face.

Darren burst into laughter. "She's a good one, Jackson. I like her. I'll make it worth your while to bring her back to my place." He gestured over his head to the waitress who had been taking care of them. "Kaylie!"

Their young waitress approached cautiously, staying out of arm's reach from her boss. Jackson's radar pinged, and he made a mental note to talk to Darren's daughter-in-law, Miranda, to see if Darren was behaving himself behind the bar with the young waitresses.

Darren yelled louder than necessary. "You go bring my friends here a platter of—"

Jackson groaned inwardly. Not again. "We talked about this Darren. I won't accept ..." Pause. Swallow. "I can't accept any free food or drinks." The line between courtesy and professionalism blurred for some, but not Jackson. He wouldn't take handouts from his family. Why did people think he'd take them from strangers? "It's kind of you, but please ... how about sending it over to the firehouse? Or the ER over at Teche General? I'm sure they would love some of your good Cajun cooking tonight."

It was an old argument between them, and one of the reasons Jackson didn't come to Gastineaux's very often. Jackson couldn't figure out what Darren hoped to gain with his *generosity*.

Darren slapped his hands on the table, causing the waitress to jump before she sidled away to see to another table. Jackson would be sure to leave her an extra generous tip.

"I'm goin' do dat just for you, my friend." The man turned to Riley, the lust-filled look in his eyes still irking Jackson. "He done tell you what he did at the bank when he came—"

"Now let's not go telling stories tonight, Darren," Jackson interrupted, tempted to just steal away now.

A lascivious twist to Darren's face passed for a smile. "I see, *cher*. You gonna want to tell her yourself."

His eyes narrowed, the lids dropping to hood the iris, and it reminded Jackson of a crocodile sitting beneath the surface of the water.

Darren guffawed. "When da time is right, I see. What dem city folk call *pillow talk*." More winking and nudging made Jackson's skin crawl.

"Oh, we've already had sex," Riley added to the mix. "Twice." She waved her beer bottle over the pile of crabs, corn, and potatoes. "This is the pillow talk."

Jackson's jaw dropped, and he saw Darren do the same. Then Riley shined a bright and innocent smile, taking a sip of her beer, and Darren nearly tipped over his chair with his great big peals of laughter.

The chair scraped the pocked-marked wooden floors as the man lumbered to his feet. He slapped Jackson on the back with more shaking. At least Jackson had time to put down his drink first. "I like dis girl ... err ... woman, sheriff. You go on and bring her back to my place again real soon, ya hear?"

Darren rejoined the crew at the bar, their voices lost beneath the music reverberating against the thick cedar plank walls. Some customers stumbled from the back room, each indistinguishable from the next, all sweaty and not enjoying the music from the pinched looks on their faces. They pushed their way through the burgeoning crowd to the bar.

Everything about the men, three of them, marked them as outsiders though they'd tried to blend in. New jeans with a crisp pleat down the front. Ironed polo shirts. The shoes gave them away if nothing else did: spit-polished loafers. Jackson pegged them as trouble and wondered if they were there for him. It wouldn't be the first time his dad had sent people to find him.

"Hey, Jackson."

The female voice dragged his attention back to the table, and he smiled at Miranda Gastineaux standing nearby with her baby perched on her hip. Jackson pushed to his feet and reached over, pinching the toes of her little boy who rewarded him with a giggle. The baby reached out to Jackson with pudgy, slobber-covered fingers. He'd missed his niece's and nephew's baby time, the only grandchildren in the family. His parents finally gave up on Jackson providing any heirs to the family name. Another addition to his long list of disappointing choices according to his dad.

"I heard what Darren promised about the food." Miranda looked embarrassed, untangling the baby's fingers from her hair. "I wanted to let you know I'd make sure it happened."

She hitched the baby up higher and motioned for Jackson to take his seat, but the kid continued to reach for him, so Jackson plucked the child from her arms and sat down after Miranda took her seat. "That'd be great."

"And I know about Kaylie," Miranda said a little lower. "I don't schedule her to work with Darren alone. We hired a new bartender, Hudson." She nodded her head to the guy behind the bar multitasking a tray of cocktails and a full line up of thirsty regulars waving for his attention. "He keeps a good eye on things when Mason or I can't be here. Kaylie knows she can trust him."

Relief melted some of the tension from Jackson's frame. "I'm grateful, Miranda. Let me know if you need back up."

She nodded once. The baby lunged for Jackson's nearby soda bottle before deciding to reach for the decimated crab claws, so Jackson scooted his chair back from the table. "This little guy is getting so big."

Miranda leaned in, thumbing away a line of drool dripping down the kid's chin. "Jackson Jr has his first tooth coming in."

At the mention of the baby's name, Riley nearly choked on a swig of her beer. Subtlety was definitely not a trait Ms. Kenner practiced, Jackson thought dryly. He liked that immensely. Always the mom, Miranda pulled a paper towel from the roll on the table and handed it to Riley without a word or second glance.

"Is his *daddy* working tonight?" Jackson asked, hoping his subtlety was a bit more obvious than Riley's. The baby lunged for his mother, and Jackson gratefully handed him over to Miranda's open arms.

"Yeah," Miranda glanced over her shoulder at the bar, and Jackson followed her gaze, her voice shaky with concern.

The leader of the three men he'd seen earlier pushing away from the dance floor snapped his fingers at Miranda's husband, Mason, then banged on the bar top with the gold ring weighing down his left ring finger. Not a smart move, Jackson noted. The air of superiority reminded him of people he'd grown up with. Rich and used to getting their way. Mason didn't move immediately, and when he finally headed toward the bar, he ambled painfully slowly. He grabbed a rag to wipe down one section of the counter. Stacked a few empties in the sink Jackson knew to be just below the bar top. Finally, he stood before the three impatient men, arms crossed.

The man leaned over the bar and spoke loudly, judging by the exaggerated movements of his mouth. Mason shook his head. The man looked back to his friends, then leaned and screamed again. Again, Mason shook his head.

Aggravation tightened the customer's shoulders, and Jackson recognized the word *fuck* cross the man's lips. This time Mason reached beneath the bar, and Jackson's hand moved on its own to the weapon secured at his waist in a gesture both practiced and new. His vision narrowed. Darren kept a shotgun beneath the bar. Would Mason be dumb enough or pissed off enough to wave it at customers while Jackson sat just a few feet away?

But Mason dropped three bottles of beer clumsily on the bar, not even bothering to open them. The man swiped his hand at the beer in a dismissive gesture and turned on his expensive, loafered heel, before storming from the bar. His two associates followed.

Jackson released the breath he didn't realize filled his lungs and re-secured the holster without moving his hand right away. When he brought his attention back to the table and Riley, he found her studying him. Given the past few seconds, he expected concern or worry to fill her eyes and face. Instead, he observed calm curiosity in her neutral gaze.

Miranda had missed him reach for the weapon, and Jackson was relieved. She looked worried, more than what he would expect watching a spouse deal with unruly customers. That was a common occurrence at Gastineaux's. This went beyond the level of concern for a typical night's rowdy customer.

As the three men disappeared into the back room once more, Mason's hard eyes locked on Miranda, flicking to Jackson briefly. His mouth tightened, a sharp slash across jaw.

"I gotta go, Jackson." Miranda forced a smile, but her deeply fretful expression told him more was going on. Mason held a grudge against Jackson. Not that Jackson blamed him.

Jackson Jr started to fuss. Miranda shushed the baby gently, kissing the top of his head, shaking her head as if to clear her thoughts. "Let me get this one home. It's getting to be his bedtime. Good to see you, Jackson."

He smiled and pushed to his feet again, ruffling the baby's head. "You two be careful getting home."

Jackson turned back to Riley, a calculating mixture of curiosity and amusement tilting her head to one side.

Chapter Nine

Riley watched the tension flow out of Jackson in a single breath as Miranda walked away. The hand she knew rested on the butt of the gun at his waist returned to her view as he adjusted the hem of his dark green shirt over the concealed holster.

"Typical night in Belle Terre?" She traced the path of the men through the bar. "Or did I just get lucky with dinner and a show?"

His forced smile told her more than anything. She'd found small towns stayed the same pretty much across the country. You belonged or didn't based on the whims of those who never questioned their place in the group. She'd never been that lucky, always the outsider looking in.

"Passions run high around here on just about any topic." He shoved the pile of empty crab shells and gnawed corn cobs into the garbage can and snagged a line of paper towels from the roll on the table. "This is mostly a local place, but it has a good rep for food. One of those food TV shows came through at the start of the year, and the clientele changed a bit."

Riley accepted the paper towels from Jacked and bussed her own part of the table. "I'd bet Darren isn't on board with the customer service expected from outsiders." She wiped her hands and pitched the used towels into the garbage.

Jackson snorted and swiped a hand across his jaw. "Darren isn't on board with customer service expected from the locals. The man can cook, I'll give him that. The locals mostly ignore his attitude. But he is …"

"A pig?" Riley finished for him.

From his silence, Jackson obviously didn't want to badmouth a local in front of an outsider—admirable to Riley. Finally, he said, "You know small towns. You fit in or you move away."

"That explains my life on the road." The admission left her lonely in the crowded room.

"Have you always been on the road?"

She looked up, feeling the weight of his scrutiny to her core. Rather than feel suffocated by it, however, she felt warmed, and let it chase away most of the loneliness, if only for the moment. There was no malice in his question, no judgement. Only curiosity, interest. So she shared a piece of herself with him; something she'd not done in a very long time. "It feels that way. I was hoping to change that, however."

"How?

"I was going to buy a house. Settle down somewhere."

"Somewhere like Belle Terre?"

Emotions flickered behind his eyes as he processed that bit of information. Had their little escapade in the work trailer been more about her eventual departure than anything else? Most of her adult life had been spent packing for the next town. She recognized the same look in Jackson.

"There are worse places." She cast a doubtful glance

over to Darren behind the bar. "Worse people." A grin tugged up the corners of her mouth; his soon followed. "Should I even ask about Jackson Jr? His daddy does *not* like you."

He groaned and shook his head. "That's a long story I'm afraid."

He leveled a look at her that filled in some of the blanks —he'd done something in his mind to hurt Miranda. Instinct told her, however, that Jackson would never intentionally harm anyone. She remembered the way he'd put himself at her back in the bank, his hand a comforting weight against her skin. The protectiveness radiating around him practically pulsed with a Superman vibe. "I've got nowhere to be tonight."

They shared a comfortable silence as the jukebox changed songs, and the crowd started singing the lyrics of something Riley didn't recognize. Jackson motioned her closer.

"The music's only going to get louder. Why don't we head outside?"

She nodded, and he signaled the waitress for the check. True to his earlier statement, he didn't protest when she dropped a couple of twenties on the bill. He did the same.

They grabbed their drinks, and Jackson led her through the back room to a side door which emptied them out into a screened-in porch area. Two wood stoves blazed in the corners and shared space with a dozen or so actual tables, but the place sat empty at the moment. Everyone else was inside with the music and warmer air.

Once again, Jackson maneuvered so he stood at her back, his hand lightly resting between her shoulder blades. The move came off as natural, the perpetual guardian and gentleman. Like in the bank, it didn't make her feel helpless. Just comfortable.

Jackson did that—made her comfortable—better than anyone in her life. He also made her extremely uncomfortable in the easy way he'd slipped beneath her defenses. She couldn't get a fix on him, and the puzzle intrigued her.

His mannerisms and speech said education. He certainly wasn't prissy or anything like that, but the culture became evident when anger added an edge to his voice and the neutralized accent slipped out. The custom-made boots said money. The comfort with which he approached people and the easy-going attitude, not to mention his public service job, said more. She wasn't sure just what it said, however.

She didn't linger overly long on that thought. Even if things worked out with the house and she stayed in Belle Terre, what could possibly come of their involvement?

Family and happiness, that secret part of her brain whispered. She didn't know if she was wired for settling down. So much time had passed since her last stable home that Riley didn't know if she could stay in one place for long. If anything could tie her down, however, it would be owning a piece of it. A place to build for herself rather than others. Now that seemed impossible.

Sex and orgasms, whispered the not so secret part, and her body ignited again at the thought of their tryst in the construction trailer. Luckily, the crew had already gone for the night so there were no witnesses to Jackson's arrival or their eventual departure together.

They meandered through the line of scarred oak tables, trailing beneath the string of bare bulbs running the length of the flat ceiling. Ceiling fans, motionless tonight, dotted the spaces in between the joists. The lights from the restaurant drifted out to the murky water just a few feet away, its reflections bobbing on the small ripples across the surface. You couldn't see below or beyond the wharf jutting out from the shoreline. Blackness swallowed it all.

Jackson looked down at her and nudged her with his shoulder. "You keep grinning like that and I'm going to start calling you Cheshire."

She didn't realize she was grinning until he pointed it out. His voice filled the large room easily, as did his body on the double Adirondack glider they commandeered. Their bodies sank into the deep angled seats facing the water. She propped her beer on the arm of the swing and had to draw one leg beneath the other to sit comfortably.

"I'm wondering what your babe patrol would think of us having dinner. Small towns and the gossip grapevine after all."

Jackson sat forward, elbows resting on his thighs, hands clasped between his knees. The jeans were washed to a faded blue, and Riley itched to find out if they were as soft as they looked. *One session of toe-curling sex and you're thinking about the man's laundry.* She rolled her eyes.

Reel it in, Riley, she chastised herself. Sex, sex, and nothing but the sex. That was all earlier was about. She'd needed the tension relief, and it worked. She'd not felt so relaxed since before her life had fallen apart at the bank earlier in the week. Riley wasn't sure she'd ever felt this relaxed at all. Not that she wanted to admit it. Not even to herself.

Jackson sat back, draping his left arm across the back of the glider. The tips of his fingertips could brush her shoulder if he flexed. Flashes of memory of what those fingers could do crowded out other less enticing memories. Could Jackson be the type to play the field? Maybe each of the babe patrol had been in Riley's shoes at some point. The realization left her cold.

"Don't worry," he assured her, the trust she felt in his statement both comforting and alarming. "I have not had a relationship of any kind with those women. They're sweet and all, but not what I'm looking for."

Which of course led to the question from Riley, "What are you looking for?" She regretted it instantaneously. "Not that I'm looking to provide it," she amended, motioning between them. "But just so we're on the same page." She released the hair band at the nape of her neck, scraping her fingers across her scalp to loosen the strands. When Riley went to put her hair up again, Jackson reached over.

"Don't." He took a section between his fingers briefly before releasing it. He studied her face, and the intensity of that perusal left Riley breathless. Jackson brushed his thumb down the line of her jaw, lost in some thought, but Riley couldn't read him well enough to know what it meant.

"More of what we had back in your office would be nice." That smirk from the bank creased his face.

The warmth of her skin had nothing to do with embarrassment and everything to do with anticipation. "I can be on board with that." The sultry purr of her voice surprised her, and she interlaced his fingers in her own, albeit briefly. He didn't apologize for their tryst. Didn't condemn her for it either.

He pulled back his hand when she let go and tucked his fingers into the front pocket of his jeans as if to keep his hands locked away. "Honestly, I don't know how long I'll be around town. And I'm not looking to make promises I can't keep."

"Fair enough," she said, glad he was being honest. It tweaked her heart a bit to think of Belle Terre without

Jackson down the road. She'd picked the town before Jackson came into the picture, however. His presence or absence didn't change the purpose for her staying: a home.

She retrieved her beer, taking a long pull while she gathered her thoughts. "Though I have to ask, if you're not sure about staying around town, why are you running for sheriff?"

He did a slow shake of his head, and Riley recognized frustration in the simple movement. "The town council put my name in for the special election to replace the retiring sheriff. I never actually accepted the nomination, but that didn't seem to matter. The election isn't until February, so I have a little time to find a replacement if I don't run."

The double-meaning on the word run didn't escape her. Jackson wasn't used to sticking around anymore than she was, and she couldn't help but wonder why.

Riley adjusted her posture, turning slightly in her seat to better see Jackson. His profile cut a sharp line in the shadows on the porch. The beach blond hair darkened out of the sunlight, making him appear more serious then she first gave him credit for.

"Based on pieces of conversation, not to mention Jackson Jr, I'm guessing there's a story behind that." She relaxed her shoulders against the back of the glider, crossing her arms, pulling one leg up, and resting her foot against the seat. "Care to share?"

He buried his face in the palm of his hand before holding it out to the night as if he could pluck an explanation from the darkness. "Everyone has blown it way out of proportion."

She gave a half-hearted laugh and nudged him with the toe of her shoe. "Now I'm dying to know. Spill it, sheriff."

Jackson dropped his chin to his chest and gave another

shake of his head. He sat back and looked out to the water lapping in the distance, his focus going with it. "I came to town in March, passing through on my way to Florida."

Images of him shirtless on the sandy beaches filled Riley's head and things in her body clenched and tightened. She finished off the beer to cool her lusty thoughts and tucked the empty between her legs.

He continued, unaware of her thoughts. "I stopped in the bank. It was lunch time on a Friday. The place was busy." Jackson recited the facts with little emotion, but Riley sensed he'd thought about this a lot. He kept his body loose, except for the muscle ticking a fast beat in the sharp angle of his jaw. "These two guys came in, and something inside of me sent up a red flag." His gaze drifted out to the darkness, probably seeing the moment he relayed to her with blunt words. "Miranda walked in just a few seconds later, and the bigger guy grabbed her, pulled a knife and put it to her throat."

Riley's eyes widened, thinking of the sweet lady she'd met only moments ago. The little boy in her arms. "How far along was she?"

"Eight months."

She saw the column of his throat work past the words, his Adam's apple sliding with the hard swallow. He'd said it was nothing, but even without all the facts, she knew that to be untrue. "You don't have to talk about it if you don't want." She hoped her sincerity on that front sounded as truthful as his did earlier. Riley didn't want to bring up a painful subject for Jackson.

He relaxed his body, crossing his left ankle over the right knee. "To tell you the truth, that's about it. They were all standing about six inches from me. The other guy went to pull something from under his shirt. I decked him. The other guy didn't even react, and I grabbed the hand with the knife, twisted it, and he went down. It was over in five seconds flat."

"That's amazing."

Jackson quirked his head slightly and turned to face her. Tight lines crinkled at the corners of his eyes and mouth. "Not really. I got lucky. Pure and simple. And it was stupid. Miranda could have been hurt. If the other guy had a gun. If I'd been two seconds slower—"

She rested a hand on his thigh. "But you weren't." The modesty in Jackson's voice and posture did not come off as false. He truly didn't see what he'd done as anything special. "I mean, you're right, you got lucky in some ways. But you reacted, and it paid off."

He gave her a slight nod, the lines in his face disappearing with each breath he took. "Anyway," he gave that dismissive wave she'd already come to recognize as discomfort on his part. The tension in his body eased, and he dropped his shoulders, scrubbing his palms across his thighs when she removed her hand.

"Miranda delivered that night, and they named the baby after me. I don't think Mason was real pleased with that." He smiled, and she could tell he was proud to have a little namesake, even if it wasn't his child. "Before Monday, I was a deputy. I passed my weapons certification a few weeks after that incident and have been here since."

Riley could understand why Jackson didn't feel like he deserved any special credit for the bank. She didn't agree. He'd saved Miranda's life, not to mention her unborn baby. True, luck played a part. So did courage. He could have just waited out the robbers and hoped things wouldn't turn deadly. Maybe he didn't see that last part and that was why he didn't plan on sticking around for the election results. He didn't feel like he deserved the accolades.

He did, and her admiration of him kicked up a notch. There was definitely more to the beach boy good looks of Jackson Guidry. For the first time in many years, she wanted to find out what that meant.

"It was just the sheriff and another deputy until I was hired, but she quit for, uh, personal reasons."

Riley leaned in, catching a whiff of the scents of cinnamon and earth she remembered from the bank lobby. "The town gossip on her, uh, personal reasons is rather interesting."

Rumor had it the deputy had found her married lover at the scene of a crime, both a perpetrator and a victim. While trying to steal a disputed camellia bush from his almost ex-wife, an overdose of the little blue pill had left him stiff in all the wrong ways. Riley knew more than most about the situation as her ex and the stiff's ex were now blissfully cohabitating. She heard the camellia was recovering nicely as well.

Jackson blushed and dropped his head into his palm. "I can neither confirm nor deny that story."

Riley waved away his refusal with a laugh. "Fair enough. So it's just you and the sheriff now. Keeping the streets safe. Protecting camellia bushes from middle of the night molesters."

He laughed, and the sound ribboned through Riley like hot chocolate on a cold night. "We've hired three more deputies. I actually have the most seniority, but they need someone with more experience. Someone who can see the problems before they get out of hand."

Jackson's assessment didn't sit well with Riley. "In construction, we consider all the factors we can control. The type of construction. The integrity of the foundation, soil erosion, groundwater, congestion. But we build in delays because not everything can be controlled. The weather. Material delays." Then she added on a laugh. "Protesters."

He shared her laugh and nodded thoughtfully as they talked a bit more. Her job with the crew. All the places he'd lived and worked over the years. They found out that other than craft beer, they shared a love of old movies and both could fit everything they owned in the back of their car. The familiarity eased around her before she knew it.

"Where will you go when you leave town?" More than a tinge of disappointment flared in Riley's gut at the thought of Jackson leaving town. *It's because of the sex*, she told herself. But she didn't believe that completely.

"I'm not sure." He dropped one hand from his leg to toy with the laces on her work boots. "I never did get to Florida, so probably there."

"What's in Florida?" What she wanted to know was *who* was in Florida. Was that jealousy behind her question? *Never*, she lied, watching his fingers and remembering where they'd been earlier. "Family?"

She'd gotten some information earlier from a conversation with her brother's secretary, but she didn't know how to what to do with it yet. It could be nothing. It could change everything.

"No. My family is actually here in Louisiana." He clinched his jaw, grinding his teeth before continuing. "A college buddy has a deep-sea fishing charter service. I was going to run tours with him."

Riley thought again about asking Jackson about the investment firm her brother worked for but let the thought slide away again as she watched his hand so near her leg. She didn't see Jackson being happy chartering tour boats but kept her opinion to herself. He was a man who wanted to build something. She better than anyone could recognize that in another. Otherwise, he'd never have accepted the job as deputy. "That could be fun."

He released her laces and folded his hands behind his neck, stretching. He unfurled his legs and crossed one ankle over the other. "What about you? You want to buy a house?"

Riley let Jackson turn the focus away from himself. She fidgeted with the empty beer bottle, never comfortable when the conversation turned her way. She liked being invisible. But Jackson deserved more than just the few details she'd provided earlier. "If you'd asked me yesterday, I would have said I wanted to stay in town for a while."

"Here?"

She nodded. "I bought a place at auction in Baton Rouge; put a down payment on Friday. I guess I've reached a point where I want something to call my own. Tired of being a boomer."

"Boomer?" Jackson plucked the empty beer bottle from her fingertips, leaning forward to tuck it out of the way.

"Boomer. Boom out. Means to travel and work out of town." Riley glanced back to the windows lining the east wall of the porch where she could see the tables of people gathered inside. Would she ever belong to a community like that? Maybe it no longer mattered.

"I have a brother living in New Orleans and thought this would be a good place to start. Build something of my own for a change. And work down here is steady. I could branch out. Be an independent contractor. I'm supposed to close on the property on New Year's Eve. Now I'm not sure what's possible."

"Did you talk to your brother?"

"Not yet. I called his office, but they said he was on vacation. His secretary hasn't talked to him since the day before Thanksgiving."

"But you didn't tell the office what was going on?"

"No. If it's a misunderstanding, I don't want to cause him trouble, and if the money's gone, it doesn't much matter."

Jackson sat up straighter and pulled a small notebook from his back pocket. He flipped through the worn and crinkled pages until he found what he was looking for, then he tore the page and handed it to her. "This is a list of lawyers you might consult. One is in town. Two in Baton Rouge. The other in New Orleans. I'm not sure of the law in your situation. Since your brother was an authorized user, it gets tricky, but they can advise you better than I can."

Riley couldn't see the list well enough in the dim light, so she folded it and tucked it in her jeans. "Thanks, Jackson."

"I don't want to pry," he began, and the earnestness in his face relaxed Riley when normally such a statement would put her on edge. People who wanted to pry usually told you they didn't. Then it was too late. Well-meaning nosiness had a devastating impact on her life, destroying her family with one phone call.

"It's ok," she assured him.

"Is there anything you can think of that would make your

brother ... react like this?"

She released a breath, slow, measured, contained. Like her life. She kept things close to the chest out of practice and self-preservation. Even after all these years out of the foster care system, it was her *modus operandi*. She didn't realize how much of her life she still lived like the foster care kid she'd been. Self-sufficient. Wary.

Alone.

"I'm not sure what to think to tell you the truth. I can't say I know him all that well," she confessed, the honesty startling but satisfactory on some unknown, visceral level. She'd not shared her family situation with anyone except JJ and her ex-husband. "We were separated as kids. We just reconnected."

"That must have been hard."

No apologies. Just acceptance of the fact. Riley appreciated that. She didn't need sympathy for her past, which is why she chose not to share it with many.

Jackson started to speak and paused as if to reconsider before finally saying, "I can still have Ricky checked out. I don't have much in the way of connections, but I can make some discreet inquiries about the firm he works for. Just give me his name and address."

Riley stayed quiet. Since the revelation at the bank, she'd tried every avenue she could think of to get in touch with her brother. No luck.

"You don't want to get him in trouble if it's some sort of—"

"Misunderstanding," she finished for him, though she didn't know how he could misunderstand her money was to stay in her account. "Still ..."

"I know you're very loyal to your family. I see that in how you deal with your crew." His read of her left her a little flustered. "It's not disloyal to protect yourself, Riley. Not every family is worth your loyalty."

The words, low and tight in his throat, told her he spoke from experience. But if you weren't loyal to your family, who was there to count on?

"Family is everything," she countered, watching the disagreement flash behind his eyes.

She'd not had that as a kid. Her dad threw them away

like they meant nothing. She didn't want to do that to Ricky. But what if he was in trouble? What if he needed help?

"But, OK." She breathed out the word on a silent wish to do the right thing. That Jackson could give her something to go on. "He lives on the North Shore. Covington. Works for a place called Fountain Lake Investments."

Even in the darkness, Riley could see Jackson's face pale. "Fountain Lake? My father owns Fountain Lake Investments."

Her skin tingled as the foundation of her life crumbled into something unrecognizable. "E.J. Guidry is the managing partner according to Ricky's secretary. I hoped it was a coincidence." She swallowed down the uncertainty climbing up from her gut. "Ricky is a partner. He married the boss' daughter."

Jackson sat up straight and turned his body toward her. "Richard Fontenot is your brother?"

Riley matched his posture, her nerves jumping to attention. "Fontenot is my maiden name. I kept my married name after the divorce."

He pulled out his phone and thumbed through to the pictures. "Is this him?"

She took the phone and angled it toward what little light eked out of the dust-covered bulbs, tilting her head side to side as she looked at the photo. "Maybe," she said noncommittally. The man in the picture wore a baseball cap, his arm draped around an exquisite looking blonde. Two kids, maybe seven and ten, stood in front, looking appropriately bored. "Hard to say with this picture."

Jackson raked his fingers across the back of his neck, his attention drifting out to the darkness eating up the bayou. "My sister is married to your brother."

Chapter Ten

The weekend rolled to a close, and even after several days spent tracking down his brother-in-law, Jackson still couldn't believe it was Riley's brother and that he worked for Jackson's father's investment firm in New Orleans.

"How can you not know where he is, Blythe?" he pressed his older sister, cradling the phone between his shoulder and ear while he signed the monthly expense report, monthly dispatch report, and monthly transportation report. Sheriff-ing was mostly about the paperwork from what Jackson could tell. Luckily, Connie kept the office, and the sheriff, organized and punctual.

"I didn't know the man had a sister and four brothers, Jackson," Blythe snapped. "Or that he'd been in foster care. There are bigger things I don't know about my husband than the location of his conference."

"Surely the office knows where he's at. Unless dad has gotten soft in his old age and stopped micromanaging the life of everyone at the firm." The mention of his father sent a twinge of something Jackson might have called regret had he been speaking about any other human on the planet.

"Go easy on dad, Jackson." Blythe stopped, unspoken words hanging between them. "You should come home. Make things right between you two."

He hadn't talked to his dad in almost a decade; though Blythe did her best to keep Jackson updated on the family. Not that Jackson wanted updates. His place in the family was crystal clear the day of his wedding.

"Dad knows where I live." Jackson shoved the final report into a folder and slapped it in the out box at the edge of the desk. At least he'd caught up on the paperwork. Until tomorrow morning when it started over again. "Back to Richard. This conference—"

"It starts with a C," she intoned, distracted by something in the background. "Chicago, Cancun. Cabos San Lucas. Who knows? That's all I can tell you. Richard has been preoccupied lately. I asked him if he had a girlfriend, but he denied it. Of course, Aunt Miriam said Uncle David denied having a mistress the morning they found his dead body in that other woman's bed. Bless her heart."

Jackson rubbed at the worry lines between his eyes. "What about Ethan?"

"Ethan's managing partner right now. I can't ask him to look into this without causing a panic."

The news caught Jackson unaware. "Ethan?" Their younger brother had not had much interest in working at the investment firm when Jackson left home. "Dad's not running the firm?"

Jackson thought of the men he'd seen at Gastineaux's the other night. Men he assumed were sent by his dad. But if his dad wasn't running the firm, would Ethan send men to find him? Maybe the firm was in trouble. His brother never had an interest in the business, preferring to spend money rather than help make it. That put a new spin on the money missing from Riley's accounts. A spin that left Jackson dizzy.

Blythe hesitated, drawing Jackson's attention back to their conversation. She stumbled over her words in a very un-Blythe like manner, setting Jackson's senses on alert.

"It's been the plan to let Ethan take over as managing partner since the merger fell through."

A merger forged in between the sheets of what was to be Jackson's marriage bed. He'd been working at a competing firm when he'd met Natalie. He didn't know she was the boss's daughter when she first started flirting with him.

At their wedding, Natalie had revealed she'd only married him to secure a merger between Jackson's father's firm and her own. Franklin Guidry had made it very worth her while. Jackson had walked out moments later, even when his father threatened to cut him off.

"Dad always said he'd quit work the day of his funeral."

"He's changed. He's taking time off right now. You should come see him."

Jackson hesitated, but pride won out. No one had wanted him around for anything but his name or what his family could bring to the table. That hadn't changed from what he could tell. "I could file a missing person's report on Richard, but there's no evidence of foul play so they won't put any resources behind it. Can you check your credit cards? See if there are any charges that might tell us where Ricky is right now?"

"I did that when I thought he was having an affair. There's a one-way ticket to Mexico and California, but Ricky usually travels like that, keeping his return dates open."

"Suspicious, yes. Foul play? No."

They finished the conversation on that note, with Blythe

promising to touch base after talking to Ethan. Of course, if Ethan were the one responsible for the missing funds, what would he do once he thought Jackson was on to him?

Jackson gathered his belongings. "I'm headed out for dinner, Connie," he informed the clerk as he passed by the front desk.

She nodded. "I made those calls you wanted."

He'd also done some asking around about the three men in the bar last night. They weren't staying in town. Jackson doubted the accommodations at the Belle Terre motel were adequate for the prima donna he'd seen last night.

"Any luck?" But he knew the answer. If she'd found something, she'd have told him immediately.

"Nothing within fifty miles. Lafayette gets to be problematic because of its sheer size."

"Remind the new sheriff to give you a raise when he's in office." Jackson teased, shouldering open the door.

"I will!" Connie's word followed him out onto the walkway where he melted into the end-of-day crowd.

Jackson wanted to tell Riley the news about her brother, so he headed to her hotel. He could call her, he told himself, even as he ducked into the car and revved the engine, but he wanted to see her. In fact, he'd not wanted to see a woman fully clothed since ... well since he'd mistakenly walked down the aisle.

The girl of his dreams turned into a nightmare before the cake was served. And she'd taken most of his family with her as they tried to save the merger. Riley showed more loyalty to a brother she hadn't seen in almost twenty years than his father who thought nothing of selling his son into marriage to solidify a business deal.

Where would Riley's loyalty lay if it turned out his

brother or father were the ones responsible for her missing money?

As he bumped the police cruiser into the hotel parking lot, Jackson noted Santa Claus hanging around the periphery of a dozen or so men gathered near two parked vans. A large, portable BBQ pit was tethered to the cab of a one-ton pick-up belched waves of smoke, heat shimmering over its lid. Moths flitted in the cones of light from the overhead lamps, lighting up the parking lot, and a hazy gauze of smoke painted the night in muted shades of grey and white. The muscles knotted between Jackson's shoulder blades, the remnants of a tension that had not dissipated since his conversation with his sister.

A placard with LCB Construction was prominently displayed on the passenger side door of each van, the bold text superimposed over a silhouette of a city landscape. Clean. Simple. Jackson liked it. He liked Will Kenner as well, LCB's owner, even though he'd been married to Riley. Something Jackson refused to name grumbled in his chest when he thought of Riley with another man.

The men, he assumed members of the LCB crew, were as diverse as a UN council meeting. Jackson knew from the gossip mill that Kenner hired recently released convicts. The new cop inside him, the one protective of the town that had given him a chance, thought about running a background check to see if any of them would bring trouble. But none of them had given him a reason to be concerned, and Jackson knew what it was like to be judged based on perception.

Death stares beneath mirrored sunglasses and baseball caps tugged low homed in on Jackson, heavy enough to bruise and break bone. Tension vibrated on tattooed muscles. These were not men fleshy and soft from sitting behind a desk. Jackson had been in his share of fights and could hold his own, but he knew without reservation these guys would kick his ass if they decided to do just that.

He backed into an empty parking space anyway, despite the ass-kickers waiting for him, stopping next to a line of Harleys. *No crotch-rockets allowed* an invisible sign warned.

An older man, his dark face impartial as he gave Jackson the once over, broke away from the others and rapped on a partially open door. Riley stuck her head out, her attention on her co-worker first before drifting to Jackson as he parked the vehicle. Her initial smile dropped into a frown as she struggled for a neutral expression, aware of the men watching her. She disappeared back into the room.

Without a visible cue, the men tightened their ranks, forming a protective semi-circle. What—or whom—they were protecting, Jackson easily guessed.

Jackson hauled himself out of the car, purposefully avoiding putting a hand on his gun belt, and shut the car door. He wished he'd changed out of his uniform, but even then, it's not like his identity was a secret. He'd been on-site during the protest, helping the sheriff keep the peace. No one minded him then. Today was a different story. He walked toward the tailgate party, and their attention shifted back to him.

"Gentlemen," he said, going for friendly and casual. Jackson concentrated on keeping his posture relaxed, arms at his side, hands open, even as his gaze jumped from man to man in rapid assessment. He nodded to the BBQ pits. "Smells wonderful. Steaks?"

"Yeah," one of the guys confirmed, the biggest man Jackson had ever seen. Jackson topped out about six-six. This guy had a few inches on him. Silently, the men marked him as one of the leaders, their posture turned slightly toward him as they stood farther back. "*Shank* steaks. My favorite." The hint of a Hispanic accent textured his words.

Jackson nodded thoughtfully, scrubbed a hand across his jaw and to the back of his neck. "Personally, I like pork. A nice, juicy roasted piece of pig."

Steak Guy's eyes widened, his smile going thin and tight in the landscape of a face probably older than it looked. Obsidian eyes catalogued Jackson, and the man's chest tightened as he held and slowly released his breath. "I'm not a fan of pig."

"I'm sure you hated every bite of those three pork chops you ate last night, Noé."

Riley pushed through the wall of testosterone, her tall frame dwarfed by the men who called her boss. She'd foregone the ponytail, instead letting the long black hair fall down her back. It curled up slightly at the ends, the late evening sun a pallet of shine in the midnight of her hair. Jackson wanted to rub the curls between his fingers. He suddenly hated the thought of leaving Belle Terre, of leaving Riley, behind. Would he miss her? Yeah. Yeah, he would.

She stopped beside Noé who looked away; not cowed, just cautious. Not an easy decision by the tension jumping in the corded muscles in his neck and jaw. He didn't want to go pissing off the boss, Jackson figured. Or maybe the man's protective instincts were sharpened on more than just keeping his job.

"Hey, Jackson." Her eyes stayed on him, but Jackson knew she sensed the anger emanating from the man standing next to her based on the rigid line of her posture. Riley took a step forward, but Noé cut off her path and Riley stopped short. A not-so-happy look tightened her face.

"He's not good for you, Seola Jae. He's sniffin' after you for the wrong reasons."

Riley went to bypass Noé, but he again stopped her progress. The first spark of anger flared to life in the jade eyes, a similar burn starting in Jackson's gut. He leaned forward on the balls of his feet, aware in the periphery of his vision the men still watching him, waiting for him to make a move.

She leveled a glare his direction. "So were you. Back down or I'll make you back down."

Despite the difference in sizes, Jackson put his money on Riley.

A staccato tic pulsed at Noé's temple. She'd hit the bulls-eye, and it gnawed at him. "I'm not *un forastero*." Outsider.

"I'm not *una fuente*," Jackson said the word *insider* quiet like, still not moving but ready to do so if needed. His fists itched to clench and lash out. He lowered his head a fraction.

"I'm not impressed because you speak my language, *cabron*."

Jackson shrugged. "I guess that puts us on even ground."

"You hurt her, I'll kill you." Noé's threat growled across the distance. The other men closed ranks in support.

"Fuck, Noé," Riley slashed the loose hair back from her face, tucking each side behind her ears in an absent gesture. "You trying to get yourself thrown back in prison?"

"If I hurt her, I think you'll have to wait in line." Jackson looked to Riley. "She can take care of herself."

"I know that." Noé's voice growled, defensive.

Jackson crossed his arms and squared off with the bigger man. Tension fused steel into his spine, and he widened his stance. "Yet here we are. You must have doubts."

It's not always about right or wrong, the former sheriff had told him his first day. *It's mostly about diffusing the situation so it doesn't explode.*

Jackson was not excited about the prospect of backing down. But he had a duty, a responsibility to the people who hired him. To those that shared his uniform. He had to let a cooler heads prevail even when he didn't want to.

"Why don't you guys just whip 'em out?" Riley stepped forward from the line of muscle, shaking her head. "I'm sure JJ has a tape measure in the work truck."

"You're not usin' my tape measure for *that*," JJ deadpanned, and a few chuckles from those farthest from the action broke through the wall of tension. Noé dropped his shoulders, and Jackson eased the breath from his lungs.

"Besides," the older man drawled, crossing his arms over the broad width of his chest. "That's the kind of thing you can measure by the smile on your partner's face."

Riley tried to wipe the smile off her face as she stepped forward, but the sound of the hoots and hollers told her she'd failed miserably. "Always trying to get out of work, JJ."

She crossed the parking lot with easy steps, having traded her work boots for tennis shoes. A faded denim jacket, almost an exact match to the jeans encasing her long legs, softened her, not that she was all the hardened to begin with. Maybe it was the company, Jackson told himself, looking back to the work crew watching them. She was a part of them, and yet separate. A quote he'd once read came into his thoughts.

Love the rose yet leave it on its stem.

His mother would be relieved to know his expensive prep school education was not a complete waste. His Ivy League education ... that was another story.

But it explained Riley. You couldn't contain her, couldn't cut her from her own way without losing the bloom.

"Is there news?" Riley jumped right to the point after she

scooted into the front seat, and they shut the doors to the cruiser.

Jackson shook his head. "My brother is acting as managing partner, so my sister is going to reach out and see if she can get answers about Ricky without setting off any alarms. Sorry it's not more, but unless you want to file a police report, we don't have a crime. Ricky's job was to manage your money, and there are reasonable explanations on where it could be right now."

He turned over the engine and pulled from the parking lot. Noé's attention followed them out as Jackson turned onto Second Street. Jackson suspected Noé would be waiting, regardless of when he and Riley returned.

He steered through town, absently watching the streets and alleys, and quickly filled Riley in on the rest of his conversation with Blythe, the uselessness of a missing person's report, and the state police's admission it wouldn't get much attention. He didn't leave anything out. Jackson didn't want to scare her, but he also didn't want to keep her in the dark. She wasn't a person who needed protecting, despite the show the work crew gave back at the hotel. But he knew that was mainly for him.

"Don't take this the wrong way," Riley started cautiously, scrubbing her hands against the length of her thigh. "But I've also considered that someone in Ricky's firm could be responsible for the missing money."

"I've considered the same thing," he replied, the weight of it heavier than he would have expected. Despite the years away, the unspoken accusation against his father and brother awakened a protective streak in him. "But like you, I can't see either of them doing this. Dad's too arrogant to think he'd need to steal, and E.J.… frankly, E.J. isn't smart enough to get away with it, and he knows it."

"But you haven't seen them in ten years."

That protective side of him flared to life. "And you hadn't seen your brother in twenty."

"Touché." Riley rested her chin in the vee between her thumb and forefinger, propping her elbow on the door. "Not telling his wife about us, it's like Ricky was trying to erase his past."

Jackson thought of his own reasons for leaving his family ten years ago. "People want ... need a fresh start sometimes."

"Is that why you stay away from your family? You wanted a fresh start."

Her question caught him off guard. He white-knuckled the steering wheel. "It's like I said the other night, not every family is worth your loyalty."

"Ours was," Riley said painfully.

He kept his eyes on the road. "I'll listen if you want to talk. No questions."

She swallowed hard. "There's not much to say. Mom died. We were at home alone one afternoon while dad was at work and a neighbor called family services. They came and took us away. I was almost ten. Ricky a year older."

He held back the apology, the *I'm sorry* people say when there's nothing else to say about a crappy situation. His sister had said it to him when he'd found out his old man had used him to further business interests. The words, even if well-intentioned, were worse than meaningless.

She thumped her fist against the door frame, and tension filled the interior of the vehicle. "I can't believe any of this is happening. I know I don't know Ricky anymore. He could be lying to me, but my gut tells me something is going on."

Experience made Jackson look at everything, and everyone, with suspicion. He wasn't good at taking people at face value. Too much experience with being fooled by ulterior motives kept him wary.

"Blythe has nothing that would point us in a direction. For now, we have to wait. Let's see what she gets from my brother. Just asking him may topple the house of cards."

Riley slumped back in her seat, crossing her legs and arms in a tight package of tension. "Patience is definitely not one of my virtues."

"Somehow I'm not surprised," he joked, pleased when she grinned back at him. "I've got to make a stop at the hardware store." Jackson offered as a way to switch gears. The two of them didn't have plans—he knew she was at the hotel the way you know things in a small town. Gossip and routine. If Riley wasn't at work, she was at the hotel. He had a few projects he needed to get done and needed to pick up supplies. Besides, he liked her company. "You want to join me or you want me to bring you back to the hotel?"

Riley let her shoulders drop and reached up to trace the bow of his mouth with the tip of a finger. "I'll go with you. Thanks."

Jackson turned left onto Federal and then right onto Highway 10, following the road beneath the overpass as they headed into the main part of town. They rode in silence, not even the radio to fill the gap in conversation, but Jackson didn't mind. His mind did its own conversation, thinking about his list of projects and needed supplies. And trying to ignore the simple scent of Riley being so close.

He hadn't noticed it when they sat together at Gastineaux's. Perhaps the day's labors—not to mention their own in the trailer, his brain reminded him as muscles low in his body clenched—had washed it from her skin with good, old fashioned sweat. Another fragrance that both suited her and proved tantalizing in its own regard.

Perhaps he'd just been too preoccupied with her being naked and so willing beneath him. But the something—natural and subtle—had his erection already pushing against his zipper. She'd left her hair loose, and the straight length shadowed her face like a curtain shielding her expression from scrutiny.

They arrived at the hardware store, and Jackson whipped into a parking space a little faster than he intended. Riley braced her hands against the dash as she strained against the seat belt.

"Eager to be here?" she joked, releasing her seat belt once the engine cut off.

Jackson pocketed the keys and met her at the rear bumper. "My second favorite place to be."

"Oh, yeah? Where's your favorite?"

"Inside you."

"Hmmmm," Riley moaned, sliding her hand subtly up the back of his thigh before reaching underneath his jacket and tucking it in the waistband of his pants. Her fingers played beneath his boxers.

As they approached the glass sliding doors to the store, Jackson caught their reflection. To an outsider, all it looked like was her arm around his waist. He knew better. So did his body. "You are a very evil person, Ms. Kenner."

"Why, Sheriff Guidry," Riley mimicked an exaggerated southern accent. "Do you prefer your females all swoony and pure as the driven snow?"

He led them into the store, reaching for her hand. "Hell, no."

Their fingers linked briefly, and their eyes connected.

Awareness zinged between them, like water on a hot

skillet. Recognition of the attraction. The sexual chemistry. The desire. They released the bond simultaneously. The emptiness lingered, a feeling unfamiliar and uncomfortable to Jackson.

Jackson grabbed a cart from its corral and pushed it down the first aisle. "Swoony females don't interest me in the least."

"Good. Because I don't swoon."

"Somehow I'm not surprised," he repeated the earlier comment, pleased to see a hint of scarlet blossom up from her neckline.

They stopped in front of a line of chains of varying sizes, and Jackson signaled to the store clerk who then measured out the needed length.

Riley leaned around Jackson's body, the smell of her shampoo teasing his senses, watching as the clerk cut the metal links with a bolt cutter. She stretched up on her tiptoes, but she still barely scraped his chin. "That's a little bit more than what we should need for a second date, don't you think?" Her breath tickled his jaw, and he grinded his teeth to keep from stealing a kiss.

The clerk's hands faltered, but his eyes never strayed from the task at hand.

"Second date?" Jackson thanked the stunned clerk, who glanced cautiously over his shoulder as he returned to the counter and dropped the chain into the cart.

Excitement coiled around his insides at Riley's hesitant grin and the way she avoided eye contact. Was she nervous? Or maybe just unused to flirting. He would put money on the latter. As bold and brash as she appeared, Riley didn't seem the flirtatious type. He doubted her life on the road with the muscle brigade he'd met at the hotel left much room—or many options-for dating and a social life.

"We haven't had a first date. My dates don't pay their own way."

He stopped in front of a display of sturdy locks and bent down to get a closer look at ones suitable for an outdoor gate. Jackson could relate to the sparse dating. He'd traveled much of the last ten years, ever since walking away from his life, never staying in a one place more than a year. It didn't lend much to developing a relationship and one-night stands left him feeling like a jerk, even when he made it clear he didn't want more. He hadn't felt like that with Riley, however. In truth, he wasn't sure what he was feeling about Riley.

When they'd started, they were both leaving town. Now that she was staying, he tried to figure out if it changed things. He massaged a tense spot at the back of his neck, watching her from the corner of his eye.

She'd moved behind the cart, putting the barrier between them. Uncertainty hooded her eyes; the first sign he'd seen she was anything but confident in her skin. Riley folded her arms across the cart's handle and leaned her weight on her elbows, turning her body away from him at an angle as if to shield her heart. Those jaded eyes bored holes in the distance.

"Having you pay for dinner after sex didn't feel right. I didn't want you to think you owed me anything. I knew what I was doing. I don't regret it."

He pushed to his feet, dropped the lock in the cart, and folded his body down to match her stance. It put them at eye level and let him study her face. Inky black hair fell forward across cheeks slashed with the colors of her discomfort. He brushed back one side and cupped her face, turning it toward him.

"I don't either. We sort of did things backwards. Started with the middle rather than at the beginning."

There was a slight crook in her nose, as if it had been broken at some point. And a scar at her temple that disappeared beneath the hairline. Work accident? Childhood injury? The thought that it could be something worse, that someone touched her in anger, spiked sharp and painful in his gut.

He was in trouble.

Chapter Eleven

Riley couldn't think of anything to say right off, somewhat lost in the way Jackson looked at her. It warmed places down deep. Swoony came to mind, and it put her off balance and set her on edge.

Damn. After all these years I'm finally becoming a girl, she thought, but no regret filled her.

That wasn't how she saw herself—some female who chased after a man for any reason. And her feminine wiles were seriously out of practice, not even something she'd pulled out of her reserves when she first hooked up with her ex-husband. They'd just fit together. They wanted the same thing. Independence. Security. Of course, she knew now he'd probably been in love with someone else which said a lot about her judgment where men were concerned.

Jackson'd told her back at Gastineaux's he wasn't looking to stay in Belle Terre, so that settled it in her mind. Even with her own future in doubt, it was clear she and Jackson wouldn't be together for the long haul. She'd just enjoy the time with him. "I'm good with middles. To quote the great philosopher Sandra Bullock, beginnings could be scary, endings usually sad. The middle was what counted."

"Hope Floats." He pressed his forehead to hers with a soft clunk, and she couldn't help but smile. The gesture, both intimate and casually playful, weaseled its way into spaces so empty they echoed.

"Are you a fan of chick flicks?"

"A necessary evil for men between eighteen and eighty." Then his grin broadened. "You like romance novels *and* chick flicks?"

Her entire body flushed at the memory of him seeing her book in the construction trailer. "We have a lot of down time on the road. Reading fills the void."

"Ms. Kenner, what would your co-workers think?"

"Nothing if they know what's good for them."

Jackson rolled his shoulders and stretched back to his full height, tugging the cart with him, forcing her to stand or fall to the floor. He pulled a few more things off the shelves as they passed through the aisles. Window caulking. Two door hinges. A filter for the AC. Door alarm. A handful of fuses. Finally, a new mailbox.

"That's quite the project list you got going," Riley peeked at the items filling the cart. "Worried about idle hands?"

His grin exposed the dimple she'd noticed in the bank while she was handcuffed in the lobby.

"Are you offering an alternative to keep them busy?"

"Maybe," she started as her lusty thoughts were interrupted by a commotion behind them.

Riley turned to see the family of foster kids from the bank spill in through the front door, their laughter and squeals of delight breaking the heaviness of her and Jackson's interlude in middle of aisle two.

Decked out in matching Santa hats, the kids began to chant, "Tree! Tree! Tree!"

Her little admirer from the bank skidded through the door seconds later, pushing a girl in a pimped-out wheelchair, the sparkly streamers on the back outnumbered only by the tiara stickers glittering on every available surface. Even the hefty helping of duct tape couldn't keep the front wheel from wobbling precariously as the kid reached Mach two around the first corner.

"*Mas rapido*, Donavan!"

But Donavan planted his heels and ground to a halt, mouth agape as his foster brothers and sisters spotted Santa Claus in the distance and took off toward the startled looking man.

"Come on, Donavan!" Tiara Girl prompted, wheeling free of Donavan's grip, streamers flying behind her as she zipped up on Santa.

Dad stumbled in behind the bunch and resettled a disgruntled toddler on his hip, pulling a clump of his sandy hair from the baby's determined grasp and settling his hand on Donavan's shoulder. The man glanced up sheepishly, looked past Riley, and waved. "Hey, Jackson."

At the sound of Jackson's name, Donavan's euphoric stupor broke, and with a sharp breath, he focused on Jackson for a split second before hightailing it after his brothers and sisters. Riley grinned but hid it behind a raised hand.

The man's attention hopped between the two of them, and Riley knew their presence would be reported to the boardwalk posse by morning. Maybe sooner.

"Sorry," he offered as he backed away, shrugging the baby up higher on his hip and trailing his eyes after the disappearing family. "They're a little excited about getting the tree. I'll try and keep the destruction to a minimum. Promise."

"No apologies needed, Patrick," Jackson quickly offered, waving away the offer.

"Javier's right behind me if he hasn't run for the hills." Patrick kept moving toward the crew of kids surrounding the poor Santa huddled in on himself protectively. "Would you point him our direction?"

"Of course. Go rescue Santa." Jackson studied the cringing St. Nick, then returned his attention to Patrick. "He looks a little out of his element."

Patrick fast-walked toward the cowering Santa, ushering the kids away and through a double sliding door.

"Patrick or Santa?" Riley asked, letting her gaze follow the kids but keeping her face neutral. She'd loved Christmas once upon a time and still found ways to torture her crew during the holiday season. Last year she wrapped the crew truck in tinsel. No one would ride with her for a month.

"Definitely Santa."

Jackson's tone broke through Riley's daydreaming and focused her attention around the rather sad looking Santa Claus as he took off through a side door.

"Did Patrick say something about a tree?" Riley asked Jackson once the noise level dropped, then the realization dawned. "Christmas trees?" Riley bounced once, twice, on the balls of her feet, then tamped down her excitement. She tucked her fingertips in the front pocket of her jeans.

Jackson grinned in that infuriatingly cute way of his. "You love Christmas."

He crossed his arms across his chest, studying her as she worked to regain some dignity. It was pretty much a lost cause.

"You're bouncing in your boots."

She stopped mid-bounce. "Construction forewomen do not bounce," she announced.

He leaned back on his heels, the now familiar smirk creasing his face. "You're an elf girl."

Riley waved him off with an upturned hand, spun slowly, and walked farther into the store. But her gaze drifted the direction in which Patrick and his family disappeared. Strains of *Here Comes Santa Claus* drifted through the sliding doors as they swished open and close.

She caught sight of Donavan stealing a peep from behind the corner of the door, his forehead pressed to the glass, the fog of his breath condensing around his mouth. He watched her and Jackson with a look of curiosity mixed with determination. She gave him a little finger wave, swallowing the lump of memories. His jaw dropped again, the kid would need a chin strap at this rate, before he pushed away from the door, leaving a kid-sized face print behind.

A man rushed into the store, a harried but content look on his face as he scanned the aisles. His eyes locked with Jackson, both hands lifting in question.

"Out back, Javier," Jackson offered to the silent inquiry.

Something stung the back of her eyes, and Riley had to breathe deeply to force air past the tightness in her throat. Memories of holidays and birthdays and Fourth of July fireworks came rushing back to crowd those empty places before she could stop them.

They weren't memories she pulled out any longer, letting them fade and cobweb out of necessity and self-preservation. The only way to survive being abandoned by your dad was to forget you'd once been happy, wanted, loved. If things could change that quickly, in the space of time it took to burn a birthday cake, then nothing was forever. Which brought her back to now. And Jackson.

She cleared her throat and turned to see him watching her, the wheels turning behind those see-everything eyes that said the cop in him was busy trying to decipher her. A deep-set wrinkle creased his forehead, but he wiped it from his face.

"You'll break something thinking that hard." She looked away, continuing down the aisle, ignoring the jitters that white-knuckled her grip on the cart's handle, but Jackson peeled her fingers from the cart.

He knocked a fist against his temple. "Hard as a rock. I think I'm safe," he joked as he pushed the cart against the wall. "What I need is out back." He crooked a finger at her and started walking backwards, abandoning their cart. "I need a tree. *You* need a tree."

Riley rolled her eyes, but her insides did a little jump, and her feet took a step forward all on their own. "I don't need a tree."

"In fact, you need two trees." Jackson now waggled two fingers at her, coaxing her forward with the silly gesture. "One for the work trailer and one for your hotel room."

He's impossible, Riley shrugged to herself, but she noticed how the teasing deepened the cleft in his chin and darkened the blue in his eyes to the color of her favorite pair of denim. "Two trees? Are you nuts? The guys would never let me live it down."

Jackson ducked beneath the upper edge of the sliding doors as they swished open. Damn, the man really was that tall. "You're the boss. Put elf stickers on their hard hats."

The snort caught her by surprise, and she slapped a hand over her mouth to stifle the sound. She hated her laugh—not the one she practiced and perfected in the mirror when another kid had made fun of her at school. This was the real one that still came out when something really got her going. "Reindeer antlers." Another snort. "With bells."

She'd been kidnapped by aliens and replaced with a stranger. Riley barely recognized herself. After only knowing him a few weeks, Jackson had her acting like ... she turned the thought over as she took the final step into the back room, overwhelmed for an instant by the scent of pine and woodsmoke, Christmas carols and laughter.

A normal person, her brain finished, and she closed her eyes against the thought.

"Hey," he was suddenly close, and she opened her eyes to see the tips of his boots. She looked up, and he reached out with his right hand to tip her chin back with one finger. The "I see everything" look in his face punched her in the gut. "I'm sorry I pushed."

Riley took a step back, cleared her throat. Everywhere she looked were things she couldn't have. Kids and moms and dads. Couples hand in hand.

The wave of loneliness chilled her, but Riley knew she was luckier than most. Even as a foster kid, she'd had a decent family. None of the horror stories you hear ever happened to her. And she had her crew, JJ and Will. Even though he had someone new in his life, Riley didn't doubt he'd be there for her if she needed him. They were a family.

Her family.

She took in the people surrounding her, the lights strung overhead connecting them in a weird way in her head. Jackson stood just a few feet away, an expectant look on his face, the penetrating stare of someone who saw things no one else did. Things she didn't want him to see. But it didn't frighten her as much. She wanted this, she realized. She wanted to stay in Belle Terre. Build something that didn't require brick and mortar and permits. Become part of the community. She looked at Jackson and something flickered she'd never considered possible.

Hope.

Chapter Twelve

Jackson watched the subtle change in Riley transform her. He didn't know what thoughts mixed around in her head as she studied the small crowd of people milling around the tree lot. The little boy, Donavan, held her interest longer than anyone, and he didn't think it was because the kid had a massive crush on her.

He recognized the look on her face, had seen it on others often enough. Even on his own. The distrust, the wariness, but it was more than that. There was a sharp edge to her eyes waiting to see when the next blow would come.

Not if, but when.

They crossed through the door that separated the tree lot from the main store, the symbolism of passage not lost on Jackson. Something had changed for Riley. He hoped it was a good thing, and he hoped he had something to do with it. Donavan straggled close behind them, staying hidden as much as a room full of Christmas trees and people permitted. Riley walked forward cautiously.

"Okay," she said to the room, catching Donavan's eye.

His tiny body vibrated with contained excitement. "Okay," she repeated

Jackson knew the answer wasn't for him or Donavan exactly. But he took it that way because he wanted to be the one to put that look of contentment on Riley's face.

He fell in step beside her. "You'll get a tree?"

She held up her hand and mimicked his two-fingered waggle. "*Two* trees. But think Charlie Brown not Norman Rockwell."

Apparently Donavan didn't need to know more than that. The kid took off like a rocket, disappearing into the fake forest faster than an over-caffeinated squirrel. Jackson laughed. "That kid'll get lift off if he moves any faster."

Jackson swept an open palm toward the array of trees, offering her the lead. Riley ambled forward, stuffing her fingertips in the front pockets of her jeans. He connected the gesture to a memory from childhood, when his mother would take him and his brother shopping. She made them put their hands in their pockets so they wouldn't be tempted to touch anything.

Perhaps Riley tucked her hands away to keep from reaching for things, things she wasn't sure would be there if she wanted them. With that thought, Jackson wanted to give her the world. He couldn't tell her that he knew with certainty. She'd disappear faster than cookies on Christmas Eve.

For tonight, he'd settle for two Christmas trees.

They joined the crowds strolling through the rows of trees. The silence between them was comfortable, but Jackson found he wanted to fill it. He wanted to know everything there was to know about Riley Kenner. "How long have you worked construction?"

"Sixteen years." She gave a half-laugh. "Wow. It sounds like an eternity when you say it out loud."

"I think you have a few good years left before retirement."

"I hope so."

The rest spilled from her without prompting.

"JJ's wife was friends with my second foster mother. When I turned eighteen, I asked him for a job, and he gave it to me. Will was already working for the crew. We'd gotten married, and the owner decided to retire. Will and I bought it from him, and when we divorced, it didn't seem to matter. We worked well together so I stayed on."

Changing the subject, he looked at her from the corner of his eye. "Can I ask you about something Noé said back at the hotel?"

Riley kicked at an invisible obstacle with her boot. "Seola Jae?" She said the name with an easy inflection.

He ambled closer, letting her set the pace and direction.

"Noé and I actually met when we were both in foster care. Not the same family but we went to the same school. Birds of a feather and all that. It's a family name," she provided, turning them toward the center of the lot. "I'm named after a great grandmother, but I started going by my middle name when ..." She paused, avoiding his gaze. "When I started junior high. My grandmother was one tough lady from what I remember."

"Just like her namesake."

Complimenting her inside his head had become second nature. It was the first time he could remember saying it out loud. She needed to hear those things, and often. "You've got to know that about yourself. Tough. Accomplished. Intelligent." He paused, and they turned to one another at the same instant. "Beautiful."

She ducked her head sheepishly, swiping back a wedge of hair.

He'd made her uncomfortable. Not what he wanted. "The name," he amended. "It's beautiful."

She nodded, and they walked in silence for a minute.

"Riley is my mother's maiden name. I kept it after...when I got out on my own."

There was more she wasn't telling him but it was ok. He felt honored that she'd opened up. It also explained Noé's protectiveness though Jackson wondered if Noé's feeling stopped at friendship.

Jackson pointed out a few trees that Charlie Brown might have put his stamp of approval on, but Riley shook her head at each.

"According to her daughter—my grandmother—I'm a lot like her." Riley trailed a hand over several pine boughs poking out from the main line of the tree. Always touching the one that didn't fit the perfect line of the tree's inward slope. "Too independent for my own good. Always looking for greener pastures."

Jackson considered that for a moment. "I guess if you're always looking for what's better, you won't appreciate what you have." The words hit closer to home than he would have liked, so he looked for a distraction from the seriousness of their thoughts.

Right on cue, Donavan burst from a side aisle, a collection of pine needles barely hanging onto a crooked branch clutched in both hands. He slapped the spindly trunk against the pavement, and a shower of needles carpeted his feet.

Jackson stuffed back a smile and swallowed the laugh beneath a cough. But it didn't matter. Donavan's eyes were all for Riley.

Jackson cleared the laughter from his voice, not wanting to hurt Donavan's feelings. "That's quite a tree you found. What do you think, Riley?"

She stepped back, giving the tree careful consideration. Riley propped her chin in the vee of her thumb and forefinger, making appreciative sounds as she circled the boy and his tree.

"I think it's perfect."

Donavan snapped to attention. "Really?"

Stunned, Jackson's jaw dropped. It was the first word he'd heard the kid utter since coming to town almost two months ago.

"Think you can find me another one like it? Maybe a little taller?"

Donavan nodded so hard Jackson could hear his teeth click. The boy slapped the tree into Jackson's hands then shot out again before they could offer another word.

Mr. Terrebonne, the store manager, appeared from nowhere and relieved them of what passed for a tree. "I'll see if I can save what needles are left," he mumbled before disappearing toward the crackling fire pit in the center of the tree lot.

Riley rubbed her arms, and Jackson saw the quick shiver run down her frame. "It's colder in here than it is outside." She pointed to the raging fire and turned down one of the tree lined aisles. "Even with that."

Jackson shrugged out of his jacket and draped it over her shoulders. She didn't protest to his surprise, just nodded and threaded her arms through the sleeves. The jacket swallowed her, and he ignored the fleeting thoughts of how much he liked seeing her in something of his. The possessiveness washed over him, drowning him beneath the wave.

Jackson corralled a toddler as he barreled through the

branches of a tree from the left, a harried woman quickly rounding the corner to snatch him up with an apologetic grin. "Sorry, Jackson."

"No problem, Miz Aucoin." He cleared his throat as the southern accent he'd neutralized through years of speech class came out. His dad said no one would take a man seriously who sounded like a hick from the bayou. So, Jackson whittled away that part of himself, like he had with so many other things until there was nothing left.

He fell in step beside Riley, thumbs hitched in the front pockets of his utility belt. He measured his steps carefully, so he didn't pull ahead of her or fall behind. Just staying even, equal.

"Mr. Terrebonne lived in Michigan," Jackson explained, nodding to the man as he pushed a tree through the baler, catching it one handed when it popped out the other side neatly wrapped and ready for transport. "He misses winter, so he cranks up the air conditioning and lights the fire pit every year." He pointed to a side table near the circle of stones containing the massive blaze. "Can I interest you in a toasted marshmallow?"

He was already headed that way, though, recognizing her love of all things Christmas with the obvious sparkle lighting her eyes. Or maybe that was just the blazing fire pit. She would follow; though she'd do so with pretend reluctance, maybe worried that the wanting of something would mean it would be taken away.

He thought of her hands still tucked in her front pockets. Jackson hated that look on her face. He'd never wanted for anything really. His father's approval, maybe, but he had better odds of winning the Powerball, so he'd learned long ago to stop waiting for that. For reasons Jackson didn't understand, he wanted ... needed ... to make sure Riley didn't have to do the same thing.

He picked up two skewers and turned just as she retrieved the bag of gigantic marshmallows. The curtain of inky hair cascaded forward over her shoulders, framing half her face in shadow while the firelight touched the curve of her other cheek in wavering gold and amber.

She grabbed his skewer and slid a marshmallow down the length. Heat shimmied its way up his spine and crashed to the pit of his belly as he watched. *They're only marshmallows*, he reminded himself.

Based on the rapt attention Riley gave to loading up the skewers, she avoided his gaze on purpose. The shit-eating grin on her face told him a lot as well.

Smugness tightened the corners of his mouth.

"Stop it," she warned, reaching into the bag again. "You smirk more than a virgin in a whorehouse."

He handed over a loaded skewer and settled beside her on the stone bench by the fire pit. "Pot. Kettle. Ring a bell?"

Donavan burst through a line of trees, startling them both. He presented Riley a new tree like a mountain climber staking a flag on Everest.

Riley *hmm-hmmed* thoughtfully but pronounced it "too fat" and Donavan departed with the new information.

Jackson laughed. "Too fat?"

"Can't let him think I'm easy," she answered, rotating her marshmallow skewer in a slow circle over the low flames at the edge of the fire.

Jackson pulled his burning marshmallows back, blew out the flames and plucked the end piece of gooiness from the skewer before holding it out to Riley. "No one who's ever met you would call you easy."

She opened her mouth and leaned her body forward

slightly, closer but still holding back. He slipped the confection between her lips, the sugary fluff stuck to the bow of her mouth, a beacon of temptation calling to every element of Jackson's psyche. Firelight danced in the dark depths of her eyes, like moonlight cresting on the silhouette of the horizon. It left him weightless and heavy at the same time.

He ran a thumb across the cleft of her chin, then to the corner of her mouth to swipe away a trace of the sweet treat. Strength. Independence. Loneliness. He recognized it in her. She touched him on all levels, a mirror to his soul. Without thinking, Jackson bent closer, brushing an almost chaste kiss against her mouth.

Neither moved.

Neither breathed.

If he hadn't heard a giggle from the sidelines of the fire pit, he'd have thought time ceased to move.

Riley pulled back, dropping her chin to her chest, the protective veil of hair concealing her face and tension pulling the line of her shoulders inward. The wariness of her body posture drew him forward, lacing his fingers with hers. He smiled and winked at her, relief washing over him when she returned the smile.

Jackson twisted to see two girls of nine or ten watching them from behind a towering Douglas fir. They were bent toward one another whispering conspiratorially until they realized they'd been caught and ducked farther behind their Christmas-y cover.

But the spell was broken, Jackson realized. Riley turned her body away, no longer touching him at any point. The guarded Riley was back and at full attention. He missed the other Riley instantly.

She swiped a drip of melting marshmallow, sucking the gooey sugar from the tip of her finger and nodding toward the store and his cart sitting just outside the sliding doors. "Are you fixing up a new place or old place?"

On to safer topics, Jackson realized, disappointed she'd pulled back emotionally as well as physically. But he understood. She was used to making it on her own, so for now, he'd let her.

"Neither really. Some of that is for a family in town. Some for my neighbor. I'm watching the place while it's for sale and she's out of town. I saw lights on the other night so think some kids may be taking advantage of her absence. I want to secure the gate."

"Very neighborly of you."

Jackson nodded in response and focused his attention on Riley. Or more accurately, her mouth as she again sucked a line of sticky sugar from her finger.

Did he mention he was in trouble?

Chapter Thirteen

As Riley licked a blob of stickiness from the corner of her mouth, she felt Jackson's attention warm on her skin. She practically sizzled with the awareness, as if his gaze held weight and heat wrapped up in a silken caress.

She also realized the intensity didn't make her uncomfortable. She'd always hated being center stage, avoiding Christmas pageants, spelling bees, court proceedings. Anything that would put her front and center of a crowd. The chance to disappoint someone, to fail at the job given her no matter how small, was a risk she'd not been willing to take. Of course, she'd failed everyone she ever loved in the privacy of her own home.

Home. The thought brought a stab of want.

Beyond the Christmas tree lot, Riley could see Donavan's foster dad, Javier, and the store manager wrestling a massive tree onto the roof of a blue minivan while Patrick marshalled the kids toward the front of the store. The American dream hogtied on four wheels. To her left, the mom they'd seen earlier now chased after her little boy as he tore off his clothes amid squeals of delight. The two tween voyeurs stole another soulfully longing glance at Jackson.

She scanned the area for Donavan but didn't find him near. Maybe her tree elf had abandoned his search. A twinge of disappointment needled her.

She returned her attention to Jackson, not sure what the look crowded behind the sparkle in his eyes meant as he watched her from beneath the arc of lashes. She didn't like the knowledge in his careful gaze. No secret stayed safe from Jackson Guidry, so she turned the conversation toward him.

"Your neighbor's place. This wouldn't be the one out on Lake Opelousas Drive? Big silver trailer on the water with the half-finished shotgun house."

Jackson nodded. "Yeah, that's it."

She leaned forward, crossing her arms and resting her elbows on her knees, unsure how much she wanted to tell him. Of course, did it matter? Whether she stayed or not, he wouldn't be around.

"I took a look at it when I was here surveying for the build. Water and land access. The trailer is good enough for the short-term, and it wouldn't take much to complete the exterior of the house to make it livable. I bought it at auction on Friday."

"I'd heard there was a bidder but that the sale was pending until close. I sort of guessed it was you after the bank incident."

She closed her eyes and dropped her chin. "This town will think I'm insane. First my bulldozer goes up in flames, then I'm center stage in an alarm at the bank."

Jackson shoulder checked her. "Nah. This town will be glad you're here once they get to know you."

"Well they may not get that chance if I can't make the final payment on the house by the deadline."

"There's still time."

"I didn't realize there were neighbors, though. The acreage is mostly to the east, and the house sits right on the western boundary."

"My uncle has the place next door. He's working offshore most of the time, so he's letting me stay there while I'm in Belle Terre."

Jackson mirrored her posture, consciously or unconsciously. Their upper arms touched, though his shoulders started at her ears.

"Camp Misfortune used to be a beauty. I spent a lot of weekends out there when I was a kid."

"You came here as a kid?" Surprise laced her voice. Beach boy Jackson was actually bayou boy Jackson.

"Yeah." He hesitated, straightening his spine and squaring his shoulders. "I grew up out near Vieux Avignon."

Riley knew the area. Money. Lots of money.

Riley tucked away her emotions like one would an old sweater you wanted no one to see. Jackson obviously came from wealth if his family owned the investment firm. Why would he be working as a deputy? The questions stuck to her brain like melted marshmallow on her fingers.

Instead of looking to her poverty-filled past, she focused on her poverty-filled future. If she couldn't recover her money... She let the thought trail off and turned her focus back to their conversation.

"An uncle. You have a sister and brother nearby, but you're headed to Florida where you have no family."

Jackson turned his attention the melting marshmallow, studying the scorched fluff with more intensity then it deserved. "Yeah."

She thought she'd have more luck dragging out the combination of the local bank. "Bad subject. Got it."

He rolled his shoulders and leaned back against the bench. "Sorry. Yeah, it's a bad subject. I haven't been home in a while."

They watched the flames for a bit. Donavan returned twice more with trees Riley labeled as *too short* before the kid disappeared back into the forest of forgotten Christmas trees.

It was the first time since meeting him that Riley felt somewhat disappointed. How could someone abandon their family? Her father had done it, and she'd never forgiven him. There was more to the story, of that she felt certain. Would he want to share it with her? Or was he as closed off about his past as she was about hers? Instead she brought them back to a safer topic.

"Why do they call it Camp Misfortune?"

Jackson stretched out the length of his frame, crossing his long legs at the ankles. He braced his hands against the bench, his fingers close enough to her thighs that the heat of anticipation ribboned silkily down her legs. "The Fortunes own the distillery out on Highway 1."

"Fortune's Brew? I know that place," Riley pushed her hair behind her ears. "We passed it on the way to town. It doesn't look like it's been open in a while."

"It shut down about fifteen years ago. The oldest son was really starting to get the brand some name recognition, but he and his wife died on the way home from a competition when their daughter was young."

A long exhale dropped Riley's shoulders. "That's awful."

"After that, nothing seemed to go right. The distillery closed. The family scattered. I think it's only the grand mother and the granddaughter left in town now. Rumor is the grandmother wants to leave town, but the grand-daughter won't sell. She's trying to rebuild the brand."

The toddler-chasing mom appeared again, this time sans toddler and sporting a look of fear. "Have you seen Tommy, Sheriff Guidry. I turned around for a second..."

Jackson jumped up, giving the harried mom's shoulder a gentle squeeze. "I'm sure he's just hiding, Lou Ann. Let's go find him." He turned, giving her a wink and telling her, "Tommy's a junior Houdini. I'll be right back," before disappearing after the mom.

Riley leaned back on her hands, thinking over their conversation about the property she wanted to buy. She thought of her own situation and the chance she'd taken with Ricky. She'd been willing to risk her future for a chance to reconnect with her brother, to rebuild her family a piece at a time.

Donavan suddenly appeared before her, another tree in his possession. Behind them in the parking lot, his foster dad called out his name. The young boy glanced over his shoulder, the struggle to obey or present his prize to Riley played on his face like dueling banjos. Patrick approached, but seeing the scene, stopped about twenty feet away. He smiled, nodding at Riley before turning back toward the van at the entrance.

Riley pushed to her feet. "That's the most perfect tree you could have found for me Donavan."

His dark eyes widened, his jaw slack at first then broadening into a wide grin. "You like it?"

Riley nodded with all the enthusiasm she could muster. "I love it. I'll get Mr. Terrebonne to help carry—"

"I'll do it!" Donavan offered and swung the tree over his shoulder.

The world crawled to slow motion in the heartbeat it took for Donavan to spin on sneakered feet. Riley's voice echoed in the vacuum of time as she shouted "No!" but it was too late. The instant the tree touched Donavan's shoulder the top dipped directly into the fire pit. A sharp whoosh drew Donavan's attention, and his eyes saucered as the blazing tree haloed his head.

She leaped forward to snag the tree, but Donavan scooted away and started swinging the tree wildly, the flames now eating up the spindly branches all the faster. Then as Donavan made a particularly wide arc with the blazing tree, the single branch snapped off and sailed over their heads to land on the nearest Scotch pine, eating a hole in the new tinder faster than she could say Smokey the Bear.

Donavan froze, then slapped the now engulfed tree into Riley's hands and disappeared. Riley froze for a split second, her eyes glued as the tree burned its way toward her hands. Memories scorched the front of her brain as the flames seared her skin. A loud gasp pulled her from the lost path of her thoughts as the manager stepped toward the fire pit, his frozen look of horror swallowing her whole. She regained her senses, dropped the tree and stomped out the flame.

She turned in time to see Jackson emerge from the tree lot, take instant inventory of the situation and hurdle over the bench toward the newest fire.

She ripped off his jacket and tossed it to him while he was in motion. "Use this!" She yelled, and he began to slap at the rapidly growing flames. Embers floated in the smoke now spiraling overhead, and within seconds, more fires burst to life as the flames jumped from tree to tree in a fiery game of dominos.

Someone yelled "Fire!" and Riley realized it was her. People echoed her scream and started a stampede toward the front gate.

"Slow down, everyone!" Jackson called after them, abandoning the growing fire to marshal the panicked crowd toward the outside. "Slow down!"

Riley scanned the interior of the lot, finding two fire extinguishers which she ripped out of their holders before tearing after Jackson.

"Here!" she yelled and thrust the device at him, pulling the pin of her own extinguisher and squeezing the trigger. Nothing. She did a quick check of the apparatus, squeezed again. Still nothing. Panic nipped at her heels until she realized Jackson was having the same problem.

"It's no use," he said and ditched the useless device. "Follow everyone out." He yelled over the growing crackle of the fire behind them. "I'm going to check—"

Two decades of fear bubbled in her stomach. She'd lost everything when she was a kid because of a fire. Not again, she promised. "I'm not leaving you in here alone."

Jackson hesitated, the argument pursed on his lips, but it was not surprise or anger filling his eyes. It was gratitude.

"Together." He nodded once. "You look left; I'll look right."

He grabbed her hand, and together they made a quick circuit of the emptying lot, finally spilling themselves into the semi-circle of shocked faces slowly backing away from the growing flames.

Riley bent over at the waist, hands propped on her knees as she coughed the smoke and burnt pine from her lungs. Inches away, Jackson did the same even as he directed people back from the lot, his voice a raspy baritone. Soot and ash darkened his blonde hair, but he issued orders, checking multiple times with the parents to make sure every child was accounted for, calling out to help reconnect those separated in the chaos.

Riley marveled at his calm control, a decidedly different

side of him from the relaxed man she'd seen so far. He knew the value of protecting what he cared about. It showed in every sweep of his eyes over the crowd. Every time a sound erupted from the fire behind them his head snapped around to judge the danger, his body coiled to take action, make decisions. He hovered without looming. A constant presence. A steadying voice, a shoulder to lean on, and Riley realized then that it wasn't the smoke that had stolen her breath.

It was Jackson.

When the fire truck rolled up moments later, every fireman on the crew seemed to pause for a split second to stare at Riley before hurrying off to contain the blaze. When Riley looked beyond the fire truck, she realized every pair of eyes locked on her. And it hit her. She'd twice now been at the center of some fiery disaster in this sleepy little town. First the blazing bulldozer incident at Thanksgiving and now the Christmas tree lot.

Judging by the looks on the faces of those crowding together in the parking lot, she couldn't have been more of an outsider if she'd worn a sign that said *arsonist*.

So many instances in her life skidded through her brain, a movie on fast forward. Parents' Day. Father daughter dances. The sentencing hearing on her eighteenth birthday. She'd done them alone, watching from the corners of what passed for her life.

She sidled away to the far edge of the lot, staying clear of the fire crew as they doused the blaze. Patrick's husband was talking to Jackson, a look of alarm clouding his face. A coil of dread tightened in her chest, and she took a step toward them, but a voice stopped her.

"Riley?"

She turned at the sound of her name, seeing Patrick

closing the distance between them. Concern etched the corners of his eyes, his mouth drawn into a tight line.

"Something's wrong with Donavan," he blurted, pointing back toward their van.

Riley's heart kicked up a notch, and she met Patrick midway. "Is he hurt?"

"I don't think so. He won't let me get near him though." They weaved through the crowd, Riley avoiding the piercing stares and grim faces. "I saw him talking to you earlier."

Guilt needled Riley, knowing what was likely eating up Donavan. "He was helping me pick out a tree." She reached out, stopping Patrick with a hand on his arm. "Donavan had a tree, and it sort of caught on fire. He panicked."

Patrick looked at the blaze a few dozen feet away. "Oh, my goodness."

"It was an accident," Riley quickly added, and she could feel her own panic starting to rise. What if Patrick and his husband didn't see it that way? No family wanted trouble from their kids, especially temporary kids. How long had it taken her own foster family to give her over to the authorities at the first sign of a hassle?

"Oh, I know that." Patrick agreed without hesitation. "He's the gentlest kid you ever wanted to meet. Couldn't hurt a fly. He's got to be so scared that..."

"That you'll send him away." Riley finished.

Patrick looked at her with a knowing eye. "You were part of the system." A statement, not a question.

Hesitation stole the answer from Riley.

"We would never send Donavan away." An urgency drew his brows into a tight line over concerned eyes. He reached toward her but stopped himself. "Please believe that."

Instinct told Riley it was true. She'd seen the way the

couple beamed around the kids and the way the kids were drawn to them.

Patrick continued, "Donavan hasn't been with us long, but we love him. The family wouldn't be complete without him."

The easy affirmation of love toward his foster son touched a part of Riley. Had her own foster parents ever felt that way about her? They were kind but never expressed love or affection toward their charges. Military stoicism summed up their approach to the large knit-together family. And once you went AWOL, judgment was swift and final.

They arrived at the Miller's van, Javier and kids standing near the front, linked hand in hand. Jackson waited off to the side, his eyes all for her as she neared the family.

Javier smiled weakly, sadness mixed with relief. "Miss Kenner, thank you for helping."

She waved away his appreciation, winking at the kids before propping her foot on the running board of the van. At the last minute, she looked over to Jackson, bolstered by his presence. The calm knowledge in his face, his unwavering hold on her gaze, said he believed in her at that moment. He didn't know anything about what had happened, but he was there. Waiting. Few had done the same in her life. She'd been replaceable. Disposable.

Why he had such confidence in her, she didn't know. Fear currently chomped on every nerve. She wanted to help Donavan, understanding better than most how kids like the two of them desperately wanted to belong and fit in. Waiting for the one mistake that would send them away. After a while, you either lived while walking on a tightrope or you pushed all the boundaries.

Riley had chosen the latter, and the self-sabotage worked. She'd not only lost a fairly decent foster family but spent a year behind bars. She didn't think Donavan was going to jail, and the Millers looked more concerned than mad. She doubted Donavan could see it, however. She hadn't when it was her turn in his shoes.

Leaning against the frame of the van's door, Riley glimpsed the top of Donavan's head in the back row where he huddled, pressed far into the corner, face buried against his knees. The *huh-huh-huh* of his cries carved a hole in her heart. She pulled herself into the dim interior of the vehicle and angled her body into the middle seat, sitting on her knees while facing the rear of the vehicle.

"Hey, Donavan," she started, leaning against the back seat and resting her chin on her crossed arms. The kid drew in tighter on himself if it were possible. "Your dads sure are worried about you."

"They're not my dads," Donavan mumbled, voice cracking.

"I know." Riley paused. "But I think they want to be."

"Not anymore. They'll send me away." The first sob shook his tiny frame. "They always send me away."

The words were coming out before she really thought about it, not used to sharing so much of herself. "My first foster family sent me away."

Donavan's head snapped up, forehead crinkling in deep furrows. "They did?"

Riley nodded. "Yeah. It wasn't really their fault though. The mom got sick, and they couldn't keep me. But I was with my next family until I was out on my own." Not a total lie, though she didn't like playing with the truth. Donavan needed reassurances tonight, she reminded herself.

The kid thought about that for a moment before his face fell again. "Bet you never got in trouble though." He gazed out the window at the smoking rubble. The red lights of the fire engines pulsed in short bursts, breaking up the night. "Really big trouble."

Riley snorted a laugh, and Donavan grinned at the sound. She leaned a little farther over the back of the seat. "Can you keep a secret?"

He scooted a little closer, attention focused all on her.

"I helped some friends steal a car."

The kid gasped and slapped his hand over his forehead. "No, you didn't!"

She nodded. "I did. It wasn't the first time either." She'd gone looking for her share of trouble back then, anything to push the boundaries of her foster parents' patience. "So the family handed me over to juvie."

The kid thought about that for a moment, forehead scrunched in concentration. "That wasn't very nice."

She swallowed, and for the first time admitted her own feelings. "I didn't think so either. At the time I didn't think they cared. I didn't talk to them for a year."

"A whole year?" Donavan rose up to his knees, and Riley could see the tear tracks on his cheeks and the wetness spiking his lashes. "What happened?"

She reached over to him and wiped away the tears with the pad of her thumb. "I went to juvie and refused to see them. When I got out, they tried to get in touch with me, but I was mad. I left and never went to see them again." Saying it now, all these years later, still hurt.

When she'd been led into the processing room at the detention center on her eighteenth birthday, they'd been waiting for her. All she'd wanted to do was run into their arms and apologize. Instead she'd ignored them, stubborn pride winning over her fears of them turning her away again.

"You don't have a family either." He lowered his head and rested it on Riley's forearm.

Riley swallowed past the lump in her throat. She cupped the back of his head with her hand and rested her chin against his scalp. "Actually, I do. I got a job on the construction crew, and the guys on the job became my family. They're like my brothers. And what I realized when I got older is that my foster family did the right thing, only I was too stupid to realize it at the time."

A sense of calm came over her, of self-realization, and it settled around her like an old sweater. Donavan sat up, his expression one of longing and hope for a better ending than what he expected.

"I was getting in more and more trouble, and if I hadn't gone to jail when I was seventeen, I'm not sure what would have happened. Probably more trouble and rather than a year in juvie, I'd have gone to prison. Maybe even worse. So, they helped me out in their own way. Even though it was tough love, it was still love."

She waited a second while Donavan absorbed her story, realizing at the same time that the truth in her words really eased some of her own pain as well. She'd never thought about the tough love her foster family had given her, how it had set her on the right path. And she'd abandoned them like she always accused them of doing to her.

Donavan stole a look over Riley's shoulder at the people waiting for him. "Is the sheriff here to arrest me?" Pools of liquid filled his dark eyes.

"Do you think you're in trouble, Donavan?"

He nodded, the tears again leaking down his face in twin streams. "I didn't mean to do it, Riley. I swear! When I saw the fire, I got so scared."

And he launched himself at Riley, wrapping his arms

tightly around her neck as he sobbed against her shoulder. She rubbed his back in tiny circles, her heart constricting at the loneliness in his sobs and the desperate way he held onto her neck. Behind her, she could hear Patrick crying, along with a myriad of tinier sniffles.

As Donavan's tears began to subside, Riley unlatched his arms from her body and pulled him over the seat to settle him onto her lap as much as possible. The scents of bubble gum and pine sap mingled beneath her nose as she cradled his body against hers until she felt him relax. His gangly legs were nearly as long as her torso, but she wanted the kid close so she could whisper the next part only for him.

"I want you to listen, Donavan, because I'm going to tell you another secret. I was an idiot to walk away from my family. They came to see me in juvie, but I sent them away. I was scared they would give up on me again, but I gave up on them."

The realization left her a little cold. She'd not trusted anyone to get close to her again. She considered the guys on the crew her family, and while she trusted them with her life, she didn't trust them with her heart.

Not even the man she married.

"Parents have to be tough on us when we screw up, even if we don't mean to screw up. That's their job to teach us and help us make better decisions next time. But what happened with you was an accident. No one is mad at you, I promise. But you have to own up to your mistake. Do you understand what I mean?"

He nodded solemnly. "I have to tell them, don't I? Even if it means they send me away."

The heartache in Donavan's realization punched a hole in Riley's gut. "Yes. But you also have to trust that they *won't* send you away. Not permanently. Because you're family. And families stick together."

"What if they don't understand?" His tiny voice cracked, a sound more painful to her than she ever believed possible. "What if they send me away forever?"

She squared her shoulders, lowering her face until they were even. "Then they aren't the right family for you. Because you deserve a family who will always be by your side."

Donavan again looked over at his waiting family but also at Jackson, and she watched the distrust of a kid in the system battling with the hope of a kid wanting to be part of a family.

He pushed himself from the protective circle of Riley's arms. Riley reluctantly let go, hoping her read on the Millers was right and she hadn't set this kid up for the biggest heartbreak in history. Because she knew this lesson—whatever it turned out to be—would be with him the rest of his life. She'd had the same opportunity only she'd learned the wrong thing.

Donavan gallows-walked toward the anxious faces of his parents and Jackson. The couple kneeled to make eye contact, but when Patrick and Javier reached out to take his hand, Donavan pulled back a little. Head downcast, he pointed to the now smoldering tree lot, his words too low for Riley to hear. When the Millers smiled gently and nodded and Donavan jumped into their arms, Riley's own breathing eased, and her heart settled back in her chest. The other kids joined in the circle of hugging, and Riley knew Donavan had found his forever family.

Jackson waited as the family comforted each other, and Riley could see the hard swallow in the column of his throat as he scrubbed a hand across his face. He hunkered down beside Patrick, putting a gentle hand on Donavan's back. Donavan rotated his head slightly, not letting go of his parents' embrace but listened as Jackson talked to him. The kid nodded then let himself be picked up by his parents as the family headed back to the van.

Riley slid her feet to the ground from her perch inside the van, meeting them halfway. When they stood side by side, Patrick put a hand on Riley's arm and gave her a hard squeeze. "There are no words..." he began, but Riley put her hand over his and smiled.

"It's not necessary. We fosters stick together." She rubbed Donavan's back one more time.

"If you don't have plans for Christmas day, we hope you'll join us. Presents are at seven." Javier scoffed, and Patrick shushed him, but they both smiled and the familiarity between them was sweet. "Breakfast is around nine. Then lunch around one. There'll be gifts and games, and who knows what else in between. Come for any or all of it. You have a place with us whenever you want."

Riley swallowed past the lump in her chest. She'd not had a family Christmas in many years. Kids around the tree. Squeals as the presents were revealed. The mountain of wrapping paper being dived under like a pile of freshly raked leaves. "I'll be there."

Patrick beamed. "Good." He took a step but turned mid-stride and whispered none too subtly. "Feel free to bring the sheriff."

Riley's cheeks burned, and she went to protest but stopped as Patrick shuffled off with his family. Riley focused on the sheriff standing just a few feet away.

Behind him, chaos made a backdrop to his calm demeanor. Fireman lugged hoses and lookie-loos pointed and gasped as the fire was brought under control. A haze of smoke hung low over the parking lot, held down by the cooler temps.

Jackson propped a hip against the back bumper of his police vehicle, pushing past the fading rush of adrenaline. His arms hung at his side, one leg cocked at the knee and the ankle resting over the other. As she neared, Riley stuffed her hands in the front pockets of her jeans, not sure how much he'd heard and not sure what he would make of all of it. She'd been a juvenile delinquent. The records sealed. Would he care?

It's not like they had much in the way of conversation about their past. Riley didn't think the look on his face, hooded eyes watching her with a gentleness smoothing out the lines of his forehead, read as anger. It wasn't pity either, which would send her in the other direction. She'd made her bed back then, lain in it, then gotten up and pulled the covers over that part of her life.

He'd pulled the shirt from his pants, the fabric stained and damp in places, while the creases around his mouth were darkened with soot. She swiped at her face, curious about her reason for the gesture even as she did it. She worked on a construction site, she chided herself. She spent most of her day covered in dirt and dust.

But with Jackson, she found herself thinking of the way he touched her hair and studied her face and throat when they talked. Even the way his fingers brushed her arm and touched her cheek. The thoughts made her self-conscious and that made her blush more heatedly.

"It doesn't do any good." After a beat, he added. "You're still beautiful."

Her step faltered just a hair as she finally came to stand in front of him, heart pounding like a jackhammer in her chest. "And you're sounding like a politician up for re-election."

Secretly though, his words touched a part of her she hadn't known existed. She knew herself capable, independent, strong. Men wanted her. But she'd never felt beautiful until he'd said it.

"I know you don't believe it, by the way." He straightened on his feet, matching her posture by stuffing his hands in his pockets. "Doesn't make it any less true."

She pursed her lips, quirked her mouth to one side, considering his words. "I know men want me." Riley conceded and scuffed a foot against the pavement, uncomfortable with the direction of the conversation. "Just like the women in town want you."

And she hated them all for what they could give Jackson.

Chapter Fourteen

J ackson nodded slowly, considering his words carefully. "Convenience and lack of options. Good points." He narrowed in on that warm gaze watching him, the depth so intense it phosphoresced in the glow of the full moon overhead and took the final steps toward her. His shadow surrounded her, the nascent warmth of her body tangible though he hadn't yet touched her.

Jackson could read her desire to flee by the tense line of her body, while he let the heat of her nearness tangle with the calm surety of his emotions for her. He'd tried to unravel the intensity of those emotions—raw desire on top of an unexpected connection built on the foundation of a deep and abiding respect. Riley wanted nothing more than to live and belong to this town, but she was willing to risk that to protect Donavan.

"Rest assured, however, that neither are the case with me where you are concerned, Riley." He reached out, and her breath hitched as he wrapped a loose strand of her hair between two fingers. The midnight strands cascaded like silk over his skin. "I have options, as you pointed out. And I don't think either of us sees the other as convenient. Probably quite the opposite. You want to stay. I want to go. You impress the hell out of me. You worry me. You surprise me. You confuse me."

"I have that effect on people. From my father to my ex, no one knew what to do with me. We know how those worked out."

He claimed those last few inches of space between them, taking her by the arms and drawing her even closer. She raised her chin, defiant, but behind the smoldering shadows of eyes, he witnessed the crack beneath the surface. He frightened her. Good. He shouldn't be the only one scared out his mind by what was happening between them.

"Don't do that with me, ok? I don't know what this is between us any more than I think you do. Don't write me off beforehand. If you don't want to do this, just say it."

She swallowed, the long column of her neck working hard at whatever words she needed to bite back. Lips slightly parted, her breath came in slow, deep draughts. Her eyes never left his, and he felt rather than saw her hands come up between them to rest on his chest. Would she push him away? Or draw him closer?

She curled her fingers into the fabric of his shirt. "Donavan's going to be ok."

Redirection. Riley's stock and trade maneuver when nervous.

Jackson smoothed down her collar which was cocked at an odd angle behind her neck. "What happened?"

She smiled secretly, even a little sadly. "He burned a birthday cake."

"What?"

She laughed. "Nothing. An accident. His dads know the

details, so I'm sure they can fill you in when needed. But the good thing is he took a chance and it paid off."

"What about you?" Jackson challenged, worried about the distant look in her eyes, the way her body seemed coiled and ready to spring.

"What about me?"

"Are you ready to take a chance?" Something like fear ate at the lining of Jackson's stomach. He knew by pushing her he was taking a chance she would bolt. The look on her face said he was right.

"Sheriff!" a voice he recognized yelled from behind, not distraught but urgent. He cursed the interruption but turned toward the sound, shocked to see most of those gathered standing a dozen feet from him and Riley. Mason Gastineaux planted himself at the front of those gathered, shoulders tightly squared over his frame.

Revenge tightened the features on Mason's face and without thought, Jackson put his body in front of Riley's. On the periphery he recognized Riley's ex, Will Kenner, and his girlfriend, Lara, walking toward the crowd.

"What's up, Mason?" Jackson asked the defacto leader of the little group given his position at the front.

Miranda Gastineaux had her hand on her husband's arm, pulling him back, whispering heatedly beneath her breath. The baby, hitched on her hip, fussed and rubbed at his eyes with meaty little fists.

Mason shook her off and took another few steps forward. He pointed at Riley, a slow snarl curling the corners of his mouth. "She responsible for this? Mr. Terrebonne said she was holding the tree that started it. I heard about what happened at the bank. You gonna arrest her now? Or does she and her crew get a free pass to destroy this town even more?"

With each word, Riley escaped the protective barrier of Jackson's body, standing beside him now. Will and Lara broke away from the mob and joined Riley and Jackson. Four against forty. Jackson didn't think violence would erupt, but he couldn't take the chance. The telltale signs were there, simmering close to the surface.

"That's not what happened, Mason. It was—" Riley touched his arm and he turned, a slow shake of her head. Jackson tightened his mouth, not sure of the exact details but knowing she was protecting Donavan. He didn't agree with her taking the fall for something that wasn't her doing, but he understood her reasoning for doing it. Donavan needed a break, and she would take the heat.

His impression of the woman went up even higher if that was possible. She wanted to belong to this town, to fit in and find her place, but she was willing to sacrifice that to keep a kid she didn't really know from bearing the brunt of this incident. He inclined his head a fraction. OK. They'd play it her way. For now.

"Well, Guidry?" Mason pushed, his voice tight.

Jackson returned his attention to the crowd, squaring his shoulders. "Like I said, that's not what happened. But I'll look into it."

A jumble of voices rose behind Mason, but Jackson couldn't tell if they agreed or disagreed with his assessment. He'd certainly hear about it tomorrow, regardless. Even if he didn't know the truth yet, he wouldn't let Riley's decision be undermined by the likes of him.

He looked to Riley. *You sure?* He asked silently with a raise of his brow.

Face set, hands tucked in the pockets of her jeans, she nodded, silent but resolute.

"Did you see what happened?" someone shouted from

the crowd, pulling Jackson's attention back to the mob gathered.

Jackson hesitated. He hadn't seen the fire start, and he already knew there was more going on based on what he'd seen with Donavan. "Not exactly. But I know Riley."

"And we know Mr. Terrebonne."

The reluctant manager was pushed up through the crowd. His gaze ping-ponged between Riley and Jackson, uncertainty wafting off him like smoke from the remains of the fire.

Jackson didn't wait, wanting to shut down the growing discontent. "Mr. Terrebonne can come to the station in the morning. I'll take his statement. If there's anything to it—"

"You choosing her over us?" Mason challenged, taking another step forward. "You refusing to do your job?"

Jackson watched the world narrow to just him and Mason as the man's hands dropped to his sides, fists clenching for wont of something to hit. It took all Jackson's effort not to mirror the gesture. "There's nothing to do right now. If an investigation is warranted, I'll do it."

"If?" the man sneered, the slash of his mouth firm, harsh. "Mr. Terrebonne saw her. And we all know what happened before Thanksgiving."

Diffuse the situation.

Jackson slowly pivoted his head to Riley, seeing her focused on the crowd. It wasn't fear or guilt he read in the set of her face, or the line of her shoulders. It was expectation.

It was like the moment in the bank when he had nothing to rely on but his own instinct. Could he take a chance with her safety? Could he get lucky twice?

He turned to her and whispered so only she would hear. "Will you trust me?"

Riley broke her gaze from the crowd, studying him with a slow perusal of his face first before crawling down his arms to where his hands rested on the cuffs at his waist. A slow roll of her eyes, an exasperated sigh. "Again?"

"Riley Kenner," Jackson announced loudly enough for the crowd to hear. "You're under arrest."

As the cuffs snapped around Riley's wrist, Jackson looked over his shoulder to see Miranda again pulled at Mason's arm. "Let's go home, honey. Sheriff Guidry is taking care of things. Jack Junior is tired and cold. Sheriff Guidry wouldn't do anything wrong. You know that."

Jackson led Riley toward the patrol car, carefully stuffing her into the back seat before returning his attention to the crowd. "Take your wife and son home, Mason. Everyone go home. Let the fire department secure the area."

Jackson and Mason squared off a few seconds longer before Mason turned and ushered his wife through the crowd. The remaining gawkers dispersed as quickly, except for the bedraggled Santa Jackson had seen earlier. He tugged on the fake beard in a gesture Jackson could only call contemplation. Had he seen something? Jackson took a step toward the red-suited man but had to stop as a line of cars pushed up clouds of dust as the parking lot emptied. When the dust settled, Santa was gone.

Shuffling footsteps drew Jackson's attention and he pivoted, surprise dropping his jaw. The entirety of Riley's construction crew stood behind them, a wall of muscle and attitude. Lara, Will, and Noé took point. Noé and Jackson eyed each other; the challenge silent but loud and clear. Noé clapped Will on the shoulder and turned without a word to blend back into darkness.

"She's gonna kick your ass for those cuffs," Noé called out.

Didn't he know it.

Within minutes, only the four of them remained with the lone fire truck. Firefighters finished hosing down the blackened lumps of the Christmas tree farm a hundred feet away. Scorched pine filled the air, and ash fell like dark snowflakes in the cones of lights surrounding the tree lot.

Lara snuggled against Will, her head resting on his shoulder. She looked tired, a feeling Jackson recognized, but he was more focused on Riley at the moment.

She'd turned her head to stare through the cruiser's window at the burned out remains of the lot, backlit by the flashing red lights from the emergency vehicles dotting the parking lot. The temperature had dropped, and although it was still well above freezing, the chill nipped at his hands as he opened the car door.

He cleared his throat, the sound breaking whatever spell had her entranced. "Let me get those cuffs off you."

She pushed from the back of the patrol car, giving Jackson her back. "Are you going to get in trouble for arresting me then un-arresting me?"

"I didn't read you your Miranda rights, so I'm releasing you on your own recognizance until you're ready to tell me what's going on."

Spine stiff, chin raised, she didn't react when the cuffs came off. Didn't even rub her wrists. Jackson didn't like the silence. He wanted her to yell. To scream at him for putting her in cuffs. Again.

Will interrupted Jackson's thoughts. "We're headed home, Jackson."

"Can you give me a ride, Will?" Riley asked.

"We're on the bike," Will shrugged, pulling a yawning Lara to his shoulder. "Jackson can you—"

"I'll get her back to the hotel, Will. Thanks. Tell your men I appreciate their support tonight."

Will waved it off. "We'll see you both tomorrow."

Lara and Will ambled off arm in arm, Riley's gaze trailing after they faded from sight.

"I'm sorry about the cuffs." Jackson scuffed over to the vehicle, leaning against the fender. "I wanted to diffuse the situation. It seemed—"

"The easiest way." She finished for him. "It made sense."

Riley crossed her arms inside the massive jean jacket draped over her shoulders, and he suspected Noé had given her the jacket. Protecting her in his own way, something Jackson could respect even if it elicited feelings he didn't want to confront.

He couldn't read the expression on her face, deciphering no anger, defeat, or anything remotely related to emotion. She'd shut down, drawing into herself. Based on the perfect poker face she wore, he suspected it was a state she'd used often.

He sidled up next to her, mirroring her posture. "Thanks for understanding. I don't know what went on tonight with Donavan. But I won't let you take the heat for him. We'll talk to Javier and Patrick. Get them to make a statement."

"No."

"No?"

"No. Donavan is still on the fence about his family. He wants to trust but..."

"He can't."

"Not yet. He'll get there. Javier and Patrick are good people. They'll help him."

"I think you're the one that helped him tonight."

From the corner of his eye, he saw Riley swallow hard,

turning her attention to the direction the Miller family had disappeared. "I'm sure the Millers could have handled it."

"Oh, me, too. But it's different when you hear 'you're gonna be ok' from someone who's been where you are."

A tightness drew her mouth into a slim line. "Yeah, we juvenile delinquents stick together."

The harsh edge to Riley's voice scraped at Jackson, and he wondered if he'd said the wrong thing. Maybe too much of her past had been dredged up the last few days. She'd obviously been in foster care at some point. Potentially betrayed by her brother. Her ex was living the happily-ever-after ending with another woman. That had to sting, no matter what Riley pretended.

Now she was *persona non-gratis* with the town thanks to the situation at the bank and now the fire. She'd come looking for the home she'd never had, reaching for something she wanted for the first time in a while from the way it sounded, and it was all snatched away.

"I know that's not what you mean," Riley interrupted his thoughts. "It doesn't matter, though. The town made it pretty clear I'm not welcome here. I can let JJ handle the rest of this build. We've got contracts for another three stores, and I can survey the sites like I did for Belle Terre. Get the wheels in motion for what comes next. The rest of it..." She cut through the air with a sharp slash of her hand and Jackson likened the maneuver to cutting out a piece of her heart. "I guess the rest of it doesn't matter anymore."

"What about your house?"

"It's not my house yet. Even if Ricky or your brother or your father didn't steal it, the money is gone. And without the money, I lose it all." She pulled back her shoulders, stiffening her spine. "Won't be the first time, I assure you. It's best if I just leave now. Save everyone the trouble of kicking me out."

Her leaving left him cold in a way Jackson did not expect. "You're jumping the gun, don't you think? Mason was just upset, more at me because of what happened with Miranda. You're just an easy target tonight with the fire. No one will hold you responsible for this fire."

"Wanna bet?"

Riley started to walk away, shrugging deeper into the coat swallowing her frame. Her comfort in Noé's clothing irked Jackson. Maybe the two of them were an item before he came along. Maybe all he'd been was a distraction. He didn't like the idea, but he could deal with it.

But the idea of Riley running away ripped a hole in his gut. He knew a little something about that, and it never provided the satisfaction you think escaping your problems would provide.

"I didn't think you were the type to run away from a fight?"

Chapter Fifteen

Riley spun sharply, feeling the rise in body temp flush along her face as she chewed up the distance between them. She wanted to strike back. Hurt him like his words hurt her. Even if they were the truth. She'd been running so long she wasn't sure she could stop. "I go with my crew. They are *my* family. The only one I've got left."

"But you want something more." His eyes pleaded with her, his voice plaintive, lost. He reached out, but she didn't get close enough for contact. "Why are you so willing to give up on it?"

How could she explain it to someone who chose to leave behind the only thing that really mattered: family. She'd destroyed hers, lost everything because her brothers and father had trusted her to take her mom's place. And she wasn't enough. She couldn't—*wouldn't*—risk the same thing happening again.

Riley scrubbed her fingers through her hair, pushing back the emotions at the same time. "You wouldn't understand."

"Then make me understand, dammit." The first hint of

anger razored his words. His hands slashed the air between them. "You act like you're the only whose ever suffered a loss, a disappointment. You can't be that arrogant."

"I can't put them at risk because the town decides they don't like me. They're all I've been able to count on over the last sixteen years. The only ones who've wanted me around. I can't risk losing even more than I've lost already."

"Money can be replaced." His voice dropped an octave as he moved in closer, but each inch he claimed, she stole back two. "And family won't desert you because you fail. You said so yourself to Donavan."

She threw her hands in the air, whirling from his plaintive expression. "Donavan's a child. He needed the lie. You have money. That bank account was everything I had." Not everything, a little voice whispered, but she silenced it, knowing want was more dangerous than need.

"Not everything," he answered as if reading her mind. A forlorn smile softened the lines around his eyes. "And your crew aren't the only ones who want you around."

"Do you think Mason is off singing my praises tonight?"

"Maybe not, but I know Donavan's parents are. Why are Mason's words more powerful? Why are you ignoring what happened with that kid? Damn, Riley." The anger was back. "You have a chance here to build something more than an AmeriMart store. Why ignore that because things aren't easy? Why run now?" He emphasized each word with a sharp jab into the earth.

She turned on him, feeling the words stick in her throat as she spit them back at him. "You want to talk about running, what about you? You're the one running from the family just a few miles down the road. You've got everything waiting for you and you toss it aside like it's nothing, like it'll always be there, so don't lecture me about running when you barely leave a footprint in the dust before you step off to the next town."

The look on Jackson's face left Riley colder than the night air wrapping them in the fog of angry words. Her words hit the mark she'd aimed for with pinpoint precision, but even she didn't know why she wanted to hurt him. She was losing everything regardless. What did it matter if she lost Jackson as well?

"You know nothing about me and my family," Jackson threw the words back at her.

Riley shrugged, lifting her hands palms outward. "You're right. But I know you have one, and you'd rather float around the country playing Jack of all Trades when you could be with them. You're not just running from your family; you're running from the responsibility of being part of that family. You don't just quit when times get tough."

She swiped at the hint of a tear in her eye, refusing to let it have life.

"That's what my father did. Quit." Words she'd held captive for a lifetime poured out of her like a carafe brimming over. The mess puddled around her life, making it sticky and leaving a mark. "I was making a birthday cake for my youngest brother only I set the dish towel on fire." Riley deflated, leaning against the back of the cruiser to stay on her feet. The bitterness of ash flooded her memory, yanking her back to the moment she'd lost it all. "Daddy came home to the police and fire department and Family and Children's Services all asking questions. Were the kids always alone? How many hours a day did he work? Why wasn't an adult with them? When the FCS lady started rounding us up, all he did was sit in his recliner and stare at my mother's picture. He didn't even show up to the hearing that placed us into state custody. He gave up on us."

And just like that she was empty.

Jackson eased closer to her, body rigid, the grim line of his mouth stealing even the dimple from his face. "My family sold me out."

The sharp weight of his words slapped her, regret flooding her body. She took a step toward him, but he held up his hand to ward her off. With a slow, disbelieving shake of his head, he finished.

"Just because people are related by blood doesn't mean they're worth calling family."

"Jackson," she started, but her voice had lost its power. He was right. She'd showed herself to be the worst kind of arrogant.

He turned to the side so he didn't face her, a tight grimace lingering in his profile as the story poured out.

"My father needed to secure a merger so he could take a competitor out of the market. The other man's daughter worked at my firm. She liked her lifestyle and didn't want to lose it." A pained laugh escaped, but he scrubbed his hand over his face, wiping away the emotion. "Dad wanted me married, settled, and she was willing." Another choked laugh. "Willing? That's an understatement. The merger fell through, but Dad paid her off when I left. No one put up much of a fuss about it. My brother wouldn't rock the boat. My sister didn't know until later. Mom ... she shrugged and said, 'that's your father for you.' Like that should explain it. I haven't been back." He stared a hole in her now, tight lines of grief framing his eyes and mouth. "Because there was nothing worth going back for. I stayed in touch with my sister."

The fire captain waved at Jackson from across the parking lot, and Riley watched Jackson square off, chasing back the painful memories with little more than stubborn pride. He started toward the scene, calling out over his shoulders. "I couldn't go back to people willing to sell out my happiness for their own security. Not every family is worth fighting for, Riley. That doesn't mean it's true for all of them."

She stalked after him, mentally beating herself for forgetting that she wasn't the only one with a painful past. Riley let herself stand apart, and in doing so, she'd forgotten what is was like to be a part of things. Until Jackson made her want that even more. Damn him.

"Maybe, but family isn't just what you're born into," Riley argued chasing after him. "You've made a family here. The people care about you, and you're walking away from them as well."

Jackson spun around so quickly she nearly collided with him, pressing her hands against his chest to keep from falling.

"I nearly got Miranda killed eight months ago and they made me a deputy. Now they want me to be sheriff." He punctuated the words with a sharp thrust of his fist toward the smoldering remains behind him. "This town needs someone who knows what they're doing. Someone they can count on."

"They count on you!" she yelled back then it dawned on her. She took a step back to see him better, to take in the tight shoulders and grim set of his mouth. "That's what bothers you. They look to you for answers, like tonight in the fire. Everyone waited on you, and that scares you."

"Of course, it scares me," he admitted, the look on his face both surprised and resigned. He stared off into the distance rather than meet her gaze. "They're putting their lives, their safety, in my hands. What have I done to earn that?"

"You put your life on the line when you didn't have to. You did it in the bank eight months ago and you did it tonight." She cupped his chin in her palm, turning his face back to meet hers. "I think that tells them everything they need to know."

He shrugged and pulled from her grasp. "That was instinct. I reacted before I really thought about it. I didn't look beyond the moment to the consequences. That's dangerous in this job."

"You can't predict the future. No one expects that." Riley sighed and scrubbed the fall of hair back from her face.

"What happens when I fail them?"

"You pick up. Do it again."

"Yet you're running. Giving up on something worth fighting for. Isn't that what your father did? Or is that advice only for me?"

The words burrowed down into Riley's core, releasing a torrent of anger on a wave of denial. "Don't confuse our situations, Jackson. I'm not running. I'm moving on to the next job."

"So am I."

"But you don't have to."

"Neither do you."

Damn the man was frustrating. But was he right? No, she scolded herself. Her time here was done. Losing her money. The distrust of the town. She'd find another town. She was making the right choice.

Is that what her father thought?

She scrubbed away the doubt. "You just refuse to see what you've built here. You've made friends, colleagues depend on you. I have nothing but a permit to build a store and when it's done ... what? Stick around and do maintenance?"

"You're the one talking about starting over. So start something new. There are people here still trying to rebuild their lives after the hurricanes and the oil spill. Build something new. Build it here."

"There has to be a strong enough foundation to build on, Jackson. And Mason made it pretty clear mine is made of quicksand. What do you think would have happened if you hadn't been here tonight when he decided to confront me?"

"Will and Noé wouldn't have let him hurt you."

"I'm not worried about me, dammit!" She focused her gaze on what remained of the tree lot before gazing in the direction of the construction lot, using the time to slow her heart rate. Harden her heart to what she wanted and what other people needed. "Will could lose everything if they revoke the building permit. And Noé would go back to jail quicker than you could spit at the first sign of trouble. I can't let them risk that for me."

"So you would give up everything."

"Not everything, Jackson. Just this. I can build a house anywhere. It's just a house."

"You don't want a house. You want a home."

"If wants and wishes were candy and kisses, we'd all have a merry Christmas."

Jackson claimed the few inches of space between them and reached over to button the jacket swallowing her frame. His fingers worked the buttons, the muscles in his forearms rippling beneath the skin like waves crashing into the shore. "And if you run away far enough and fast enough, people stop coming after you."

Chapter Sixteen

Four days.

Four days since she'd left town.

Jackson ignored the raw burn in his gut, the hole left by her absence still a gaping wound, and instead focusing on the myriad of mundane duties that kept him and the other deputies busy as the holidays crept closer. He'd not called or texted her. He'd not reached out to Will or JJ to find out where she was. She was running, so he let her run.

Though it killed something inside of himself to do that.

She had to learn, and stubborn as she was, it would have to be the hard way. Riley feared failing those who cared for her, as if a failure would take away all she'd earned, and worse, endanger those around her.

Sadly, there was nothing he could do to convince her otherwise. She'd have to figure it out herself.

He moved into the growing crowd milling about city center for the tree lighting ceremony being staged at the Spirit of Belle Terre. A local and much-loved monument, the double-rig shrimping trawler had been delivered on the hurricane force winds from the Atchafalaya River to the town center in the 1960s and now played center stage for every holiday from July fourth to Mardi Gras. White twinkling lights covered every available surface on the decades old boat, from the top of the mast to the rusted-out propeller still clinging to the stern. A live Rudolph waited none too patiently for Santa to arrive, munching hay from the kids willing to pay a buck for a handful of dried grass.

Small groups walked around the closed off avenue as Jackson weaved his way through the crowd, looking for one face in particular but knowing he wouldn't find it. His resolve weakened with each passing day, however. Maybe they'd both said too much that last night. He'd put her in handcuffs. For the second time. Most women would be put out about that alone. But he'd accused her of running away.

Now it looked like he'd chased her away.

"Dumbass."

A choked cough came from his left.

"Did you say something, Sheriff?"

He avoided the curious stare of the deputy who'd managed to walk up at just the wrong time. "No, Matt. And don't call me sheriff."

The young kid had the nerve to salute before walking away. Jackson swallowed the growl rumbling in his chest, but it vibrated down his torso until the very ground started to shake.

The shaking cascaded outward, parting the crowd in the streets as a crane lumbered from beneath the bridge overpass a half mile down the highway. Relieved not to have his own discontentment shaking the foundation of his world quite so literally, he waved the people closest to the boat back toward the perimeter, watching as the other deputies did the same.

JJ walked in front of the slow-moving crane, making a

series of hand signals to the operator. The rest of the crew walked the flanks, keeping away nosey kids and selfie-taking adults.

The crane's lowered boom began a slow rise as the behemoth machine came to a grinding halt at the tip of the center island which housed the shrimp boat. As the crane continued its rise, a massive Christmas tree upended from the bed of machine, lifting higher until it dangled over the shrimp boat.

The crowd watched with rapt attention as he surveyed the area, making sure no one wandered too close. The mayor ushered a reluctant—and noticeably disheveled—Santa through the crowd toward the stairs leading to the boat's deck, grabbing a microphone with one hand and a retreating Santa with the other as he launched into a welcome speech.

As Jackson's eyes swept over the crowd, he saw Riley watching him from above, isolated in the crane's cab, her lips pressed into a thin, hard line. Not even the distance could hide the distrust. His heart thundered in his chest, his breath a painful lump in his throat. He'd feared she'd left town for good without saying good-bye. It left him colder than he would have thought. They barely knew one another. It didn't matter, however. She'd wound herself around his life.

She exited the crane's cab, descending the ladder with quick steps before settling in a quiet, shadowed spot away from the crowd. Dark and light surrounded her but revealed little outside of the wariness in her stance, arms crossed protectively in front of her. He checked his deputies, strategically stationed around the perimeter and motioned to his senior officer that he was taking a break.

Riley rested a hip against the back of the crane, a sudden

breeze catching the loose hair escaping her ponytail and whipping it across her face. She swiped it back absently, her gaze focused over the crowd.

"I wasn't sure if you were still in town," Jackson sidled up next to her, leaving an arm's length of space between them. Her shoulders tightened a fraction, and the motion squeezed sharply his chest. Was he now the enemy?

"Did you need someone to arrest to make your monthly quota?"

He cocked his head to the side, waiting to see if her face revealed any emotion. Joking? Serious? He reminded himself not to play poker with this woman. Then a slight twitch at the corner of her mouth hinted at a smile.

Something like relief washed over him. "You're safe." He rolled his shoulders to let the tension ease from his body. "I'm not allowed to arrest the same person more than twice a month."

The smile quirked higher. "But it's a new month. My last two arrests were in November."

"I'll keep my handcuffs ready."

She kicked at a patch of grass, the tell signaling her discomfort. But she didn't back down. Or run away. Progress?

"I've opened an account at the bail bondsman just in case."

The silence grew between them, a heavy cumbersome thing Jackson wanted to swat away. "Javier and Patrick brought Donavan by the station to make a statement about the fire."

Riley's posture stiffened. "It was an accident, Jackson. The kid freaked—"

Jackson waved her down with a slow press of his hands. "I know. So does Mr. Terrebonne. He wasn't going to press charges or anything, but Donavan wanted to pay for the damages."

"I'll cover it," Riley blurted, eyes narrowing as she met Jackson's gaze. "I know Patrick and Javier probably don't have that kind of money. I'm good for it. I'll sign over my paychecks to Mr. Terrebonne until it's paid for."

Damn the woman was loyal. When she called you a friend, she'd go to any lengths to protect you. It was one of the many things Jackson admired about her. He'd seen so many people over the years willing to sell out a friend for the price of cup of coffee. But not Riley. She'd give away her world for someone she cared about.

"It's a little pricey. You sure you want to do that?"

"I'm sure."

Jackson let the smile crack his face, seeing the confusion crinkle momentarily at the edge of Riley's eyes. "Mr. Terrebonne said the damage to the tree Donavan was carrying equaled a little over ten dollars." Riley sucked in a sharp breath. "Luckily, the money in the swear jar Connie keeps on the front desk covered it. I used a few choice words when I went to check. Just in case."

Riley's eyes widened, and she ducked her head until her emotions were safely tucked behind her walls. It took her two tries to speak.

"Remind me to send Mr. Terrebonne a very large supply of marshmallows." Her posture relaxed, and her attention went back to the crowd as she settled her body against the back of the crane. "Did Donavan–"

Hesitation stole the words, but it was the unease Jackson watched settle over Riley like a thunder cloud. She closed her eyes for a second, sighed.

"He still wouldn't say what you told him in the car that night."

She released the breath lifting her shoulders.

"But if you wanted to talk about it, I'm willing to listen."

She lifted her face to him, squared her body with his, and nodded. "Soon?"

She'd tried to make her expression blank, wipe the weight of the old pain, corral the ghosts, rebuild the wall of indifference. It failed, so he just nodded. "Good enough."

An uproar from the crowd interrupted them, and Jackson watched as the mayor turned to introduce Santa, momentary surprise registering as Santa was trying to sneak away. As the mayor retrieved Santa from disappearing down the boat's ladder and urged the not-so-jolly St. Nick back to center stage, the fake beard skewed slightly to the left as Santa tried to pull from the politician's determined grasp.

Jackson squinted against the glare of the portable spotlights. Recognition tickled the back of Jackson's brain, and he took a step toward the commotion.

Chapter Seventeen

Riley fell in step beside Jackson as he moved back toward the crowd, her skin suddenly prickling with gooseflesh. "Everything ok? You look tense all of a sudden."

He stopped and scrubbed a hand over his jaw before skimming it to the back of his neck, massaging the space there. A tell for deeper thoughts and concern she'd recognized when they were in the hardware store.

"Santa doesn't seem really happy to be here. Reminds me of the guy at the hardware store dressed like Santa. Why does a man dress as Santa at Christmas if he wants to be ignored?"

She widened her stance, leaning back on her heels. "Maybe he thought he'd blend in. Not stand out."

"Exactly what I was thinking."

Their conversation died as the mayor welcomed the town over the squeals of an ancient sound system. The town gave a collective gasp and covered their ears while Santa once again tried to sneak away. The mayor reached back and gripped Santa's arm just in time to yank him back to his side.

A movement overhead caught Riley's attention, drawing her eyes to the thirty-foot tree swinging slowly above the crowd. The tree wasn't meant to be held in that position long, only secured by a cable wrapped around the massive trunk. With the added stress of the movement, the soft wood wouldn't hold out.

"Jackson—" She started, but he'd taken off at a good clip toward the crowd, his eyes also glued on the movement of the Christmas tree. A grinding sound from behind spun her around to see a man fiddling with the gears on the crane. From there, things happened simultaneously.

The boom dropped down a few feet, sending a shower of pine needles like falling snow over the crowd. She dropped to a crouch as the tree bobbed sharply overhead, people scattered in all directions with shouts of warning and screams of fear. Jackson and his deputies waved the bystanders away from the crane, but the rushing crowd knocked over the ladder that allowed the mayor and a nervous Santa to descend from the boat's deck. Jackson took off for the fallen ladder.

Rising to her feet, she sprinted back to the crane as Jackson's voice shouted above the cries of alarm. Her own voice joined the chorus, shouting at her crew to help clear the area around the crane. Bodies moved as one, a wave of motion pouring outward from the epicenter of the crane.

She clamored up the ladder and yanked open the cab's door as the man inside maneuvered the levers haphazardly, his bulk filling up the interior of the crane. A moment of recognition—it was one of the angry customers from Gastineaux's—and confusion slowed her reaction, but she recovered and slammed her body into his shoulders. He barely flinched, shoving her back out the small cab's interior.

She teetered on the edge and stretched her arms overhead, grabbed the door top frame, lifted her legs, and rammed her two feet into the man's head, rewarded with a resounding crunch of his nose beneath her heel. He pitched sideways, grasping his bleeding nose in both hands while a wail of curses filled the interior of the cab. As he tried to right himself, he accidentally hit the correct lever to release the massive tree. The two of them paused in surprise as the giant pine spiraled toward the ground.

She held a breath and traced the large tree's rapid descent, somewhat relieved when it crashed into the empty shrimp boat rather than the people gathered around it. Off to the side, she could see Jackson ushering the shaken mayor into the retreating crowd.

She had little time to contemplate that minor miracle, or even recover her footing, before the man grabbed her around the waist and pulled her into the cab as he dove past her to freedom. She crashed into the crane's control panel, the metal digging painfully into her side as she slumped to the floor, reaching futilely for the retreating vandal's expensive loafer only to be left with the shoe as the fleeing man disappeared.

She pulled herself to her feet just as JJ stuck his head inside the door.

"Who the hell was that?" he shouted, giving her a hand up. He lifted the side of her shirt to peek at the angry red scrapes already visible across her waist.

"Cinder-felon," she answered, waving away his inspection of the injury and holding up the shoe in her possession. "I was hoping someone got a good enough look to describe him to the sheriff for me."

"Why can't you describe him to the sheriff?"

She pointed to the crowd below gaping up to her

standing on the crane's chassis. A palpable aura of anger and distrust shimmered in the faces closing in, especially Mason Gastineaux's.

"Because I'll likely be in handcuffs and sitting in the back of his car." She huffed her frustration in a short burst of air. "Again."

Chapter Eighteen

Jackson released the cuffs and shoved them back into his utility belt, ignoring the inner voice that wanted him to take her hands in his and massage the angry red marks circling her wrists. But it was unprofessional.

And she'd likely smack him.

"I'm—"

"Don't."

The clipped word silenced him immediately.

She kicked at the ground, fists stuffed in the pockets of her jeans, staring anywhere but the space he occupied.

Two EMTs stood near the perimeter and he gestured in their direction, wanting any reason to keep her near. Keep her safe. "At least let the paramedics look at you." Swipes of blood had seeped through her shirt, and he couldn't help but stare.

"It's nothing." She pulled the shirt away from her torso to examine the marks. A few tangles of hair fell over her cheek and she absently swiped them behind her ear when she lifted her head again. "Just a couple of scratches. I've had worse."

"That doesn't exactly make me feel better."

She swallowed hard and finally let her gaze meet his. Uncertainty was the only thing he could read in her eyes.

"I'll clean up at the hotel later."

"Riley..." He bit back the rest of the sentence, not knowing how to approach her. He was sorry he'd hurt her the last time they'd been together but not for pushing her buttons. She needed to be pushed. To see that she had to stake a claim in order to have the rights of ownership. So instead he said, "I need to get a statement about what happened. JJ said there was a guy in the cab of the crane."

"Yeah. I'm almost positive it was one of the guys that night at Gastineaux's. The lead asshat giving Mason a hard time wore a ring that he banged on the counter and this guy was wearing something similar."

He tried not to smile at her description but failed.

"But I can't be sure. I did get a good look at his shoe."

She handed over the shoe and gave him a quick rundown of the events, skimming over her attack of a man three times her size to keep him from dropping the tree. If only Mason could see this side of the woman who earned more and more of Jackson's respect every time she was near. She'd kept Donavan's accident out of the spotlight. Now she'd let everyone ignore her own selfless actions that likely saved many people from injury tonight. He looked at the broken tree laying in the rubble of the trawler's stern. Maybe even saved a few lives.

"You shouldn't have gone after him." He narrowed the distance between them, inhaling the earthy musk he now associated with her. "You could've been hurt."

"There wasn't time to call the cavalry." She turned her head to the side, shutting him out, but not before he saw that the ghosts were back, chasing away the light in her eyes and replacing it with shadows.

Unable to resist, he placed a finger under her chin, drawing her back to him. Her eyes searched his face, for what he couldn't say specifically, but more than anything he wanted to find the right words of reassurance that would erase the doubt and isolation hidden in the shadows in her eyes.

"You count, too, Riley." He had to swallow back other words that tripped over his heart on the way to his tongue. Words he knew would send her running once again in the opposite direction. "Somewhere along the way, you've forgotten or you've allowed yourself to believe you don't. But your health and safety and happiness count just as much as the rest of us."

He thought about his earlier assessment about her staking a claim. He wanted very much to pull her into his arms and kiss the daylights out of her in front of everyone milling about. Let them know she was off-limits to their scorn and distrust. But doing that would only make her mad. Riley needed to earn her spot in this town's fabric on her own. Otherwise, she'd never believe it was real.

She sure as hell wouldn't believe that he'd started to fall for her. He barely could believe it. And fall hard. She challenged him. Angered him. Pushed him. He wanted to know more about Riley. He wanted to get to know this confounding, confusing, exceptional woman. Actually, he wanted to know everything about her.

"I appreciate that, Jackson," she started, and a knife plunged into his gut driven by the look in her eyes. She retreated a few steps. "But I can't stay here. I'm moving on."

He tried to swallow past the lump stuck near his Adam's apple. "Will you be back?"

She shrugged, turning away from him again. "I'm sure I'll touch base with the crew between surveys like today. I promised Donavan I'd be here for Christmas day. But after the build is completed..." The sentence trailed away into the dark. "There's nothing for me here."

"Everything you want is here." *I'm here.* Even he could hear the desperation in his voice, but he didn't care. He was going to fight for her and for the chance to make her a part of his life wherever that may be. "You're just not looking hard enough."

"Says the man with a plan to leave town."

"That's the thing about plans; they're made to be changed." He didn't even know he'd changed his mind about leaving until he said the words. He could be happy here. If she was with him.

He reclaimed the space she'd put between them but didn't know how to knock down the walls around her heart. "Take a chance with me, Riley. Here in Belle Terre. Fight for what you want. Don't make the mistake your dad made. Fight for your family. Fight for your right to belong here. That's the only way you'll ever be a part of this town."

Something like doubt flickered on her face. Her eyes narrowed as if she were looking beyond what she could see in front of her. Was she looking for something or trying to block it out?

"You should run for sheriff," she said, a sad smile weakly lifting the corners of her mouth. "You'll be a good protector for the town."

A combination of dread and anger wormed its way through his system, finding his heart with pinpoint accuracy. They began to squeeze. "Riley don't—"

"Good-bye, Jackson."

Chapter Nineteen

Riley'd driven back to town in the final hours of Christmas Eve, avoiding a pass by the sheriff's office, instead going straight to the hotel. Most of the crew was already gone, headed back to their own families scattered around the country for the holiday. She'd missed them before she arrived, missed them even more when she found them gone. She refused to think about who else she missed.

Even now, the accusations stung. He'd had no right to accuse her of being like her father that night at the tree lighting. The situations were completely different, she kept telling herself. Her father refused to fight for them. She'd fought.

And lost.

She found her room key tucked in the visor of the company truck just as her ex had promised, along with a card from JJ.

Outside: *Everyone wants to be on Santa's nice list.*

Inside: *I think the naughty list is more fun.*

Taped to the bottom was a key that could only fit a pair

of handcuffs. Scribbled at the bottom in JJ's serial killer-handwriting was a note:

Stop finding excuses. Make reasons.

In her room, a tree that would make Charlie Brown proud sat in the corner by the television, a collection of paper ornaments weighing down the spindly branches. An aluminum foil star nearly pulled the top down on itself. Another note waited, Jackson's familiar handwriting on the folded cardstock.

No elf should be without her tree on Christmas.
- J

Riley looked into the cracked mirror over the dresser and ignored the tears crawling down her face.

～

R iley helped Patrick corral the kids into the dining room, pulling bits of paper from her hair left over from the crown of Christmas ribbons she'd been wearing most of the morning.

"This town is tough," he advised, his arms crushing together a mound of wrapping paper before stuffing it in the garbage bag at his feet. "But that's also what makes it good. People weren't unkind to me and Javier when we arrived. They were cautious, quiet."

"That's just polite southern judgment," Riley interpreted. He'd been trying to convince her, however subtly, to give the town another chance. And though it went unspoken, she knew Jackson fit in the second chance category as well.

Patrick gave her a one-armed squeeze. "That, too. But we're part of the fabric of the town now."

Javier stuck his head into the living room. "We're the neon pink silk in a tapestry of sturdy cotton blends. Y'all get in here. The food's ready."

She'd wanted to fit into the town, but events had put her on the outside looking in. It was a familiar view. Even if she wanted to change it, where to begin? Destruction seemed to follow her around. The bank. The hardware store. The tree lighting.

Birthday cakes.

She sighed, wishing she could release the uncertainty just as easily.

Riley looked back at the heap of destruction under the tree, a snort of disbelief at the bikes, skateboards, doll houses and assorted clothing draped over handlebars and rooftops. The toys may have been secondhand, but no one noticed or cared. They had reason to be happy, so they were.

"Beep beep, Riley!"

As seven-year-old Lordes zipped by in her brand new wheelchair, a gift from Santa that had appeared on the porch that morning, Riley scooped up three-year old Jin from the kiddie stampede and jumped out of the way.

"The Tiara Express coming through!" Lordes *vroomed* past the duo, taking a corner on two wheels as her new bell echoed against the high cracked ceilings and scuffed hardwood floors of the massive but ancient home.

Jin giggled and threw her head back, arms wide as she waited to be tickled. It had been their game since Riley's arrival, and she didn't want to disappoint the little girl. She traced her fingers up to the child's ribs to her armpits, rewarded with a deluge of squiggles and high-pitched squeals.

Jin relaxed in her arms, tiny fingers signing something with great joy, but Riley could only smile and wink. She didn't recognize the sign as one they'd taught her that morning.

"She's saying you're silly," Javier translated as he buzzed into the room with an armful of sausage, eggs, and pancakes piled on a giant platter, sliding the food to the center of a table already laden with pitchers of juice and milk, not to mention the jelly, butter, utensils and plates.

Riley noted the kitchen door was missing. In fact, most of the downstairs doors were missing. Bits of plaster dotted the hardwood floor like snowflakes every time someone walked upstairs. When she'd walked in that morning, a chime had greeted her from the new door alarm installed at the front entrance. It was the one Jackson had picked up that day at the hardware store. There was also a new line of caulking around the front door windows. Another item she'd seen in the good sheriff's shopping cart.

She put the brake on those thoughts, knowing it would lead to nowhere but more frustration, doubt, and disappointment.

Patrick began handing out plates and silverware to the older kids as Javier disappeared back into the kitchen.

Riley settled Jin into a booster seat as the kids all squeezed around the large oak table, chairs, the wheelchair, and highchair lining every inch of the ten-person table with barely enough room between them and the walls. Patrick flipped the light switch on the wall, but the overhead didn't come on. He flicked it a few more times before giving up with a shake of his head. Mid-morning light filtered in from the large living room windows, along with a healthy breeze that ruffled the ornaments on the tree. Riley noted no windows were open, however.

"OK, who can teach me the sign for *am not*?" Riley asked as the kids slowly settled. Donavan waited for her to take a seat then quickly snagged the one next to her.

Collectively, every child at the table made the simple sign, thumb under chin thrusting outward with a firm shake of the head then an index finger to the chest. Riley couldn't help but laugh and repeated the sign to a giggling Jin.

When the entire family was finally gathered around the table, Javier and Patrick bowed their heads, each child following suit without so much as a word. Patrick led the simple *God is Great* prayer in sign language and English while Javier added his own rich baritone in Spanish. The kids followed, speaking the prayer in both sign and either English or Spanish.

Then calm chaos ensued.

Patrick passed the plate of eggs to Riley with a warning. "Better grab what you want now because there will be nothing left. These little guys eat like a band of starved lumberjacks from Survivor."

"We're growing kids!" a collective shout responded to the apparently usual jab as butter and jelly and syrup passed from hand to hand, older kids helping the younger without any prompt from the dads.

Riley scooped a serving of eggs onto her plate and another serving on Jin's, plopping a pancake onto her own plate before signing an unsure, "You want?" to Jin and pointing to a pancake.

The little girl nodded enthusiastically, one small fist signing *yes* around her clutched fork while she grabbed at the eggs with her other hand. A quick and eggy thank you followed as Riley passed the plate down to Donavan and Javier.

Javier beamed at his foster daughter, his handsome face truly glowing with love. He signed, speaking aloud at the same time. "Slow down and chew. There's more for later."

Riley's heart sank, but she pulled a poker face up from her emotional vault and kept busy with passing things from Patrick to Javier. She'd not asked about each child's story. Some of it was obvious. Lordes' chair. Nathan's Down Syndrome. It was the other scars she worried about that caused a tremble in her legs, a mushroom of emotion bubbling up from her core.

She'd never felt loved or truly wanted in foster care, but she'd never been starved either. Her gaze touched on Donavan's face before bouncing around the table to the other kids. She'd mostly ignored the challenges faced by these kids because they didn't seem to be an issue for the family. Everyone belonged. Everything worked, not always smoothly, but in just the few hours she'd spent with the family while Christmas unfolded, unwrapped, and unraveled, nothing had fazed any of them.

The steady clink of silverware against plates, the laughter of kids as they talked of new toys and clothes filled in the gap in the conversation while Riley tried to swallow the lump in her throat.

Patrick wiped a smudge of butter from baby Nathan's chin. "Jin was about a year and half when she came to us." His voice caught, and he cleared his throat, relaxing when Javier gave him a wink from the other end of the table. "Not too late for us to work on her signing, but she'd already learned that food wouldn't always be there."

"It's gotten better," Javier quickly added, cutting into his own pancake with one hand and putting his other onto five-year-old Sam's back. The small boy was rocking quietly at the table as he separated the food on his plate with his fingers. Sam stilled once Javier's hand made contact, and he accepted the fork his dad handed him.

"Eggs come from chicken butts," Sam announced quite seriously, before continuing to eat. Only when Sam began to eat did his older sister, Selena, also pick up her fork and eat. No one reacted to Sam's odd announcement, but his straightforward approach to the truth was part of what Riley loved about the little boy.

"I'm ... I..." Riley couldn't find the right words to Patrick's explanation about Jin. *I'm sorry* didn't seem adequate. And Jin looked like a happy, healthy little girl, her dark silky hair swinging back and forth as she bopped to a song only in her head. She signed to one of her brothers and the bowl of fruit came her way. Riley grabbed the spoon before Jin could get to it and put some of the strawberries on the child's plate. "I don't know what to say."

"There's nothing to say." Patrick stood, putting a hand on her shoulder while reaching for the milk to refill glasses around the table. Matter-of-factly he added, "She's happy. We're happy. Everything else will work itself out in time."

Riley absorbed that for a minute as food disappeared at an alarming rate. She nibbled at her own plate, amazed that Patrick and Javier got more than two bites each while helping, pouring, passing, cutting, serving, or cleaning up something or another every few seconds.

"Don't you get overwhelmed?"

Javier laughed around a mouthful of pancake. "On an hourly basis."

"Hourly?" Patrick gasped, his one free hand clutched to his chest dramatically, the feigned shock widening his eyes as he scrunched his brows together into a single caterpillar-like line. "I thought we agreed to the half-hour schedule."

Javier gave his husband an exaggerated eye roll and a dismissive wave. "I renegotiated with the kids. Only one crisis per hour at least until Nathan is out of diapers."

Nathan gave a chuckle at the mention of his name, extending both meaty fists over his head like a ref calling a touchdown.

"Nathan!" the kids called out, mimicking the touchdown gesture.

Then all motion stopped and all eyes turned to Riley, who sat a little stunned in her seat. When Donavan elbowed her in the ribs, she realized what they wanted and quickly lifted her hands over her head and cheered, "Nathan!"

The fit of giggles round-robined around the table as everyone went back to eating. A hint of goosebumps pimpled her flesh as realization made its way through her brain.

The two dads were a dream come true for many foster kids. A stable, loving home. Acceptance and patience. Was anything else really important in a family?

Or a home?

But she didn't have acceptance in Belle Terre. The town's patience had been tested between the incident at the bank and the hardware store, not to mention the tree lighting ceremony. Three strikes. She'd thought it better to leave before they ran her out of town.

Next to her, Donavan chatted across the table with Sam and Selena, though the younger boy didn't always respond. He spoke his truth quietly and selectively while Selena watched everyone with a stoicism that tugged at Riley.

Donavan, Riley's little shadow, had really come out of his shell in the weeks since the fire, and now you'd never know he'd once felt insecure about his place in the family. Riley knew that would surface now and again—it was a constant battle with foster kids.

Even with herself now as an adult.

Was that why she'd resisted attachments? Riley always blamed her job as the reason she'd not found a relationship after her marriage. Had she really been secure with Will? Will had been a good husband, but they'd been convenient for each other rather than a true match. He'd found that with Lara when he returned to Belle Terre and dived in headfirst into her life and family. Riley had heard a rumor they were expecting a baby after only a few weeks together. They seemed ecstatic at the news.

She thought of her own families—biological, foster, chosen—and found the common element missing. Engagement. At first it was her father who'd checked out. Then it was her. Had her own father been too afraid to lose more than he already had if he failed? *When* he failed, she reminded herself.

That day with CFS all over the house, the fire department, neighbors, he'd not looked mad. He'd looked lost and embarrassed. That had been her as well when she stepped out of the juvenile facility the day of her release, her foster family waiting. She couldn't face them. Not for their failures, but for her own.

Wasn't that what Jackson had told her? That she was too afraid to fail and wouldn't put herself out there.

"I was noticing the door to the kitchen," Riley indicated with a slight nod of her head, the weight of risk pressing against her chest. "I happen to know someone with construction experience who would be happy to look at that for you. I happen to have a connection that specializes in salvage from older homes. It would match the decor if not the time period of the house."

Javier multi-tasked a negotiation for the last two pancakes and a new glass of juice and glanced over his shoulder, surprise registering briefly. "Oh, they're not missing. We had to take them off the hinges for Lourdes' chair. Though it would be great if the kitchen had a door while I was cooking to keep the tasters at bay." He threw a pointed look at Patrick, who ignored him with a smile. "And as you can tell," he plopped one pancake on two plates held aloft by Selena and Donavan and picked up the juice pitcher in a continuous flow of motion, "I'm always cooking with this gang."

Riley didn't hide the smile as the table erupted in a chorus of hoots and bell rings and cheers for another touchdown from Nathan.

A knock on the front door interrupted the celebration, and the kids yelled, "Santa!" as they almost jumped to their feet before collectively stopping mid-hop and looking to Javier and Patrick.

Javier swallowed the laugh and struggled to hide the twitch of his mouth. "OK. You're excused."

The words barely made it from his lips before the kids spilled from the table like water over a cliff, running en masse toward the front door. Riley helped a bouncy Jin down from her booster chair and watched as she followed only a few steps behind Lordes and Sam as they skidded around the corner. The two older kids, Donavan and Selena, yanked at the door with some boisterous grunts, the door sticking to the frame with stubborn intent before an ear-splitting creak sounded and it broke free, opening with the chime of bells. She added that to her mental list of repairs she and her crew would undertake before they wrapped up the build downtown.

"Sheriff!" the announcement was followed immediately by a healthy "Ho! Ho! Ho!" in Jackson's strong bass.

Riley gulped down the spike of adrenaline short circuiting her brain as Jackson edged into the house in the center of a swirling Category Five hurricane of children. The kids jumped at the two sacks he held suspended over their heads, a wicked grin connecting the dimple in his cheek to the desire tugging at Riley's insides. He handed the two bags to Javier, who'd gotten up from the table while Patrick tended Nathan.

"C.A.N.D.Y." Jackson waggled his brows conspiratorially, waiting as the kids fell silent.

Then they erupted, "Candy!"

Riley giggled and lifted Jin onto her hip as the toddler reached up both hands plaintively, but she'd noted that Selena had fallen back a few steps as the other kids did something related to dancing around Jackson's long legs.

Javier rolled his eyes, taking the bags from Jackson. "Thanks, bud. I'll remember this in a few weeks at the election. I'm going to stuff the ballot box with your name."

"My pleasure." Jackson motioned to the two bags. "There's some sugar-free stuff in there for Selena."

Riley's attention fell back to Selena whose face lit up like the star on top of the tree in the living room. She pointed a finger at her chest, the new medic alert bracelet on her wrist appropriately bedazzled by blue and green sparkle gems.

"For me, Mr. Sheriff?"

Jackson dropped to a squat, balancing like a pro as the kids clamored to sit on his knees. His eyes met Riley's briefly but focused on Selena, giving the little girl his full attention.

"Absolutely, kiddo. I wouldn't forget my favorite girl now, would I?"

Selena's hesitation melted on the flash of Jackson's brilliant smile, and she launched herself into his arms. "I've never been anyone's favorite girl."

Jackson curled one arm around her tiny frame. "I think your dads would disagree, but you'll always be my favorite nine-year-old."

Selena pulled back, a seriousness drawing her eyebrows together. "But I'll be ten next month."

Jackson clunked his forehead against hers. "Then you'll be my favorite ten-year-old girl."

It was official, Riley realized beneath the spike of adrenaline. She'd fallen for Jackson Guidry.

"Alright kids," Patrick clapped his hands, Nathan joining in the fun from his spot on his dad's hip. "Let's get back to the dining room and clear the table, ok? Everyone pick up their plate and fork and put it in the sink."

"Yessir!"

"Carefully!" Javier added as eight feet and two tires squeaked across the hardwood back to the table before piling into the kitchen.

"Holy cow." Riley released a heavy breath as the kids disappeared into the back. She could hear more giggles from the next room but not a single crash, break, or wail.

"You have no idea," Javier agreed, taking Nathan from Patrick as he planted a kiss on his husband's jelly-coated cheek. "Merry Christmas," he whispered as if they were the only two in the room.

"Merrier every year," Patrick whispered back, brushing his thumb across Javier's stubbled chin.

Riley watched the loving exchange with a mix of envy and excitement for their happiness. The hobbled together family reminded her of the construction crew. Everyone belonged in their own way and with their own set of challenges. But it worked. *They* worked, better together than apart.

So why had she left?

Her gaze sidled to Jackson, who watched her with a curious tilt to his mouth.

"What's so funny?"

He reached over, plucking something from her hair. His knuckle scorched her cheek and set off a fire storm in the pit of her belly, not to mention a place lower on her anatomy. He held bit of silver tinsel before her. A prize? A peace offering?

"What?" she mouthed as the kids came crashing back into the dining room.

The kids pushed at Jackson's legs, and he nearly had to shout over the chaotic din of excited kids' voices. "Your elf girl is showing."

"Come see, Mr. Sheriff!"

"We got new toys!"

"And clothes!"

"You even have a present under the tree!"

The chorus ping-ponged around them, but the last one grabbed Jackson's attention and his head snapped to the left while a grin grabbed one corner of his mouth. "Santa left me a present at your house?"

"Yes!" the chorus answered, and together they ushered Riley and Jackson into the living room. Javier was already reaching beneath the mountain of crumpled paper and passed the box wrapped in the Sunday comics over to Patrick who then passed it to Jackson.

Riley laughed at the awed look on Jackson's face as he carefully examined the package, turning it this way and that, touching the ribbon and paper with an abundance of appreciation.

"I love it, kids," he held up the wrapped box and examined it as if the finest treasure. "I'll put it on my shelf so I can see it every day."

"You have to open it, Mr. Sheriff," Selena interrupted, hands on hips as Jackson pretended to consider her words. "The present is *inside*."

"Oh," Jackson nodded thoughtfully. "That would make more sense. Let's see what's inside!" His deep bass sank even lower and turned gravelly as he mimicked the Hulk ripping into the box, and Riley joined the kids as they laughed uncontrollably at Jackson's faux snarl. Her heart did a little two-step when he tore into the box, his face washed of color and expression while he examined what was inside.

His jaw dropped, and with infinite care, he traced a finger over the homemade plaque decorated with painted macaroni and a variety of stickers and beads.

Our hero.

He opened his mouth to speak but could only clear his throat. His attention snapped to Riley, the gaze simultaneously clouded with a desperation to escape and a hungry need to believe.

Even now, hours later, the emotion wrapped inside the simple gift welled inside Riley, crowding out lesser things like doubt and suspicion. She gave him a half-smile and a shrug filled with understanding of the emotion. "I got one, too."

She knew the battle inside of Jackson right now because it was one she waged as well. Wanting to belong. Wanting the family. Wanting.

Jackson dropped to his haunches, his eyes shifting from the gift in his hands to the kids circling him. "I don't know what to say kids," he croaked hoarsely, his gaze touching on each of the kids' faces as his throat worked hard. "It's the best present I've ever gotten from anyone."

"Even Santa?" Selena pushed forward a little, then took a step back, the momentary elation on her face replaced with the more usual wariness.

"Santa's elves got nothing on you guys."

He opened his arms, encompassing Lourdes first as the rest of the kids swarmed into the hug, knocking Jackson to his backside with squeals and giggles as they piled on top. Even Selena and Sam joined in the fray until Jackson was begging for rescue.

"OK, kids, let's not assault the nice policeman on Christmas morning," Javier joked, offering a hand to Jackson while Riley did the same. Once on his feet, Jackson's hand lingered a bit longer than necessary in Riley's, the current between them warm and pulsing.

"I actually needed to see you, Riley." He pointed back toward the door as the kids and dads returned to the living room.

"What's up?" she asked, trying to ignore the tingling feeling on her skin where Jackson had touched her.

"A call came in this morning indicating a possible break-in out at the Fortune place. I thought you might want to ride out there and take a look. I cleared the scene, but you probably know the place better than anyone and can tell if anything was damaged or taken."

Riley's senses went on alert. Even though the place wasn't hers yet—and likely wouldn't be—she still thought of it as her future home. Hopefully, there wasn't too much damage.

She and Jackson made their excuses to Javier, Patrick, and the kids and, despite the protests and demands for promises to return, it only took her a few minutes to grab her jacket and meet Jackson outside.

As they trooped down the front steps, she couldn't help but check him out, cataloging his relaxed uniform in honor of Christmas, she assumed. She let her eyes wander up the dark jeans riding low on his hips before following the uniform shirt from where it tucked in at the waist to where it strained over the wide shoulders. Things got warm in her body, low in her body, and she did a mental slap to steer her mind to the right path.

Trouble was, the path it was on was just fine with her.

Chapter Twenty

J ackson could feel her watching him. He wanted to turn around and catch her in the act but feared he would chase her away. She'd just gotten back in town after several weeks of being on the road. He didn't want her to leave again. He was content to ignore the reasons for now.

He stopped on the passenger side, opening the door for her but leaving her to close it on her own. He knew better than to help her too much. It was things like that that kept his mind occupied the last few weeks. How would she react to his sister wanting to meet her? What would she think of joining him in Florida? Would he get to kiss her again?

He stashed his gift from the kids in the back seat, and by the time he squeezed his frame into the mid-sized sedan, she was buckled in, holding the two pies that had been resting on the seat. They balanced on her knees, and he couldn't help but follow the path of her thighs up to her hips. He breathed deep, realizing he liked the smell of her shampoo better than the warm apple pies in her possession.

The grin tilted up one side of her mouth. "The board-walk posse I presume?"

"They've been especially attentive the last few weeks."

He said it, knowing she'd understand. Knowing she'd guess his reaction to the posse without telling her. Did she care? Judging by the shit-eating-grin on her face, he didn't think so.

She bent down and laid the two pies on the floor of the front seat, tucking them back enough so she wouldn't step on them later. "How many of them invited you for breakfast, lunch, or dinner today?"

"I don't remember," he muttered, focused way too hard on making the three-point turn onto the highway rather than the way Riley's attention made him both too aware of his entire body and totally relaxed at the same time.

She laughed, the full throaty sound wrapping around insides. Riley angled her back against the door, facing him and crossing her arms. "That must mean all of them."

He relaxed his body, driving with his left hand while draping his right arm across the back of the seat. "You're having way too much fun with that information."

She sobered a little more than he wanted, tipping her head slightly to look out the window at the sky overhead. "It's lonely on the road. Nearly the entire crew has gone somewhere for the holidays. I have to give someone a hard time or my skills get rusty."

"We can't have that." He tried for lighthearted, but his words were flat.

The subject was a sore spot. Her disappearance hadn't really given them a chance to resolve their fight over her plans to leave. Or his admission that his plans were amenable to change. He figured that had been the reason she took off. Did she see it as pressure? Or would any hint that he wanted more be enough to send her running even faster in the other direction?

It was his turn to change the subject. "There's still no news on Ricky. He left a message at home that he was safe, but we have no way to get in touch with him. Cinder-felon," he glanced her way in time to see her smile at the use of her nickname for the man she attacked, "and his buddies have been notably absent from town, and my description didn't ring any bells with my brother. He said it sounded like half the account managers at the firm, but he's had a forensic accountant going over the books. It's a lot of transactions to audit and the balance sheets show no money missing. Your money is there."

"Just not where it's supposed to be."

"Still, if we call in the authorities thing get complicated according to Ethan. You're the only one complaining of missing funds so far."

"Have you talked to your dad? Your brother?"

Jackson hesitated. The underlying accusation was understandable, but it still needled him to know she thought his family capable of the deception. He didn't think long on why it bothered him—they'd deceived him enough in the past to make their motives suspect even to him. But while his dad was a prideful man who might sell off his son to secure his business, he wouldn't steal.

"No, but my sister has, and I trust her."

They rode in silence for a bit, passing by the lake on the way out of town. Campaign signs littered the side of the road; unfortunately, most of them were for him.

With the election just a few months away, he needed to make a decision. Leave, and meet up with his buddy in Florida. Spend his days running fishing expeditions for tourists until he got bored. Or stay and build something here in Belle Terre.

Our hero.

That gift had nearly been his undoing. For the first time in a decade, he wanted to settle down, maybe try and live up to the macaroni-shaped words on that plaque. Sure, it terrified the hell out of him to think of the expectations that came with this job. But, in truth, he'd never felt more at ease.

A few others had thrown their hat into the ring for sheriff. Mason Gastineaux was pushing himself as a write-in candidate. Jackson wasn't sure Gastineaux had the right temperament for the role. The man liked to pull his shotgun on customers.

Maybe Mason would win and the choice would be out of Jackson's hands. Or Jackson could withdraw, leaving Mason as the only candidate. A decision by default didn't sit well with him, however.

"I hear your name's still on the ballot for the election." Riley turned her attention back to him, pulling him from the direction of his thoughts.

Jackson tugged at the collar of his shirt. "Yeah. I didn't officially withdraw."

"Is that an admission that you want the job?"

He shrugged one shoulder, allowing himself to think through his response before giving it, even though his answer had come to him a few days ago. "There are worse things than having people look to you for help."

"So, you're sticking around?"

He thought about it, the choice more than just putting down roots. "It's the first time, maybe in my life, that people have looked to me without seeing my dad first. If I fail them, I'll have no one to blame but myself. The thought of what could go wrong terrifies the ever-loving shit out of me, but yeah, if elected, I'm sticking around."

"What if you're not elected?"

Jackson gave his head a slight shake, letting the grin

pushing at his lips have its due. "Do you think I could get that lucky?"

She tossed the silken weight of her hair over a shoulder. "Hell, no. Congratulations, Mr. Sheriff."

Jackson made the turn onto the dirt road that led to the Fortune camp. Crime scene tape fluttered on the gate, and a muscle in Riley's neck pulsed as they passed from the highway to the private property.

"Those kids are something else, aren't they?" He spoke around the lump in his throat.

"They're amazing," Riley admitted. Then added with a smirk, "And Patrick and Javier have done wonders with Donavan. He won't stop talking."

He slowed the car to a crawl, parking behind the house under the dense overhang of a large cypress tree. Boards covered the windows and front door but it wouldn't take much to get into the house. His eyes met hers as he cut the engine, noting the tense line of her shoulders, the thin set to her mouth. A mouth he still wanted to taste and tease.

He wrangled his focus back to the topic at hand. "Patrick and Javier are amazing, but Donavan's change is because of you."

She gave a quick shake of her head as she gathered her dark hair into a ponytail, snapping the band from around her wrist to secure it. "He just needed to know they wouldn't desert him. I couldn't give that to him. His dads had to. They're the reason he's ok."

She opened the door and stepped out of the vehicle before he could answer, leaving him to follow her out and stop her in front of the vehicle. "But Donavan was willing to take a chance on them because of you. You gave him the courage to take the chance. Without that, he wouldn't be a part of that family like he is now. He might live there, but they wouldn't *be* his family."

"You make it sound so simple."

"It is and it isn't simple. My guess is you shared something of your past with him."

The shield Riley used as a weapon snapped across her face so quickly and so completely Jackson felt the disturbance in the air flow.

"I still don't know what you told him," he added, palms held out in surrender and reassurance. "That's between you and Donavan. But Javier told me that Donavan said it was ok for them to punish him because tough love was still love."

A wetness shimmered over her eyes, but she looked away and cleared her throat. She punched her fists against her waist, shoulders squared into a taut line. Jackson gave her a minute while he went to open the door to the house. From his earlier walk around the perimeter, nothing looked broken. The door jam and lock were intact, so it was likely whomever had gotten in found an open window.

He felt her presence before anything else. The heat of her body branded his, her essence merging with his to raise his temp just short of spontaneous combustion. The scent of her shampoo filled his senses. The steady sound of her breath in perfect rhythm with his own.

"The trailer was locked up tight." He gestured to the silver bullet of aluminum sitting at the edge of the water, the canopy of cypress overhead brushing the top. A makeshift porch hugged one end, jutting into the water where boaters could tie in after a day on the water. "This place had easier access and was more concealed by the trees."

"Did you find the entry point?" Her voice, steadier now, was still softer than normal.

He pushed opened the door and stepped between the boards nailed to the frame and into the home; the interior light muted with dust. "Nothing obvious. There are no brick-induced opened windows. Either they were very careful, or the door wasn't locked."

Riley filled in the space he'd vacated and jiggled the door handle. "There's no bolt on the door and no molding around the frame, just a spring lock, so a credit card would be easy enough to flip the lock."

He let her walk around the living room, still mostly a bare structure except for a ragged couch flush in the corner. A bulb topped a lamp held together by duct tape. It was the lamp that drew her attention first.

She lifted the dilapidated thing, tilting it sideways to look at the bottom before holding it out to him and showing him the exposed wiring and electrical tape. "They hacked the lamp. Attached an eight-pack of double-A batteries."

"Anyone with a smartphone can find that on a DIY website though."

"Yeah, but it's not likely kids are going to go to this much trouble for a night. They'll bring flashlights or a lantern. The lamp is more permanent."

He couldn't fault her logic, so he didn't. He lifted a corner of a cushion, then removed it altogether. Underneath, he found a piece of plywood over a hole in the couch's deck and motioned her over as he examined what was hidden inside the bones. "We've got quite a supply here. Food. Water. Batteries. First aid kit." Using a plastic glove which he removed from his utility belt, Jackson pulled out the first aid kit, opening the lid, adding, "which has been used." He peered under the other cushions. "Sleeping bag. Clothing." He picked up a weighted sock and shook it, the sound of coins clinking. "Piggy bank."

"Home sweet home." Riley turned from the sofa, moving farther into the heart of the house then doubling back toward the south wall. "Our vagrant will come back eventually."

Jackson followed her into the kitchen, peering out to the back deck. He opened a few cabinets. "The kitchen actually looks like it's been cleaned. A few Sterno cans for cooking. A portable grill. No food or trash. Either our squatter is eating in town or they're taking the trash with them."

"Very considerate."

The rear of the house was more complete. The deck and eat-in kitchen mostly finished from what he could tell.

"It'll be a great place once you get it finished," he said out loud, wanting the words to convey the faith he had in her. In her ability to overcome anything thrown at her. How she could doubt that was the only thing that confused him. He didn't think Riley doubted anything about herself. Then again, maybe it wasn't her she doubted. It was just everyone else.

He heard the sigh, then her feet scuffing the plank flooring. "The house has good bones. And that," she pointed to something, but he didn't take his eyes off her face. "They mirrored the Greek key designs."

He watched as she pointed out different aspects of the architecture, telling him what she'd do to this corner in the gallery or how she'd miter that angle near a hole in the wall for a seamless match. Her body was in constant motion, but her eyes, it was her eyes that really painted the picture because Jackson could see her visualizing the house in her head. What it could be with a little love and plaster and paint, turning the house into a home.

Beneath that, though, he recognized her passion, a soul-deep desire to build something where there was nothing.

Or, more importantly for Riley, to fix something that was broken. Jackson's chest squeezed around the word *broken*. Riley thought she was broken, which is why she had such unwavering loyalty to her crew and her friends. They took her as she was—broken bits and all—so she gave them everything she had. Her loyalty. Her faith.

"I was going to add a jewel box where you're standing now." She pointed to the wall looking over the deck.

He had to clear the emotion from his throat to speak. "A jewel box?"

"A poor man's conservatory." She smiled at the explanation.

He approached her while she spoke, taking a step every few words so not to spook her.

She stilled, a wariness darkening behind her eyes. "Removable windows so you can use it year-round."

Her eyes widened a touch, and he risked life and limb to reach out and push a strand of hair behind her ear, running his thumb down the curve of her jaw and across the bow of her lip.

"With a rooftop deck to see out on the water." Her voice now a hoarse whisper, her eyes locked with his, and he saw them fill with the need to flee.

She didn't flee, however, and Jackson knew it took every ounce of her considerable willpower to stand there and be admired; be desired.

Because that's what he did. He admired the hell out of this woman. Desired her almost as much. Strong and vulnerable. Passionate and fiercely loyal. And oh-so-blind to the beauty that started inside and worked its way outward.

He took a cautious step forward. She mirrored the step back.

"Jackson." The word said caution, beware.

"I know." And he did. With every fiber of his being. He knew it was a mistake, an error in judgment.

Another step forward for him.

Another step back for her. But smaller this time.

But it was an error he was going to make. And he'd not regret one damn moment of it.

Her backside hit the countertop and she braced her hands on the edge. He pinned her with his presence and placed his hands slowly next to hers on the edge of the counter, his thumbs rubbing tiny circles on the back of her hands.

Her chest rose and fell in slow, measured movements, her lips parting as if the escaping breaths were too big to leave any other way. They hovered that way, faces close, bodies curving around each other but still not touching, as if their heat recognized the danger and pushed back. He scented the sweet bite of wintergreen that he now associated with her. The flowery perfume of her shampoo or soap.

As he lowered his head toward her, he heard the sharp intake of breath a second before he pressed his lips to the small vee at the base of her throat. He trailed his tongue lightly up the small ridge of flesh over her collarbone.

"I've missed you," he whispered when he reached the shell of her ear, burying his mouth behind the lobe and pressing another kiss there. A raspy breath shuddered from her.

She moved her arms to his neck, leveraging her body against his to arch farther back for better access.

"I've missed talking with you." Another kiss down on her neck. "I've missed fighting with you." This time his lips pressed to her temple. "I've missed seeing you in town with a hard hat over your hard head." Her chest rumbled with suppressed laughter. "I've missed putting you in handcuffs." A smile sharpened the angle of her cheeks. Her eyes fluttered closed as he pressed his lips to each lid. "I've missed knowing you were here even if I didn't see you." He gave similar treatment to her other ear, licking and scraping his teeth along the edge before gliding his mouth down her throat until he was back at the starting point at the base of her throat. Her pulse thrummed beneath the skin near her jaw, and he flicked his tongue over the spot.

His hands found her waist, circling it easily as he hooked two fingers in her belt loops and pulled her closer, grinding the swell of his erection against her stomach. She hissed and leaned in, the pressure exquisitely tortuous.

"What are you doing, Jackson?"

"If you can't tell, then I'm doing something wrong." More soft kisses. More gasps of pleasure. "I'm going to touch you so tell me to stop."

Jackson skimmed his fingertips beneath the waistband of her jeans, pulling her shirt free so he could touch her skin, feel the warmth of her flesh. His own body was on fire and he wanted hers to be the same.

He found the spot beneath her ear that made her hum in pleasure. "You're not telling me to stop." Jackson pulled back enough to look into her eyes, the lids half closed. He could feel the ragged release of her breath on his neck, feel the tight grip of her fingers on his forearms. "I need you to say the words, Riley. Tell me to stop and I will. I'll walk away."

Her eyes opened fully and he saw the hope warring with experience in the tremble of her lips. "I don't want you to stop."

With slow movements, he unsnapped her jeans and slid the zipper down, easing his hand into the envelope of space between her and the clothing.

He followed the curve of her body beneath the soft fabric of her panties, through the silken curls at the apex of her legs, until his fingers found the heated folds of her sex. He cupped her intimately, and she rocked her hips forward as he eased his middle finger into her flesh, skimming along the edge but not delving inside.

A delicious groan of frustration and desire rumbled out as she clasped her hands on either side of his face and drew him down to press her forehead against his chin.

"Tell me what you want, Riley." He made slow circle with the tip of his finger against the seam of her body at the same time his teeth caught her lower lip and tugged ever so lightly.

A sweet moan gasped from between her lips. "That." She gasped again as he gave her what she asked for, and she moved her hips against his fingers. "More of that."

He gave her what she asked for, brought her to the edge, eased her back from the precipice while his tongue played chase with hers. He left her mouth, his teeth scraping along her jaw, the tip of her nose, the ridge of her collarbone. She leaned forward, resting her forehead on his chest, her breath a raspy, desperate sound.

Riley dropped one hand from his face and started pulling at the waist of his jeans, and it was his turn to gasp and moan.

"No," he stopped her, reluctant as a starving man before a world class buffet. "Let me."

Her body tensed, and she studied him beneath the fan of her lashes, the flecks of silver in her eyes sharpened on the edges of doubt and suspicion. Her face was flushed, their arousal scenting the air. "Why?"

He slipped a finger inside of her body, then added

another, the clench of her muscles pulling him in and holding him there. "Because this is what I want."

Jackson claimed her mouth, her body already his as the orgasm convulsed across her muscles. Her breath bathed his skin in hot waves as the ripples receded.

Her hand pressed over the bulge in his jeans, and he bit out a curse beneath his breath. "I don't have any condoms."

"I'm on the pill."

"I was tested earlier in the year. Clean bill of health."

"Ditto."

When she reached again for his jeans, he didn't stop her this time. She opened his fly enough to palm the length of his cock before pushing down the band of his boxer briefs and wrapping her hand around the base. Her hand took a dangerously slow journey up, and her thumb swirled over the head. He looked down to see her swipe a bead of fluid off the head and bring it to her lips.

Her tongue darted out, swiping the drop from the pad of her thumb, then sucking the entire digit into her mouth. While his mouth fell open, hers broke into a wicked grin, and she retraced the path of her fingers up and down his shaft again.

On unspoken agreement, they fumbled for each other's clothes, pushing and pulling until their jeans bridged across their thighs. Riley turned in the circle of Jackson's embrace and pressed her bare ass against his groin. He latched his right arm around her waist, drawing her closer while his other hand reached between them and guided his cock to the opening of her body.

He positioned himself against her opening, feeling the warm liquid of her arousal, and pushed into her with a single thrust.

She arched back against him, and he held her closer. As

her body tightened around him, his swelled to fill her. Jackson nuzzled the nape of her neck, licking the exposed line of her shoulders, throat, and neck as he pistoned into her body.

"Damn, Riley," Jackson bent his head over her shoulder, touched his tongue to the hard line of her jaw.

She arched her hips higher and met him thrust for thrust, guiding the hand around her waist to the juncture of her thighs. He found her clit, the nub swollen and slick, and teased it with the tip on his finger.

"Yes," she hissed and tried to press his fingers against his flesh, but he resisted. "Please, Jackson."

He nipped at her shoulder, her neck, her ear, demanding, "Say that again," while moving his free hand to encircle her throat, wanting to feel the words as they poured from her body like her desired poured onto his fingers.

"Jackson."

The word vibrated beneath his touch, deep, throaty, full of the passion he loved so much about her.

He moved faster, harder, chasing the pleasure, both hers and his. Felt the pulsing begin in the lowest levels of his body as her muscles clamped tighter around his shaft. He weaved his hand into her hair and arched her back, wanting to see her face. Her eyes, glazed and dilated, met his in the periphery of vision. The sharp pull of passion constricted through his muscles, and he felt the release pour from his body into hers, her own release shuddering around him

He floated on the waves of adrenaline and spent passion, so tightly intertwined that only the opposing force of her presence kept him on his feet. As strength returned to his limbs, he felt shudders make their way through her body. Still pressed against her, unwilling to let her go just yet, he stripped off his shirt and gave her his undershirt to clean up with.

They adjusted their clothes in silence, trading glances here and there, a smirk, finally a kiss as they fell back against the counter, weight braced on their elbows.

Just as Jackson opened his mouth to speak the front door opened and in walked Santa.

Surprise and recognition crinkled between Santa's eyes, and he dropped the red sack in his possession. Pulling off the beard, he asked, "Jackson?"

"Richard?"

"Ricky?"

"Riley?"

Together, "What the hell are you doing here?"

Santa Ricky sniffed the air. "And why does it smell like sex?"

Chapter Twenty-One

"Where's my money, Ricky?" Riley demanded, crossing the living room in a few determined strides to get in her long-lost and feloniously-inclined brother's face. The war between trusting her brother and watching her future go down in flames clashed in the pit of her stomach.

Ricky's posture shrank back from her approach, and he snatched the red Santa hat off his head, revealing the balding crown of dark brown hair that reminded her too much of their father. He'd always favored their dad the most. The rest of them looked like their mom.

"Take it easy, sis." He scooted the sack against the couch with the toe of his boot, dropping onto one of the cushions with a huff of air. "I had to move it to keep it safe, but it's all there."

Jackson pushed a hip off the counter and joined Riley's looming presence. "Keep it safe? Why is it in danger?"

"Now, Jackson, I'm not sure I want to tell you while you're wearing that gun." Ricky gave a slight nod to the holster on Jackson's hip. "Someone is embezzling from the firm. Your dad and your brother were my first two suspects."

Despite having similar thoughts, Riley gasped at the accusation, and her gaze snapped to the right.

Jackson drew back his shoulders, his spine going ramrod straight. "Dad's an asshole, but he's not a thief. And Ethan—"

"Ethan just isn't smart enough to pull it off." Ricky rummaged through the Santa sack, pulling out a large bundle wrapped in newspaper. He opened the paper to reveal a fried turkey, the aroma filling the small room quickly. "Then someone is setting your dad up to take a massive fall."

"But my money is still around? You're not financing a mistress or two on my savings?"

"Geez, Riley," Ricky rolled his eyes, unwrapping the turkey and digging back in the sack and retrieving a knife and fork. "I'm a married man. I love my wife. Plus, my brother-in-law carries a gun." His shoulders drooped a little. "Do you really think I'd cheat you? My little sister?"

"I wasn't sure." Guilt nibbled at her insides. "You disappeared. With my money. No word. No contact. What was I supposed to think?"

"You're supposed to think you're my sister and I wouldn't screw you over like that." Ricky sliced off a chunk of turkey and shook it at Riley like a parent waggling the dreaded finger of disapproval. "Trust issues much?"

The accusation hit a little closer to home than she wanted to admit. It was easier to not trust others than to give them the power and be disappointed. It's what she'd done in foster care as a kid. It's what she'd done in almost every relationship, not that there had been all that many. She used the excuse of others not being trustworthy as a reason not to trust anyone. She even recognized she was doing it now with the people of Belle Terre.

But most especially with Jackson.

"We hadn't seen each other since we were kids, Ricky." She scooted around Ricky and the turkey to plop on the sofa next to him while Jackson took up a spot on the far wall, resting his tall frame on the width of his shoulders and crossing his legs at the ankles. "You married money. I wasn't sure what to think." She leaned over, resting her shoulder against Ricky's, the relief at sharing some of the burden on her shoulders making her breathe a touch easier. "I'm sorry. It's just my first instinct."

Ricky lifted his arm—the one without the turkey—and put it around her shoulder, pulling her in close. "I get it. Given the circumstances, I probably wouldn't have thought any differently."

The bonding moment was broken as Ricky took another mouthful of turkey and groaned in duet with his growling stomach.

Jackson filled in the silence while she pushed down the guilt about not trusting her brother. "Am I going to get a report later today about a turkey that went missing from someone's backyard?"

Ricky had the decency to look ashamed. "They had two." He took a bite. "I've been living on peppermint sticks and stuff I get from the cook at the River City Cafe. But he's been on vacation the last few days. I've kept a list. I'll pay everyone back when this is over."

Riley settled back in the sofa. "I feel like the theme song to Twilight Zone should be playing. What's going on, Ricky? And why the hell have you been dressed like Santa the last few weeks? That was you, wasn't it? First at the bank, then the hardware store, and the tree lighting."

Ricky finished chewing and reluctantly put his fork down. "Yes. This was the best way to hide out. Sort of stand out to blend in. I knew you were in town, and I wanted to tell you what was going on, but you're surrounded by very big men all the time. The guys after me are dangerous, and I thought it was safer to just stay away. I knew the construction crew and Jackson would protect you. Then you left town, and I was worried they'd come after you."

"Why not just put the money back where it belongs?" Jackson pressed.

"They'd just steal it again."

"Can't they do that now?"

Ricky shook his head. "No, I disabled the algorithm. They had the money tagged to move it en masse with the right code. But I added a code on top of their code. Without me, they get nothing."

"That's why the accountant the firm is using is not finding anything missing. It's not actually missing." At Ricky's nod, Jackson continued. "Why not just go to the police? And what's my dad got to do with it?"

"I wasn't sure who I could trust." His appetite undisturbed, he continued to eat. "And I wanted to protect the money if I could, so at least the honest clients wouldn't be totally screwed if the feds got involved. That can take years to sort out." At their continued confused looks, Ricky explained. "You remember in the movie Ghost how Patrick Swayze found too much money in his clients' accounts?"

Jackson and Riley nodded.

"Well, I started finding deficits in some of the bigger accounts. Nothing that would really go noticed unless you looked hard. Those accounts can fluctuate daily. But all the deficits were in the exact same amount between all the accounts on each day."

"Someone was stealing?"

"And someone not too bright at that." Ricky shrugged. "It's called lapping. You have to understand, so much of the cash we deal with is just numbers on a screen. We don't physically have hundreds of billions in a bank vault somewhere."

"Should I be happy or sad that my money isn't physically where someone can steal it?" Riley asked, and Ricky patted her knee.

"It's just as real, honey, even if you can't touch it. The money is invested. It earns a return. The return is credited to the appropriate account. We reconcile the incoming and outgoing on a regular basis to make sure all the accounts are properly credited."

"But," Jackson interrupted. "Someone found a way around it."

"Oh, there are always ways around it." Ricky waved off Jackson's next question. "Especially if you have the right people in on the scheme. You steal from account A." Ricky picked up a full water bottle and put it on the floor next to an empty one. "And move the money into account B." He opened the full water bottle and poured a little water into the empty one. "You record the transactions but just not with the right account numbers." He put a third bottle down and emptied the remaining water into it. "When you reconcile the accounts all the money is there." He indicated the three bottles now holding the contents of one bottle. "Just not where it's supposed to be. But the balance sheet looks good."

"Could one person do it?"

Ricky shook his head immediately. "No. It takes several, unless management is completely clueless, which does happen in smaller companies. But not a firm like your dad's.

They keep the duties divided in accounting to avoid such events. The person who records the transactions is never the person who receives the money who is never the person who deposits the money. It's all separated out so there's not too much power in one person's hands."

Jackson stilled, and Riley turned her attention to him. "You just realized something."

"Those three guys at Gastineaux's we saw. Expensive shoes. Short tempers. You said you recognized one at the tree lighting incident." Her expression must have relayed the shock waves pulsing inside because his gaze slid to her, not Ricky, as he explained the info he'd found out after their first date. "I thought they were here for me at first. My dad has kept tabs on me over the years but never anything so direct as sending people."

Riley watched Jackson, his face hard as granite, holding in whatever emotions strained against his insides. Not that she could tell what ate at him. Anger? Elation? Relief?

"But they didn't seem to even notice I was around. Then the night of the tree lighting, I was on alert, but everything happened..." He rolled his shoulders, and Riley recognized what ate at Jackson's insides.

Failure.

She'd been hurt, although a minor wound, because he'd not accounted for all the scenarios that brought those men to town.

Jackson looked away. "You could have been killed."

"They can't kill me," Ricky dismissed Jackson's words with a wave of his hand, apparently unaware they weren't meant for him. "I'm the only one who knows where the money is."

Riley ignored her brother, pushed off the sofa and went to Jackson's side, resting her hand on the corded muscles in his forearm where she felt the tension pulse beneath the skin. She leaned against him, her forehead to his shoulder. "But I wasn't."

"It never occurred to me that they would hurt anyone. Not for a second. Just like with Miranda. I didn't see it coming."

She gave him a half-hearted shrug, but inside she was crumbling, falling to pieces, because in that instant she realized she'd lost her heart to the guy. Love? Maybe. She wasn't sure she knew what that really meant. But yeah ... she'd fallen for Jackson Guidry.

He wanted somewhere to belong as much as she did, but he was more worried about her than his place or security in the town. "You're not supposed to stop crime before it happens, Jackson. That's not failure. And no one expects that, by the way. Except maybe you."

"But they'll keep coming back. We have to stop them before they either find out where Ricky is hiding or that you're his sister and figure they can use you to get to him."

"I know how to draw them out," Ricky added around a mouth full of turkey. "And it won't be that hard."

Jackson pushed off the wall, walking to the center of the room. "What do you mean?"

"I have the money safely tucked in the petty cash account in the firm's legers. No one ever thinks about those because they're not for client cash. They're not connected to our books, and because of the way I have it entered into the system, it shows on the balance sheet without identifying the location. Only if you look at the transactions will someone notice there's more in there than there should be."

"Ethan is doing that now. You can get to it?"

"Yeah. I'm probably the only one who can."

"Why is that?" Jackson's head cocked to one side.

"It's key coded to my biometrics. Without my thumbprint, the money stays in the inbetween. No thumbprint. No money."

Jackson huffed. "The thing is, they don't need you, just your thumb."

Ricky slumped forward. "Yeah. I didn't think of that at the time. It's why I've been hiding out trying to figure out my next move."

Riley joined Jackson in the middle of the room, hands tucked in her jeans. "Why not just go to the authorities?" To Riley this seemed the quickest end to the mess. "The FBI or some other three letter agency? Why not tell the firm's owner?"

"You think my father is involved." The words sounded pained, and Jackson's eyes refused to meet hers or Ricky's.

Ricky put down the now bare turkey leg, wiping his hands on a pile of napkins. "I did at first. But he's not been involved in the firm much lately. And honestly, after thinking about it the past few weeks, if your dad was involved, I don't think I'd have ever found the money. He's too smart for something this basic. This was a smash and grab. He would have finessed the money out of the system."

The smile on Jackson's face looked reluctant. "Never thought I'd be glad to hear about how smart my dad is. What about my brother?"

"He's a good kid." Ricky took a drink from one of the water bottles on the table and wiped his mouth with the back of his hand. "He's still learning the ropes. Ethan's not savvy enough to carry something like this off without a lot of help."

"That leads us back to my original question," Riley interjected. "Why not just go to the authorities?"

"Because technically," Ricky made a see-saw gesture

with his hands. "I'm the one who has hidden the money. I made a screen shot of the accounts before I did the little accounting magic with the petty cash, but I'm not sure if that's good enough. If I can get access to the system again, I think I can find the audit trail they'll need. That part is almost impossible to delete. And once the authorities are involved, all the money gets frozen. It'll take years to sort it all out."

Riley choked on the words about to leave her throat, even thinking them causing a lump the size of Mt. Rushmore to seize up in her lungs. "It's not worth it."

Ricky pivoted his body to face her. "Keeping my thumbs attached?" But a grin teased the corners of his mouth.

"No, doofus," she shoulder-checked him. "The money. I won't risk your life for some money."

"That's your life savings," Jackson said low. "Everything you've worked for. Your security, your future."

"No," she shook her head, adding, "it's money. It comes and goes. My family. My crew. My job. Friends." *You*, her inner voice whispered but didn't have the courage to say aloud. Not yet. "That's my future. The money will be returned in time hopefully. The rest can't. I let the other stuff go once. I won't do it again." She slapped Ricky playfully upside the head. "Besides, if he loses his thumbs, I'll have to cut his steak again like when we were kids. And that's just not gonna happen."

Rickey smiled. "You did break my arm. You owe me."

Riley flung out her hands, palms up, at the old childhood argument between them. But inside, elation was filling her with a new sense of hope. "That was your fault. You should have fallen like we practiced!"

"Yeah, probably." Ricky scratched his head. "And I appreciate your moment of selfless nobility over the money and don't think your sacrifice doesn't touch me, but your account is probably the smallest that would be impacted if we let them get ahold of that money."

Jackson didn't move, but Riley could see the wheels in his head churning as he assessed the situation and his ability to deal with it. "How much are we talking about, Ricky?"

"One hundred million at last count."

Her jaw dropped. "How can they hope to get away with that kind of scam?"

"Ricky shrugged. "The firm manages over three trillion dollars. If I hadn't stumbled across it, no telling how long it would have taken for someone to notice."

"So, what do we do now?" Riley watched Jackson closely, her own sense of foreboding lessened as the tense lines bracketing his mouth turned to determination.

"We keep Ricky hidden until the New Year's Eve fireworks display and parade. Then we serve him up."

Riley was certain her face mirrored her brothers, who looked rightfully concerned over Jackson's words. "Serve him up? What do you mean?"

Jackson pushed off the wall, legs splayed shoulder width apart. A decidedly devilish grin tilted up the corners of his mouth. "How much dynamite can you get a hold of?"

Chapter Twenty-Two

He and Riley ran in to town and retrieved some supplies for Ricky. Now that his brother-in-law didn't have to scrounge for food, they could keep him hidden and worry less about his thumbs remaining attached to his body. That was the easy part of the plan.

Jackson idled the police cruiser outside of the motel where Riley's crew was housed. The workers would trickle back to Belle Terre over the next few days, and in that time, he would pull together the resources he needed for his plan to go off without a hitch. At least that was the hope.

Riley exited her room and stalked to the car, her shoulders a tight line. Even with the grim set of her jaw, she was more beautiful than anything he'd ever seen. He'd known back at the cabin he'd fallen for her, and he fell a little harder when she was willing to give up everything she'd worked for to protect her brother. That said something about a person in his mind.

From there, it didn't take much to accept that his feelings for her went deeper than lust. The best part, however, was that she was falling for him. He couldn't push

her, though. That would send her running in the opposite direction.

The stubborn woman would just have to figure it out on her own. And she would, Jackson was certain of that. He had all the time in the world for her to get comfortable with the idea that he loved her.

Now he had to decide whether it was better to let her make the first move or to make it himself, showing her he wanted her around for more than hot sex and her willingness to walk into the fires with him. Riley wanted to belong. It was a basic need he recognized in himself. But belonging was a choice. One she had to make and understand others accepted it without ulterior motives.

Well, he had ulterior motives, and they were purely selfish. He didn't want to go a day without her in his life.

Now to convince her of that.

She snatched open the door, dropping a hefty binder on the seat before sliding in and closing the door. "OK," she started as she turned to yank the seat belt across her chest.

He revved the engine and did a three-point turn out of the parking lot. "OK?"

"We have a hundred plus cases of construction-grade gelatin dynamite leftover from the build in Virginia. They're only eight sticks to a case, but it'll make an impressive show. What are we going to blow up?"

"Your brother."

She cocked an eyebrow at him, and he could see the machinations in her brain try to piece together the strange puzzle he was assembling.

"And your bulldozer."

She tossed her hands up in the air. "You can have my

brother, but if you think I'm going to let you near my brand-new bulldozer with that much dynamite, you're nuts."

He laughed, unable to stop himself. His plan was risky, but he'd played out the various scenarios in his head and couldn't see another way to flush out the truth without a confession. He'd need to have all the players in place long before the primary actors took the stage, however. And that required more hands than he had at his disposal.

"Think some of your crew would be willing to lend us a hand?"

"To blow stuff up?" Riley snorted. "I think you'll have more trouble keeping them away." She paused, angling her body to watch him drive. "How much danger is my bulldozer in?"

Jackson dropped one hand from the steering wheel as he eased the cruiser onto the empty road and made quick work to the highway. "The dynamite is for show. We need to force the men after Ricky into action, and the only way I know how to do that is threaten their payday. They seem to like public gatherings."

"Easier for them to blend in. Disappear in the crowd."

"We know they're looking for Santa Claus." He turned slightly to watch her face. "So, we give them Santa Claus. Or, in this case, someone they can think is Ricky in a Santa suit."

Her brows knitted together. "We give them Ricky?"

"Not exactly." He paused, both hands back on the steering wheel as he made the left onto Highway 90.

He gave her a brief outline of his plan, finishing just as they pulled up in front of the station. The station building was designed to look like any other storefront on Main Street. Clapboard shingles in a respectable color of gray. Gingerbread trim. Nothing really spectacular; although to

Jackson, it had become a symbol of independence. He'd broken away from the need for revenge against his father and found a place he'd carved on his own.

Jackson slammed the car into park, leaving the engine running. He tipped his head back against the seat and closed his eyes for a moment, overwhelmed with gratitude to the people who'd trusted him. Him. He'd never done anything worthwhile in his life. He'd not been a total prick. Not intentionally, anyway. But until he'd found Belle Terre, he'd been sort of aimless.

Eyes open, he reached over to Riley and threaded his fingers through hers. It was unexpected to him as to her, based on the way her mouth fell open. He made little circles on the flat of her palm with his thumb, memorizing the warmth and the silky way her skin felt beneath his. Her pulse sped up a touch—he could feel the steady thrum of it against the heel of his hand—and she held a breath.

His plan was probably nuts. It endangered her brother, not to mention her. Maybe it was just sane enough that he could catch the bad guys without anyone getting hurt. He vowed to protect them all, come hell or high water. No one was going to hurt what was his.

When his focus drew back once more, Riley was watching him, her head tilted to the side, leaving her hair to fall in a curtain of black against her shoulder. "Deep thoughts?" She released the seat belt but kept her hand in his as she slid closer, her warmth and the subtle scent of her shampoo wrapping around him and drawing him forward.

He reached out and tucked some of the hair behind her ear, grazing his thumb from her temple to her chin before dipping his head and pressing a chaste kiss to her lips. His forehead resting against hers, "Would you be surprised if I said yes?"

The smile crinkled her nose. "I'd be more surprised if you told me no. Care to share?"

A deep breath for bravery lifted his shoulders and tightened his chest. "I like you, Ms. Kenner."

She stuttered a gasp, eyes ping-ponging in their sockets as she searched his face. Her fingers tightened around his, pulling his hand against her thigh.

His heart soared. It was a subtle gesture. He would have missed it if every cell in his body wasn't in tune with what she did on a microscopic level. The heat infusing her body a deep pink from the tip of her nose to the collarbone barely peeking out from her t-shirt. The pinprick retraction of her pupils. The muscles tightening. The breath fanning his face.

He drew back enough to see her entire face. "And when this is all over, I'm going to take you on a proper date. One where I pick you up. I'll be wearing something other than jeans, and we'll go up to Lafayette or New Orleans for typical date stuff. And I'm paying. No arguments."

She nodded once, and he couldn't help himself as he leaned down and kissed her from her temple to her chin. He went in for something less chaste when a knock on the window provided *kissus interruptus*.

With a growl, he turned, but the sound died in his throat at the helmet of perfectly teased and tamed blondeness filling the driver's side window. Disapproval narrowed a pair of heavily made up eyes, accentuating the beginning of crow's feet at the corners of his sister's cobalt eyes. If he told her that, she'd be in the plastic surgeon's office before sunset.

Riley leaned forward, looking around his body at the Peeping Tomalina. "Who is that?"

Jackson scrubbed a hand across his face then through his hair. "Meet your sister-in-law."

Riley cursed and snatched her hand from his. The lost contact dug a well of emptiness in his gut as she slammed her back against the seat, spine ramrod straight, fists curled against her knees. "Did she just catch me making out with … oh, shit … are you my brother-in-law? Are we related in some Louisiana way?"

"Welcome to the family."

Chapter Twenty-Three

Riley knew she and Jackson weren't technically related. Still, as she pushed her reluctant body from the cruiser to meet her sister-in-law for the first time, she couldn't help but worry what the woman was thinking.

As she rounded the hood of the car, Blythe Fontenot watched her beneath raised brows, her mouth a firm line of crafted neutrality or bad Botox. Riley didn't know her sister-in-law that well, but between old money and new money, the woman could afford the best in Botox out there.

Jackson made quick introductions and waved them inside the station.

"I didn't know Richard had a sister," Blythe said without inflection as they climbed the few steps to the boardwalk.

"I didn't know Ricky had a wife." Riley let Blythe enter the building first through the door Jackson held open, wanting to smack him for the barely contained smirk. How could he remotely think this was funny? "We hadn't seen each other for a while."

And then like the parting of the Red Sea, Blythe's face smoothed out and something Riley could only call compassion filled eyes the same color as Jackson's. "I heard ... why ... Richard explained why you hadn't been in touch. Why he didn't tell me. I'm sorry you had to go through that." Blythe reached out and took Riley's hand and for once, Riley didn't feel the need to pull away from the connection. "And I'm really glad that you and Richard found one another again."

Riley didn't know what to do with Blythe's comment, so she filed it under things to think about later. She squeezed Blythe's hand then let her own fall by her side. "Thanks, Blythe. I'm glad he found you, too. He's a lucky man."

They reached Jackson's office, and Blythe took the chair he held out while Riley propped her hip against a filing cabinet in the corner.

Her sister-in-law crossed her legs, smoothing out the blue wool pants, hands shaking slightly. "I wish you'd been able to know Richard while you grew up. He's an idiot some- times," a quick grin lifted the corners of her mouth, "but he's a good guy. I appreciate you being willing to help him out." She leaned forward, elbows on the knees of her expensive slacks. "You'd have always been welcome at our home, just so you know. You're welcome there now. I know you may not believe that, but please give us a chance. I want my kids to know their family." She shifted her gaze to Jackson. "*All* of their family."

The weight of her statement hit Riley in the gut. The edges of her vision went blurry as her loss and loneliness clouded her mind, swimming to the surface of her being with broad, sure strokes before dissipating beneath the knowledge she had a place to go when she wanted.

She stared down at her feet, uncomfortable but wanting to wrap the elusive feeling of belonging around her like a warm blanket. It was a different feeling than what being with JJ and the crew gave her. They were a family she'd made after joining them, getting to know them, and letting them get to know her. They were a family of choice, no less special, just different.

Blythe's simple words gave her a new angle on the word family, however. One she'd not considered possible for a long time. Unconditional acceptance. It's what she remembered having as a kid, with her brothers and dad, her vague memories of her mom. She'd never questioned her place in the family back then, and when it was gone, nothing ever seemed to match it. Until now.

"Thanks, Blythe." Her attention wasn't on the meticulous woman with her manicured nails and not-a-hair-out-of-place updo. It was on the man behind Blythe.

Jackson studied her beneath hooded eyes, trying to pretend he was looking at the paperwork he was shuffling on his desk and failing miserably as a ghost of a smile haunted his mouth.

She'd accepted the fact that she'd fallen for the man back in his car when he'd told her he liked her. She suspected he'd chosen his words carefully so as not to spook her and that just upped his standing in her book. He knew her that well already and didn't want to change her. Jackson accepted that she'd need time to come to terms with his feelings, not to mention her own, and he didn't press it.

Blythe's curious expression indicated she'd noticed the silent communication going, but she kept quiet, her eyes jumping between them. "I'm tired of waiting at home," she announced, breaking the silence. "Ethan hasn't found what you're looking for from going through the books. Richard's probably the only who can find it. It's time to make a move."

"You said something about a plan." Riley went for the distraction, not ready to examine the mix of emotions whipping her insides like a tornado.

Jackson cleared his throat, leaning back in his chair. "Let's turn the tables a bit. They like sneaking in during the city celebrations. Let's clear them a path this time and see what they do when opportunity presents itself."

"And will opportunity be disguised as my brand new bulldozer?"

"Let's just say your bulldozer is the serving platter."

J ackson laid out the details of his plan to Blythe. They'd put Ricky on display to draw out the three men looking to detach his thumbs from his body, using the empty boxes of dynamite as a deterrent to simply killing him. If they could lure the men away from the crowds under the guise of providing the codes they needed in exchange for Ricky's life, Jackson's men would be waiting to make the arrests.

His sister studied him, one leg crossed over the other as her foot tapped to an invisible rhythm. "What if the authorities think Richard was involved? I really don't want Richard to go to prison."

"Which is why we wait to call in the three-letter people," Riley explained, doubt and worry weighing down her posture until, causing her to slump against the cabinet where she'd braced her body. "Even if he can prove he's not guilty later on, the FBI'd never let him near the accounts."

"Plus, he has the firm's owners to vouch for him." Jackson didn't know this for certain this would impact a federal investigation.

Blythe nodded, her expression so much like Jackson's that it tugged at Riley's insides. "OK. We'll go with Jackson's plan. Keep me posted. I'm staying out at Uncle Greg's."

Jackson rose to his feet. "That's where I'm living."

"I know. And you're a slob. There are dishes in the sink."

"One dish."

"And clothes on the floor."

"In a laundry basket."

"And I still can't find all the pieces to Monopoly you lost when we were kids."

"I needed the houses and hotels for Godzilla to crush."

"You need to go see dad."

This time Jackson didn't respond. He looked away, the muscles of his jaw twitching as he ground his teeth. This was as close as he'd been to his family in a decade and the pull to have that connection again settled around him. But he and his siblings had been talking for days and his father had been noticeably absent. Maybe the message was loud and clear: he wanted nothing to do with his son.

Blythe smiled, a mirror of Jackson's. She gave a half-wave to Riley before leaning over the desk and pressing a kiss to her brother's cheek. "I'll see you later, Jacks."

She left, and Riley slid into the seat she'd vacated, taking her turn to study Jackson as he folded his body into the ancient leather desk chair. Her insides jangled, hot wires skittering over a puddle of nerves. "I like her."

"She's always been a good big sister," Jackson admitted, pushing some of the file folders on his desk around until they looked stacked, if not organized.

"And your brother Ethan is younger." Riley wrapped a hand around the ankle crossed over her right knee.

Jackson tilted his head to the side a little, watching her beneath hooded eyes. "Yes. Mom's therapist friend said I was the classic middle child. At first, I tried to please. Then I tried to rebel."

"I was good at rebellion myself."

She dropped her head, the first hitch of reluctance weighing down her voice. She'd decided to tell Jackson more about her past when they stood together at the tree lighting ceremony. Riley couldn't put into words why she wanted to do this. When she'd met her ex the first time, he knew she'd just gotten out of juvie. He'd had his own brush with the law as a kid, and it was a connection with a shared understanding of why they'd chosen that path.

Jackson, on the other hand, didn't have such an understanding. Riley didn't know how he'd feel about someone who'd broken laws; laws he'd now sworn to protect. She'd had her run-ins with him acting as sheriff, but they'd been minor skirmishes, none ending with her behind bars.

"I spent a year in juvenile detention." She lifted her head, waiting to see a quirk of a brow, a tightening of his mouth, disapproval, shock, something. He gave her nothing, however, except patience while she laid out her story. "I was a foster kid from the age of ten. I ran away a lot initially, trying to find my brothers. I thought it was my fault we'd been split up, so it was my responsibility to bring them back together."

Breathing got a little bit harder for Riley, mainly because her heart was lodged in her throat. She tamped it down with determination, but it didn't stay.

"Then I met some friends."

The first break in Jackson's quiet patience: a huff.

"Yeah," Riley shrugged. "*Friends* is a stretch but it's how I met Noé. We were outsiders together. Long story short, we ended up stealing a car one night. My foster family turned me in, and I spent almost a year at a detention center in Shreveport."

Jackson leaned forward, planted his elbows on his desk

and propped his chin on the tips of his steepled fingers. But still he waited.

"I refused to see my foster parents while I was there. Refused to see them when I got out. They eventually stopped trying."

Without moving an inch, Jackson spoke. "I'm sure there's a lesson in there for me."

Riley stood, adjusted the sleeves on her shirt, swiped her hair back. "JJ has told me—repeatedly—that I'm still really good at running away from people who want to get close to me. So maybe there's lessons in there for both of us."

"What are you trying to say?"

"Soon as it opens, I'm going to go by the bank. Talk to Mr. Michel about a mortgage on the Fortune place."

Jackson was on his feet and around the desk so fast Riley didn't have time to blink. "You're staying?"

She didn't step back from the space he'd stolen, didn't look away. "Let's see what happens." *I'm not sure if I know how to stay.* The unspoken words crowded around the ones she'd said out loud, trembling on her lips.

At least until Jackson kissed her.

Chapter Twenty-Four

J ackson watched from the boardwalk outside the
sheriff's station as Belle Terre's population filled Main
Street for the New Year's Eve celebration to welcome Te
Bonhomme Janvier, a Cajun-equivalent Santa character that
delivered fruits and candy to the good boys and girls and
replaced Christmas presents with coal to the not-so-good-
ones during the year. Jackson hoped to deliver a sack of coal
to the men looking to fillet Ricky's thumbs from his body.

He'd thought about this for the last week, figuring every
angle. He didn't want to be caught unaware. He'd also spent
a lot of time thinking about his date with Riley a few nights
ago. He'd worn a tie.

Noé, a menacing guardian angel, was watching from the
corner of the building when Jackson knocked on Riley's
door. Jackson thought of saying something to the man, but
then Riley had answered, and all thoughts of others floated
from his mind.

She'd worn a bronze blouse, the color bringing out the
honey in her skin, over black dress pants with ankle boots.
They'd had dinner, talked until they looked up and saw they

were the last customers in the restaurant; the manager looked bored and sleepy at a table up front.

He'd also spent a considerable amount of time thinking about his family. His dad, to be more precise. When this was over, maybe he'd go home for a weekend. See if they could find neutral ground, if not common ground.

Tonight, people spilled out to the docks behind the sea wall that protected the city from the ever-present danger of floods during hurricane season. Jackson prayed silently that if the worst happened tonight, it would shield them if his grand plan backfired.

He rested a shoulder against a post, arms loose at his sides. Jackson had to work to keep his fists from bunching, the tension humming through his body like an over-caffeinated hummingbird. His gaze jumped to the uniforms dotting the street. He had called in reserve deputies for crowd control, stationing the men and women along the parade route that would serve up Te Bonhomme Janvier on a bulldozer-sized platter.

They'd made a very big deal throughout the week of announcing that Santa Claus had retired for the year, but his *younger brother* would be around for the New Year's Eve parade and fireworks. Hopefully, it was obvious that Santa and Te Bonhomme Janvier were the same person in this case, and the bad guys would take the bait.

The bulldozer was parked in the alley behind the station, the front blade already fitted out with empty boxes —the word DYNAMITE scorched on each side—beneath a layer of fake snow. The costume was stashed in his office so as not to give away that someone other than Ricky would be riding dead center, a calling card to the men likely stalking through the crowd.

The plan was risky, but he wasn't stupid. He would lead

217

the bad guys away from the crowds to a spot beneath the bridge where "Ricky" could be off-loaded. The dynamite would keep them from endangering their payday, seemingly unprotected except for the bulldozer driver.

When they made their move, Jackson would make his.

Or at least the deputies waiting at the end of the route would make their move, arresting the bad guys with the town none the wiser about the excitement.

Ricky was stashed safely away, hiding on the barge tethered in the middle of the river where the pyrotechnics for the midnight fireworks display would be launched.

Riley had argued for the job as the bulldozer driver, but Jackson convinced her to help with crowd control instead, using the LCB construction crew as back up to keep the three men on their radar. He wanted her as far from the danger as possible, though he couldn't tell her that.

Jackson laughed at himself. He didn't really believe his motives had been unclear to her. She was too sharp for that. Keeping her actively involved in the search for the men looking to hurt her brother, however, fulfilled her need to help and his desire to keep her out of the danger zone.

So far, though, no luck with finding the bad guys in the crowds of families and parade watchers. They were blending in better this time.

"Jackson?"

The familiar voice raked down his spine with the combined talons of dread and anticipation. Jackson's body tensed, and without turning around, he said, "Hey, Dad. Here for the fireworks?"

Footsteps scraped the wooden slats behind him, slow, deliberate ... and hesitant. The emotional tangle threading itself around his insides kept Jackson from moving, though his heart rate was trying to make up for the stillness by beating out of his chest. How could a man he didn't like and hadn't seen in almost ten years cause the fire and ice reaction in his brain?

"I'm here to see you."

The rush of anger propelled him forward a single step before he pivoted one-hundred eighty degrees, ready to stalk toward his father. But he froze on the spot, and his anger dissipated on a single rush of breath beneath the pained look of a weary, aged man. His father leaned heavily on the cane in his left hand, and Jackson's gaze took in the slight frame beneath the normally well-tailored suits.

"Thyroid cancer, to answer your first question." Franklin Guidry drew his shoulders back, trying not to lean so heavily on the cane. "I'd have been here sooner but I was in Switzerland for treatment. I'm in remission, if it matters."

Something in Jackson tightened in his throat: frustration that he couldn't hate the man who'd caused him such pain, a mourning for the years lost. Maybe Riley was right. He'd had a family, good and bad, and he'd walked away rather than stay and fight for it. That stopped now.

"It does matter." Jackson moved to stand in front of his dad, looking over the man's shoulder to see his mother and sister farther down the boardwalk. Bathed in the soft whiteness of the Christmas lights, their faces, so similar in appearance, mirrored a look of hopeful wariness. He returned his attention to the man before him. "Blythe never said anything."

"I asked her not to. If you were going to come home, I wanted it to be your choice."

"We have a lot to talk about."

His dad's shoulders slumped a bit, the lines on his face smoothing out as relief eased the tension riding his frame. "We do, but first you have a job to do." His voice regained some of the strength Jackson remembered. "And I don't want to interfere. Blythe told us what was going on. I've notified the authorities, and Ethan is working with the forensic accountant at the firm. We put some safeguards in place, just in case. But I had to see you. You look good, like you belong here. You've done well on your own. I'm glad. I'm proud."

Jackson tried to numb himself against the small flicker of hope those words gave life to inside of him. The first notes of the high school band's warmup clattered up the street, off-key and haphazard like the emotions clanging around inside his head. Guilt. Relief. Regret. But mostly hope.

Jackson shook off the thoughts rooting his feet to the boardwalk. There'd be time later to deal with all of this. Unless he screwed up and got Riley's brother and his sister's husband killed. That dragged him back to reality pretty quickly. "You're right. I've got to go to work, but we'll talk later."

The elder Guidry nodded and turned, joining his wife and daughter. Jackson caught Blythe's attention and inclined his head once in acknowledgement, then went inside to get into disguise. Moments later he exited through the building's back door into the alley, ready to end this once and for all.

He might have made it, too, if Noé hadn't been waiting for him with a plan of his own.

Chapter Twenty-Five

Riley paced the length of the seawall walkway, the lights on the main street's boardwalk the only break against the inky blackness of a starless sky. She'd been searching the crowd from her vantage point, easily spotting her crew among the families enjoying the festivities. But couldn't find the man she'd gone toe to toe with the night of the tree lighting. By the time she felt the heat of someone standing behind her, heard his breath wheeze out of the broken nose she'd given him, she knew it was too late.

"Where's your brother?" he rasped, his voice nasally and strained. The sharp, cool edge of metal dug into her kidneys while his fingers bit into her arm. "Is that Ricky down on the street, dressed up like some knockoff Santa Claus," he wheezed, and Riley saw a costumed figure emerge from the corner atop her new bulldozer. "That's how he's been hiding out from us. Maybe I'll just have my guys shoot him and be done with it."

Riley scrambled for a moment. "Ricky thought of that which is why he's standing on enough dynamite to make sure his thumbprint's useless."

Riley turned slowly, surprised when he didn't stop her. He underestimated her. Good. It might buy her the time she needed to signal someone below. She eyed his puffy face, the bruising still a yellowing stain across the bridge of his nose.

"Aww, did you break your nose? Hurts like hell, doesn't it? Even weeks later." She planted her feet wide for balance, knowing if she went off the twenty-foot wall she'd not be walking away. "Wait until you get hit there again." She rolled her head skyward and huffed. "Man, you'll think someone grabbed your balls and pulled them through your nostrils." Then she shrugged and met his eyes once again. "Or so they tell me. I don't have the requisite body parts for that particular pain." She shifted her eyes in the direction of his lower torso, letting the promise of pain leak into her smirk. "But I'm sure it hurts like a mother."

"Shut up, bitch." He twisted his fingers into the fleshy part of her upper arm, the ring digging in painfully, but she wouldn't wince. He twisted harder. "Where's your boyfriend?" he demanded this time, yanking her around to face the crowd.

Riley jerked her arm against his grip. "Sure, I tell you where he is, then you'll tell someone, and they'll tell someone, and before you know it, we have a whole convention of assholes walking around." She cut him a look out of the corner of her eye. "Oh, too late."

He cursed her again, nothing imaginative, but it took his attention away while he fiddled with his phone.

She focused on the crowd below and saw the other two bad guys. One stood close enough to JJ that she knew he was aware of the presence as well. JJ looked up at her with grim determination. Riley extended her right arm, thumb pointing down. The signal to lower the boom. He nodded, ready for whatever she did, and disappeared into the crowd while a few of the scarier members of the crew formed a picket fence of muscle when the tail attempted to follow.

Not twenty feet to the right, the last bad guy shadowed Miranda and Jack Jr., but Riley didn't think Miranda was aware. Riley wanted to keep it that way. Miranda seemed to search the crowd, hitching Jack Jr. higher on her hip and winding her way through the gathering until Riley lost sight of her.

Her focus lasered in on getting the bad guys away from the crowd below. It was her fault, once again, that the townspeople of Belle Terre were in danger. She wouldn't let anything happen to them. Jackson had Ricky protected out of the river barge, safely away from harm. She could take care of the rest and hopefully no one would get hurt. Once she got them all away from the crowds, she'd figure out some way of keeping them occupied until JJ could bring reinforcements.

"Beck," the bad guy screamed into the phone as the first chorus of Auld Lang Syne squealed up the street and snapped Riley's head in that direction. "Why don't you see if that nice lady can tell you where the sheriff is?"

The crowd surged toward the sound as a single wave. Behind the marching band, Riley saw the bulldozer lumbering down the street. A half dozen deputies flanked the machine, and Santa stood in the bucket, but it wasn't Jackson. Riley would recognize Jackson regardless of his clothes. Jackson was nowhere to be seen. Something had gone wrong. Their careful plan to keep the action out of the way was going up in smoke.

"The barge." Riley said flatly, thinking of the river barge anchored in the middle of the river, home to tonight's fireworks show. She hoped somehow JJ could get word to Jackson, wherever he was. Maybe JJ had guessed the full scope of the problem, but even then, she didn't want him putting Jackson's life in danger for her and her brother. Ricky was her problem. No one else. She'd take care of it. Somehow. "Ricky's out on the barge." Her heart thudded in her chest while her mind raced to come up with a new plan. "The guy in the suit is a decoy and all the elves are cops. I think the FBI even showed up."

The man holding her cursed a blue streak and yanked her away from the edge of the crowd, pushing her toward the stairs leading out to the marina. He put the cell phone back to his ear and spoke in gruff half-sentences. "Beck. Goodloe. East end of the wharf. Ricky's out on the barge. Find a boat."

Riley's mind jackhammered around the possibilities, trying to cut through the ones that would get her killed immediately and find the one that might delay her demise long enough to manage some version of a rescue or a distraction. At least they'd be away from the public. And by moving them out on the water, she'd buy some time if JJ managed to alert Jackson their target had moved. If not, maybe the bad guys would just take her and try and negotiate later with Ricky, leaving the rest of the townspeople alone. It wasn't much to pin a hope on, but it was all she had at the moment.

The two men Riley recognized from that night at Gastineaux's slithered through the opening in the sea wall, both checking over their shoulders with guilty regularity. Clearly not men used to being bad guys. They'd traded in their three-piece suits for ugly holiday sweaters and baggy sweats. One came in their direction while the other slinked in the shadows further down the wharf.

"What the fuck, Dan?" the new guy asked, pointing to Riley with a shaky finger. "What's she doing here?"

Hoping to rile Dan enough to get him to loosen his grip, Riley answered, "Your friend here liked his broken nose so much he thought you might want one."

Dan backhanded Riley quicker than she thought he could move but didn't release her. She bent at the waist, one hand propped at her knee, her hair falling in a curtain as she shook her head to clear the stars from her vision. A warm trickle seeped out from her hairline where his ring had cut her scalp. She wiped it away with her hand and saw blood.

Riley pulled out her loosened hair tie. "I'd say you hit like a girl, but I broke your nose. All you did was mess up my hair."

Dan reared back his hand again, this time with a closed fist, and Riley planted her feet to pivot away from the punch. The other man hooked both his hands around Dan's raised elbow and jerked hard. Dan barely moved, but it stopped the momentum of his fist.

"You're wasting time. We know where Ricky is. Why do we need her?"

"She's insurance in case that sheriff comes along. They got a thing going on," Dan answered, jostling Riley by the arm and yanking her along as he followed the wall to the end of the wharf. A slice of light from an overhead streetlamp caught the sneer on his face. "Guy at the office heard the old man saying Ricky'd found his sister down here. Two for one."

The new guy scratched a hand through his hair. "Then let's get him. I want this done with. I didn't sign on for kidnapping or ... worse." The new guy looked worried. Riley could use that. "I just want my money. Then I'm gone."

"Stop whining, Beck." Dan nodded over Beck's shoulder, and Riley saw the third man signaling from the end of the pier. "Goodloe found us a boat. C'mon."

The three of them headed toward Goodloe.

"Dan was saying what he was going to do with his eighty percent, Beck," Riley taunted. "You got big plans for your cut of my money?"

"Eighty percent?" Beck screeched.

"Shut your mouth, bitch." Dan waved away Beck's outrage. "She's yanking your chain, dumbass. No one's getting eighty percent."

They passed the opening in the sea wall, and Riley could see the deputies passing by with the bulldozer. She thought of screaming, but the rumbling of the bulldozer coupled with the cacophony of the marching band would just drown her out. And it might draw the attention of someone in the crowd enough they'd investigate. Riley couldn't take that chance. At least on the barge she could get in the water, disappear in the swirling murkiness that made up the Atchafalaya. It was the only option she'd come up with in the last few minutes.

"I'd be careful, Beck." Riley continued, wanting to throw the dynamic between the men off as much as possible. "He said he was the brains of this operation and all you and Goodloe did was punch a few keys on a keyboard."

Beck huffed indignantly. "I designed the algorithm and—"

"Shut. Up. You. Moron." Dan punctuated each word with a death-grip pull on Riley's arm until she thought her shoulder would pop out of its socket.

They arrived at the end of the pier, Beck and Dan fuming but for different reasons.

Goodloe motioned to the twenty-foot trawler docked

against the wharf. "Found one," he explained uselessly, pointing to the boat in case they didn't know what he meant. He looked even less sure than Beck about his role in the snowballing list of felonies. "Even has the keys in the engine."

Dan shoved Riley toward the boat, ordering Beck and Goodloe to release the tie lines before boarding. Riley bided her time, watching Beck whisper heatedly to Goodloe as they untied the ropes, moving to the stern to stand against a wall of tarp-covered crab traps. The two men finally jumped onto the deck while Dan fiddled with the controls much like he'd done on the crane. Eventually he got the engine started, and they idled through the marina, heading straight to the barge anchored in the center of the river.

The current was stronger than Dan anticipated apparently, and he missed the barge on first pass as the river carried them beyond their docking point with the barge.

"Not real good at hitting what you aim for, are you Dan?" Riley needled, gauging the distance between the trawler and the barge as they glided by. "Must make you popular in the men's bathroom."

Dan growled but kept his attention on the bow of the boat. He swung the trawler around, gunning the engine against the swift moving water and made a rough but successful docking the second go round. Riley jumped to the barge ladder hanging over the edge and scuttled up the side, hoping to find a place to hide before the others disembarked. But just as she poked her head over the top, she saw her brother standing near the starboard aft, his eyes crinkled before going wide in recognition.

"Ricky!" She called out, scrambling along the deck, weaving in and out of the barrels of pyrotechnics set up for the midnight fireworks show. She sprinted across the flat surface the length of a football field, hearing the three men chase after her. Before she could get to Ricky, however, Dan was behind her, slamming his weight into hers and carrying her to the deck.

"You're starting to piss me off," he growled into her ear, tangling one hand in her hair and pulling her back from the door by her roots. Pain stung the corners of her eyes, her scalp on fire as instinct lifted her hands to grasp the hand in her hair.

"And I'm not even trying yet. Wait until you've known me a bit longer," she snapped between grimaces, knowing the smart-assed remark was foolish. She wasn't going down with a whimper, and if she could manage to get Dan off-balance, she might have a chance. Beck and Goodloe would crumble at the first opposition.

"Let her go, Dan!" Ricky bellowed, charging from behind until Riley's shout of pain pulled him up short as Dan yanked her back against his chest and dragged her behind a railcar stationed at the far end of the deck.

"All we want is the money, Ricky." Beck found a backbone and stepped forward, but not enough to escape Dan's shadow. "Make that happen and this all goes away."

Riley snapped her eyes to Ricky, knowing if he gave them what they wanted they'd both die. "No, Ricky."

Ricky's gaze cut to a spot over the three men's heads, then right back to her. "No choice, sis. It's only money, right?"

"Yeah, but it's my money, and the thought of this idiot wasting it on strippers and cheap beer is criminal."

Dan shook her so hard her teeth clacked together in her skull. "Shut up! Do it, Ricky, or I swear I'll end her now. You'll get to miss out on the little family reunion you been whining about. Think about what your brothers will say when you tell them little sister died protecting your sorry ass."

"Enough, Dan," Ricky spat between clenched teeth. "Beck, get out the tablet I know you have stashed somewhere. You don't go to the john without it. Bring up the software. I'll do it."

"Give him the account, Beck." Dan ordered, pulling Riley tighter against his check. She hissed between her teeth.

Beck hesitated. "Three accounts, Dan. Not one. I want a separate account transfer for each of us."

A growl rumbled from Dan's chest. "That's not the plan, Beck."

"It is now."

An eternity of seconds passed as Riley stood with Dan's hands still tangled in her hair.

"You're costing us time, Beck. Goodloe, take the tablet."

Goodloe see-sawed between Beck and Dan. "Uhh, I don't know his passcode."

Dan swiveled the gun in Beck's direction. "If you don't let Ricky make the transfer, I'm going to shoot you myself."

Beck straightened. "And do what with it? Without my passcode, you got nothing."

Against her better judgment, she prodded Dan, wanting to buy them some time. Maybe someone was riding to the rescue. "If you piss him off no telling where he'll send your money. And you'll never find it. You should listen. I know something about the reliability of online transfers. Better let Beck handle the hard stuff, Dan. You don't look like you can handle the math behind this, even if you counted on your fingers and toes."

Dan tightened his grip, making her wince, and twisted her around to stare down into her face. Bad breath bathed her nostrils. "Sweetheart, a hundred million buys a hell of a good accountant." He jabbed himself in the chest with the gun gripped in his right hand. "I just needed those two in transfers and acquisitions to make it all look copacetic on the balance sheets."

"Copacetic," Riley sneered. "That's a big word. Don't hurt yourself."

Dan nuzzled her cheek with his own and revulsion did a slow crawl down her spine. "Keep talking and I'll show you something else big."

"I knew it!" The man named Beck stepped forward, then retreated beneath the withering stare from Dan. "You're going to cheat us."

"Don't be stupid. You have the code. How can I cheat you when you're the one transferring the money?"

That seemed to confuse the other man momentarily.

Ricky stared at the three men with something close to fury burning behind his eyes. "Let her go. She's got nothing to do with this."

Dan gave a half-laugh. "She's my version of the FDIC, man. Insurance against a bad decision on your part."

"What's our insurance against you screwing us over, Dan?" Beck demanded, swinging the tablet with too much *oomph* in Dan's direction.

Everyone on deck watched as the tablet went flying out of Beck's grip and over the side of the barge, plopping into the water and sinking like a stone.

"You fuckin'–"

In that brief instant, Riley felt Dan's grip loosen, and she dropped to her knees between one heartbeat and the next, driving her elbow up into Dan's groin with every ounce of strength she possessed. Things happened in rapid-fire succession, but she saw the events unfold in slow motion as

Jackson and four deputies spilled from the sides of the rail car amid shouts of "Sheriff's Department!" and "On your knees!"

Dan released her hair completely to pivot the gun toward Jackson with one hand and cradle his wounded privates with the other, tottering on one leg as Riley launched herself at his chin, grabbing the barrel of the gun and slamming her weight behind a jab that sent him crashing backwards. Jackson reached her in two long strides, shoulder-checking Dan's arm to redirect the gun's aim. Dan's bulk won out over balance, but not before he squeezed off a round that went wide, the random shot taking out the electronics panel on the other side of the boat.

Ricky dived behind the display as the pyrotechnics exploded in a deafening bouquet of heat, light, and sparkles.

Beck and Goodloe dropped so fast Riley thought they'd been shot. Dan crashed like a felled tree, curling into a fetal position. The burn of electrical circuits filled the air with ozone, and the roiling smoke from the sudden blast bathed the deck of the barge in a roiling mist.

Jackson wedged a booted foot against Dan's chest, exchanging his gun for a pair of handcuffs, which he waved at Riley in a *I-should-slap-these-on-you* kind of gesture since words were useless beneath the roar of the fireworks show filling the night sky.

Then he smiled, and she decided since she loved him, she'd let him put her in cuffs anytime he wanted. She'd make him pay for it, but she didn't think he'd mind the price.

Chapter Twenty-Six

Now that the fireworks were over and some of Jackson's hearing had come back, he paced the twenty-two-foot length of the ambulance parked outside his station and waited for the federal agents and EMTs to release Riley. They'd had her sequestered inside his office for the last half hour since she wouldn't let them take her to the hospital to check her over.

It's a good thing he loved her, he decided, otherwise he'd have her cuffed to the stretcher and let them to haul her down to the emergency room. But because he loved her, he knew she'd have none of that. So he had to trust that she knew what was best for herself. Didn't mean he didn't worry. Stuff was prone to blowing up around that woman. He'd have to take that into consideration after he asked her to marry him.

In the meantime, there other things to worry about.

Off to the side stood his family, including Ricky who'd not been allowed to wander more than an arm's length away from Blythe since she'd gotten her hands on him. Inside the ambulance, his dad was answering questions from the federal agents who showed up. Given his health, they weren't being overly aggressive. He'd called them, Jackson reminded them when they showed up in the blue windbreakers and black SUVs. And he'd cleared Ricky of any wrongdoing, telling them Ricky had moved the money on his orders.

But it wasn't his family that kept his focus. It was the entire town lined up in the street, waiting with him. Jackson just didn't know if they were a cheering squad or a firing squad. Seeing Noé Tam in the holiday suit Jackson had intended to wear to distract the embezzlers gave him another thought to focus on. Noé's news about seeing Riley with the man now identified as Dan Steward had put a little crimp in his plan. Luckily, Noé had his back. Jackson owed the man a beer.

As the possibilities rattled around his brain one more time, the door to the station opened, and Riley stepped tenderly onto the boardwalk, a bandage over her hand from the burns she'd received grabbing Dan's gun, and another on her temple from where Dan had backhanded her.

He rushed toward her, skidding to a stop, but the words on his tongue didn't get the halt message. "Are you ok? You really should go to the hospital and let them check you over. JJ and the guys are worried. Ricky is fine. Why didn't you—"

She silenced him with a kiss, and since that was also on his mind, he didn't really care. He kissed her back, cradling her face between his palms and letting his mouth slide over the seam of her lips.

When they finally broke loose, he let her smile warm up those places ice cold from worry. Still, he scanned her face for injuries, seeing too many to his liking. But he'd also seen Dan. His woman gave as good as she got.

"My bulldozer better be safe."

Jackson gave a half-laugh, then held up three fingers in the Boy Scout salute. "It is safely locked inside the fence at the construction site." Jackson wrapped his arms around her waist and drew her closer, pulling her up to her tip toes. His voice wavered as he spoke. "Noé said he saw you with an unfriendly. We'd already stashed Ricky out on the barge, thinking it the safest place for him. But we knew you'd try to lead them away from the crowds, so I swapped out my place on the bulldozer with Noé and went out to the barge to wait."

"I think you were there before we were."

Jackson shrugged this time. "It's the basin. Everyone and their mother has their own boat docked down at the marina. And we knew you'd be a smartass and delay them getting out there."

"I'm not sure I like you knowing so much about me, sheriff."

He clunked his head to hers, then whispered against her lips. "Too bad, Ms. Kenner."

"Guidry!"

The harsh voice interrupted his kissing, and Jackson wondered if a review panel would believe locking up Mason Gastineaux for being an ass was justified. Breaking from the kiss, Riley melded her long body against his and a groan tore up his throat.

Riley grinned at him, brushing her thumb across the moisture on his lips. "You can't arrest him," she chided, as if reading his mind.

"I'm saving my handcuffs for you," Jackson teased, biting the pad of her thumb.

She pulled back a touch and widened her smile, but even the small space between them felt like a gulf, so he wrapped his arm tighter around her shoulders and dragged her closer.

"I need to keep you close," he warned lightly. "For the safety of all concerned. You're a dangerous woman."

"Mmmmmm, Sheriff Guidry." It was her turn to groan. "I surrender."

The throaty growl went right to his heart. And a little bit lower if he was being honest. "Smart woman. We'll talk about your sentencing later tonight." He nodded toward the waiting crowd. "When there aren't so many witnesses."

"Guidry!" Mason yelled again, this time peeling away from the safety of the crowd and planting himself at the bottom of the stairs leading to the boardwalk. It was also within Jackson's reach, which is why Jackson figured the other man looked a little uncertain.

"What is it, Mason?" Jackson reluctantly turned to face Mason, whose face was screwed into a mix of frustration and hopelessness.

"That woman," Mason started, pointing at Riley in case anyone was uncertain which woman he was referring to, "is a menace to this town."

"Don't I know it." Jackson agreed. "I'm going to keep a very close eye on her. Don't you worry. She'll have twenty-four-seven police surveillance from now on."

Undeterred, Mason turned and moved closer to the crowd, looking for the support he wasn't finding in Jackson. "She threatened Tiffany down at the bank!"

"No, she didn't." All heads swiveled as Mr. Michel pushed from the crowd, looking both dapper and Christmas-y in his bright green suit and red tie decorated with a flashing Rudolph nose. "That was all a misunderstanding. Tiffany overreacted, but Ms. Kenner was very gracious about the bank's error."

Mason tried again. "Then she nearly burned down Mr. Terrebonne's hardware store!"

"No, she didn't." Like a synchronized swim team, the entire town pivoted to watch as Donavan stepped from the crowd, his fathers, brothers, and sisters quickly following him out of the crowd. "That was me." Donavan squared his shoulders, stuffing his hands in the pockets of his jacket. His gaze was only for Riley, and Jackson could feel the love coming from the kid. "I done told Mr. Terrebonne and the sheriff what happened. It was an accident. Riley took the blame 'cuz I was scared, but I'm not scared no more."

Jackson turned to see Riley dash away a tear.

"Then her carelessness destroyed the Spirit of Belle Terre at the tree lighting!" Mason tried again.

"No, she didn't." This time it was Miranda stepping forward, and Mason seemed to lose steam. His shoulders slumped as his wife moved next to him, handing him his son. "That big guy the deputies took away was the one trying to drop the tree. Riley jumped into that crane to stop him. She tackled him, a guy as big as that. He tossed her into the controls. That's when the tree dropped. Riley probably saved a lot of people, giving them extra time to get away."

Jackson walked down the steps and clapped Mason on the shoulder. "I get it, Mason. She drives me a little crazy too."

"Hey!" Riley cried out, punching her fists into her waist.

"But," Jackson held up a finger to silence Riley's inevitable argument, "she's risked life, limbs, and her bulldozer for the safety of this town. You won't find a better citizen for Belle Terre than that woman right there."

A chorus of "I agree" rose from the crowd.

Mason hefted his son to his shoulder, his eyes skating over Riley with a blend of confusion and frustration, then turned with his wife to blend back into the disappearing crowd.

Riley's crew stood against the sea wall, the thinning crowd finally revealing their presence. JJ, a broad and toothy grin splitting his face, gave Jackson a salute.

Noé nodded once. "We've got some brisket cooking in the smoker. You two should come by."

Jackson nodded once back, watching as the crew ambled down the street.

His manly truce with LCB Construction cemented, Jackson focused his attention back on better subjects. Namely, Riley.

"Looks like there are a lot of people who'd be disappointed if you didn't stick around town." Jackson scuffed a foot against the pavement, easing his way slowly back toward Riley. He was going to convince her to stay in town and she was going to probably freak a little. She wasn't used to good things, but he could be patient. He'd found something he hadn't been looking for when he came to Belle Terre. Now he couldn't imagine life without it. "I know one in particular that will be sticking around town on the off chance you decide to make this a home."

Her face fell a little. "But I never got the mortgage from the bank, and tonight was the deadline. I don't have a home here."

"Yes, you do." Franklin Guidry shuffled forward on the boardwalk. "I paid the auction company. The property is yours. Without you and your brother I'd have lost everything today." The older man's eyes found his son's. "You saved more than my money. I'm forever in your debt, Ms. Kenner."

Since Jackson was within arm's reach, he twined his fingers with hers, pushing her arms behind her back. Then he held her close, trapped between the dual embrace. "Looks like you got what you wanted. A home. Family nearby. Friends."

Riley tipped up on her toes and pressed her forehead against his chin, then leaned back and met his gaze. He felt the love pour from her heart, even if she wasn't ready to say the words.

"I think I love you, Jackson Guidry."

The shock dropped his jaw.

Riley laughed. "I wondered what it would take to leave you speechless. Good to know." She spun in their embrace and led him toward their waiting family. "Come on. Introduce me to my future in-laws."

Left speechless once again, Jackson and Riley joined the combination of their family on the boardwalk, both feeling for the first time like they were truly home.

THE END

Thank You For Reading

Reviews are the lifeblood of an author. Please consider leaving a review on any of your favorite review sites.

If you enjoyed *Second Chance Romance*, keep reading for a sneak peek from book two in the Hearts of Louisiana series, *Love and Miss Fortune*.

Subscribe to the newsletter for release day information, prizes, and more!

Love and Miss Fortune

HEARTS OF LOUISIANA, BOOK THREE

Hearts of Louisiana Bay

Love and
Miss Fortune

MAGGIE PRESTON

Chapter One

Charlotte Fortune was born bass-ackwards on the unluckiest day of the year according to the family history kept by their long-time housekeeper, Miss Perla. Things had gone downhill from there and weren't looking particularly bright this morning.

Harley jerked the car to the shoulder of Highway 70, careful not to plow down the rubberneckers jostling for first position in the disaster that passed for her life. She shouldered her way through the Robichaux family reunion then slinked around a woman taking a selfie with the scene of the accident in the background. She turned just as Harley drew even, holding up the picture to examine it closer.

"Rainbow filter," Harley deadpanned in the woman's ear, then craned her neck over the spectators to see the demolished pallet of her distillery's signature product swirling into the cracks of the blacktop road. "Nice touch."

The woman jumped and swiveled her head like an agitated bobblehead doll. "I know, right?" Classic valley California dripped from her accent and bottle tan. "With the lake in the background? Someone in the crowd said the company's nickname is *Misfortune's* Brew so the rainbow seems, like, I don't know, *apropos*? It's like that dude Confucius says, everything has beauty you just sometimes, I don't know, gotta fake it." Her fingers danced over the screen. "My followers will love it."

"Glad we could provide entertainment for your day," Harley snapped, her voice drowning beneath bitterness crawling up her throat.

Miss California's jaw dropped and she clutched the phone to her chest, eyes wide. "They are *soooo* right. You southerners are just the sweetest. Thank you!"

On cue, Brownell Belle Tower chimed a slow, haunting peal. To Harley, the funeral dirge pounded home the last nail in the coffin of her five-year struggle to rebuild her dad's distillery. They even had a dead body: one pallet of her great-great-great-great-great granddaddy's finest corn liquor, crushed nearly beyond recognition in the middle of the highway.

Misfortune's Brew, Harley repeated the name bitterly, biting her tongue and blending further into the spectators huddled along Lake Opelousas a few miles north of Belle Terre, Louisiana. *Mix one part Harley Fortune with two parts bad luck. Stir until it foams over the rim.*

She was out of time.

She was out of money.

She was out of ideas.

Harley struggled to remember how to breathe. Panic pulled at the last threads of her sanity, hope already a frayed and worn tapestry in the ongoing battle against family and fate.

"Can my life get any better?" she asked herself, hoping there was no one paying attention to her talking to herself. No sense being known as unlucky *and* slightly touched, as her Granny would say. The family had enough of a reputation to live down.

Pity party, table for one. She blinked back the burn of tears and when that failed, Harley closed her eyes.

"Are you alright?"

The calm voice, a cocktail blended of concern and sexy rumble, flowed through Harley like the twelve-year-old Dewar's her Uncle Everett brought to Thanksgiving last year. She snapped to attention and opened her eyes to find the source.

The mid-morning sun blinded her for a moment, or perhaps it was the glint of copper and honey in the fringe of hair waving at her from the man who'd managed to move silently into her personal space. At just five foot two, Harley was used to people standing over her. But this guy didn't loom. He just...was.

She couldn't see much against the glare. Just the solid male form, broad shoulders squaring out the frame and tapering down to long legs.

"No," she forced out the word then turned her back on her future *literally* going down the drain, stomping further away from the crowd and back to her car to grab her phone. She needed to take pictures for the insurance claim. Her steps faltered, skidding across the gravel. A groan creaked out of her throat. She'd cancelled the collision policy last week. To save money and give them more time until August.

The blood drained from her body leaving her skin cold in the wake.

"You really don't look good," the man said, following her movement, worry raising the pitch of his voice. "Kind of pale. Like you've seen a ghost or gotten a notice from the IRS of a pending audit."

Harley narrowed her gaze, feeling the brows over her

eyes knit into a single line. He was near enough the aroma of his cologne mingled with the scent of the sweet peas blooming at the Tower gardens, the intoxicating fragrance carried by the early March breeze off the lake.

"You don't have much luck with women, do you?"

Mr. Helpful shrugged, those very broad shoulders looking solid enough to lean on. But there was a mischievous glint as he whipped off the sunglasses and gazed at her down the bridge of his nose "Depends on the woman."

A heavy dose of invitation laced his voice, like a generous dollop of cream in her coffee to sweeten the bitter chicory brew. Was he flirting with her? Her face burned beneath the awareness in his light brown eyes. But what did he see? Did he see beyond the dirty ball cap and wrinkled button down? What put that glint in his eyes, crooked that grin just so? It sure as hell couldn't be *her*. Not today.

She didn't need to know. Harley had enough problems of her own.

Harley spun and continued to her car, snatching her phone from the front seat and propping one hip against the dented bumper of her twenty-year-old Mercedes. The car had belonged to her father, just like the distillery. At least it was still running.

What am I going to do now? she wondered. Harley dropped her forehead into her palm. If they didn't deliver this purchase order, they wouldn't qualify for the Crescent City World Spirits Competition in August. Of course, to get to that she had to get past her family and her birthday-slash-do-or-die deadline on April 13. The thirteenth was on a Friday this year. She'd been born on Friday the 13th. How appropriate her future would be decided on the same day.

The sound of footsteps crunched against the gravel. Harley squinted between her fingers. Shiny loafers appeared in her field of vision as she counted the blades of grass.

"Nice car. Mercedes F-class. The fastest coupe they ever made for the public but the first with side airbags." The facts rolled off his tongue in an absent-minded flood.

Harley looked up. He scrubbed the wind-blown hair from his forehead and tilted his head slightly left as he examined the car.

Then he refocused on her, a sharpening that constricted in his pupils. "Seriously, though. If you're not feeling well the ambulance is still here. Would you like to let them check you out? The truck driver seems to be, uh —" he paused, looking back toward the flashing red lights, the slow smile tilting up one corner of a very nice mouth to flash the perfect amount of straight white teeth, "well, just using up oxygen if you want to know the truth."

Harley huffed out a laugh before she could stop herself. "He's not going to get a bill for it, so I guess he figures why not?"

Mr. Helpful mulled over her bitter remark but must have decided to ignore it. Instead, he repeated, "I'm sure the EMT would be happy to check you out."

More innuendo for Harley to decipher. Either amusement or too much sun crinkled the corners of his eyes. "The EMT likely has his hands full right now. The driver looks to be a bit of a drama queen."

She propelled herself off the hood as soon as a thought filled her head. Maybe they could salvage a few boxes to keep the customer happy until they could distill another batch. She eyed the crushed pallet then scooted around the ancient Mercedes to open the trunk.

The Good Samaritan followed. "True, but I think he's

worried about facing his boss. He said a hungry gator is nicer and more fun to work with."

That stopped her short and she pivoted, her eyes dragging up from the shiny loafers to the pleated grey slacks and simple black t-shirt fit snugly across the chest and what Harley suspected were washboard abs. She'd never dated a guy with washboard abs. Damn. She needed to stop thinking about that.

Dating. Not washboard abs.

Thoughts of dating again made her nauseous.

There was probably a jacket somewhere nearby waiting for this guy. Harley would bet it had one of those little hankies folded precisely in the front pocket. Her life was filled with people like this guy. With quick motions, she opened the trunk. "Yeah, I hear she's a real piece of work."

"Oh, do you know her?"

Again, that huff of sound cracked from her lungs. "Belle Terre is a small town. Everyone knows everyone." *And everything about everyone*, she added but only to herself.

Anyone local probably knew the details of Harley's life. And what was at stake. She'd dropped five grand into the mail less than an hour ago in the hope of changing the expected outcome. As usual, it was the wrong decision. *Sorry, mom and dad.*

"I'm hoping to meet up with her today." The man's attention zeroed in on the wrecked truck, the front end sitting cattywhompus in the ditch. The Fortune's Brew logo displayed prominently on the tailgate. *Fortune's Brew. Where good fortune meets good whiskey.*

"There's some business I'd like to discuss with her."

Just another salesman, Harley figured, slamming the trunk closed. They were always coming out to the property, most trying to convince her to sell her lease on the hybrid corn her daddy and granddaddy had developed with their supplier. No way. That was what made Fortune's Brew special. Without that corn, they were just another whiskey.

"From the sounds of it you might want to avoid her," Harley warned. "Especially today. She doesn't sound like a really nice person."

That lazy smile again and Harley had to admit it was a damn good smile. If she had time to think about such things, and she didn't, she'd definitely see the appeal of being on the receiving end of a smile like that.

"I'm not worried." Mr. Helpful slipped the pair of designer sunglasses back on his perfectly aquiline nose. He pointed a key fob over Harley's shoulder and beeped open the door to a sporty little coup the color of a Tuscan sun she'd seen on the slideshow from her granny's computer. One of those car deodorizers hung from the rearview mirror in the shape of a four leaf clover. "If you're sure you're feeling alright then I'm going to head out."

"Watch out for hungry gators," she warned as he started to turn.

The grin stretched back across his face, sharpening the angle of his cheeks without making his face appear hard. "I can hold my own against any wild creature I might meet today."

Harley didn't doubt that. He could likely charm the clouds from the sky.

He gave her one final lopsided grin. "Best of luck to you."

Harley rolled her eyes. Luck. If she had any luck she'd have listened to her instincts and driven this order to the supplier herself. But Uncle Everett had called a family meeting at lunch and she needed to be there.

What else could go wrong today?

She needed a minute before facing reality any closer so

she stomped up the dirt road to the top of the levee, part of the system that protected Belle Terre from the unpredictable waters of the Atchafalaya. Here the river was fed by Cormorant Lake which nibbled on dozens of smaller tributaries further north which finally nursed on the Mississippi. That was the problem -- melting snows and heavy storms in other parts of the country and dumped their problems down to the basin. Everything rolled downhill and Harley and Belle Terre were there to greet it.

The gates were open and she crossed through to the calmness of the other side. Like magic, the rush of passing cars dissipated, leaving only the occasional call of a whooping crane or whistling duck to remind you life went on. The damp earth with its musty perfume of algae and decay, unpleasant to many, were a balm to Harley. They were the smells of a legacy of life that had been there long before today arrived.

Most loved the lake, the rough water giving skiers a good ride while not being too much to sit and enjoy an afternoon of fishing. But for Harley, the choppy whitecaps ruined the spell and the wide open space let everyone know where you were and what you were doing. She preferred the bayou; calm dark waters hid a myriad of challenges and the endless channels provided solitude and privacy when you wanted it. The land, what there was of it anyway, was thick with cypress and oak but you could find enough solid ground to plop a one or two room cabin. She'd spent time with her granddaddy and daddy on the waters, fishing, trapping, running trout lines. They were some of her best memories.

"Harley?"

The deep bass filtered in through her subconscious and she dragged her eyes up as the town's newly elected sheriff crested the small rise to the top of the levee.

"Sheriff Guidry," Harley acknowledged with a nod, mentally pouring some steel into her spine to mimic a confidence she had to fake. She had less than six weeks before her family voted to sell the distillery. And her bargaining chip - the only pallet of Fortune's Brew *Lucky Lady* - now watered the weeds along the highway behind them. "Congratulations on the election." Not everyone's future was as uncertain as hers, she admitted and jerked the green-eyed monster into submission. "I heard it was a landslide victory."

Unlike her, Jackson Guidry was a transplant to Belle Terre, arriving almost a year ago while passing through to somewhere else. Fate had stepped into his life but delivered true love and a new job. Not for the first time, Harley wondered what she'd done to piss off the universe. She didn't expect true love or a perfect life, but a few less knocks would be nice.

"Thanks, Harley."

Sheriff Guidry matched her posture, his weight resting on one leg while he scratched a line in the ground with the toe of his boots. "I need your signature for the wrecker to hook up to the truck."

Harley took a mental snapshot of the peaceful waters then headed back with the sheriff to the scene of the accident. Their feet scraped against the dirt as they descended the small hill, and the roar of traffic enveloped them as they neared the road.

"Do you think it's a total loss?" He gestured absently to the broken pallet of boxes in the middle of the road, the boxes a darker brown at the bottom where the cardboard was drunk on her whiskey. But even the boxes on top had the telltale markings. So much for her plan to salvage.

The words knifed her gut and a huff of pain escaped before she could stop it. "The Fortune luck holds true."

He grimaced, like he'd known the answer but asked anyway out of politeness or a false sense of hope. "Will you still be able to meet the entry requirements for Crescent City?"

Of course he knew, Harley reasoned. People in town knew what was at stake. You didn't hide much in a small town, even when you lived twenty miles outside its borders.

The Crescent City World Spirits Competition was being held in New Orleans in a little over four months. It was the biggest for the smallest, those looking to break into the market. It was the first time in fifteen years Fortune's Brew would be represented.

The wave of nausea swamped Harley's senses and she locked her knees to keep from falling to them. "I put my entry application and application fee in the mail this morning."

It was the very last of her money. She'd hit the point where she'd promised herself she'd stop if they hadn't made it yet. Going further put everything in jeopardy: the house, the property. Everything her family had worked generations to acquire.

"But I'm not sure if we'll qualify. The final bottles to meet the ten-thousand-unit quota are perfuming the air as we speak." The heady aroma of moonshine mixed with the mulberries and dewberries ready to blossom as the weather started to warm. The next words strangled on her pride. "Uncle Everett wants to meet at lunch."

The sheriff watched her, waiting, then prompted, "Did he say why he wanted to meet?"

"'*To discuss the future of the company and what was best for all concerned.*'" She repeated the words as Uncle Everett had delivered them that morning when he dropped by, though she doubted they'd tasted as bitter on his tongue.

Probably more *suggestions* to change their operation so they tasted like every other whiskey out there. Cheaper corn. Shorter distillation run. *No thanks*, Harley had told him. *We've used the same recipe for two hundred years. There's nothing wrong with our product.*

She didn't let herself think too long about whether or not the problem was her.

She loved him but Uncle Everett didn't have a vision for Fortune's Brew. He had a vision for himself and his husband retiring on the proceeds from the sale.

Ready to change the subject, Harley inclined her head toward the accident and she and Sheriff Guidry walked down. She pointed to the man sitting in the back of the ambulance, wrapped in a blanket not even winter in Louisiana required. She stuffed back a length of hair that escaped the ball cap on her head. "Is Dean ok?"

The sheriff waited for the roar from a passing semi to die down, then scrubbed a hand across his jaw. "His vision and reflexes are just fine based on the rate of his texting and posting to social media. You have insurance, right?"

"Liability." The word came out sharper than Harley intended, so she cleared the attitude from her throat.

It was all they were required to carry by state law. It wasn't Sheriff Guidry's fault she'd cancelled the collision part of the policy to try and save a little money. Money she needed to pay their suppliers so they could ramp up production. Production, she noted with a pained looked, currently getting this part of the highway sloshed.

If there was a wrong way to go, Harley would find it. Her last name had become an oxymoron. Or maybe *she* was the oxymoron.

She sighed, sucked in a breath, let it out slowly. "Sorry. That came out —" but the sheriff waved her off with a sad smile.

"Dean's going to be a problem for you."

Her eyes snapped to follow the slight incline of the sheriff's head. "He's been a problem since we broke up last year." Then at the man's worried quirk of a brow, Harley quickly clarified, "Nothing extreme but my grandmother was right. You shouldn't fish off the company pier."

Sheriff Guidry gave a short laugh empty of humor. "Well if Dean tries to bait your hook with his worm, let me know."

"I appreciate that," Harley shoulder bumped him, though her shoulder barely reached his upper arm. "Dean's not a bad guy."

"Are you trying to convince me or yourself?" His tone challenged but remained respectful.

"Myself probably. I hurt his pride when I turned down his proposal. I couldn't fire him on top of that." She'd forgiven him for cheating on her, but she'd not been willing to wait around for a repeat performance. Some things didn't deserve a second chance. Harley tried not to wallow in the past although her entire life seemed to be centered around fixing it. Her parents. The distillery. Dean.

They stood in silence while a few more cars passed the accident, the vibration of tires on pavement dancing up her calves. The sun was high enough in the sky to be noticeable, the weather warmer than usual as the Mardi Gras season went into full swing.

A nails-against-chalkboard screech of metal against cement brought her upright as the pickup truck was hauled back onto the road, the front wheel's rim bare of rubber.

When the truck rested quietly on the road, Sheriff Guidry turned to Harley, face grim. "Dean is saying another vehicle, a gold sports car, swerved into his lane and caused the accident."

Gold sports car? "I saw a car like that when I pulled up." Hope flared in Harley, at least until she glimpsed the sheriff's furrowed brow. "But?" she prompted, knowing there was a but coming. There was always a but.

Sheriff Guidry shifted his weight and crossed his arms. "The skid marks don't start until the shoulder and they're in a straight line. Like the vehicle was drifting and the driver realized it when the front tire went off the road then slammed on the brakes. If the driver had swerved to avoid another vehicle, the skid marks would likely swerve. Of course, there are no cameras out here, nothing to contradict Dean's statement. Unless a witness comes forward, I really have nothing to either support or refute Dean."

The sheriff pushed off the back of the Mercedes. "Sorry to deliver more bad news," he added then went to manage the accident scene, leaving Harley with thoughts she'd rather not think.

Her heart raced with a mixture of anger and adrenaline as she stalked toward Dean and the ambulance. Dean was a screw up; always had been but like so many other things at Fortune's Brew, he came with the property. He'd been working summers for the family since they'd been in junior high school. His family owned the farm where Fortune's Brew grew their patented corn. Not even his dad would hire him. That should have told her something.

"Glad you're —" Harley breathed deeply as Dean flashed the palm of his hand at her then texted one handed faster than she could with two. She shoved the tips of her fingers in the front pockets of her jeans so she wouldn't rip the ever-present phone from Dean's hands. When he finally looked up at her, his expression was blank.

"Yeah. What is it Harley?" The blank expression slipped slightly, eyes Harley once looked into with affection now narrow and hard. The flush of anger deepened his breaths and darkened the walnut tone of his skin. Dean's attention shifted almost immediately over Harley's shoulder and she had to resist following the gaze.

"You just totaled our only truck and destroyed three weeks' worth of work. Perhaps you could —" She opened her mouth to continue, but snapped it closed. It wouldn't do any good.

"Wasn't my fault." Dean lifted the oxygen mask draped over his lap and took a hit.

"It's never your fault Dean." The muscles in her arms tightened at the shoulders until her upper body was a tense line. "It wasn't your fault when you forgot to clean out the malting barn and we had to replace the floor because of mold. It wasn't your fault when you missed cutting the head from that last batch and ruined the run. And it wasn't your fault when you hooked up the propane tank incorrectly and nearly destroyed the still house." Even now her lungs burned from the smoke inhalation trying to put out the fire. "It's never your fault."

Dean drew the blanket tighter around his shoulders. "I can't help it if you won't provide adequate resources. I'm the only one out there and can't be expected to be everywhere at once."

The sheer arrogance of his words punched Harley in the throat and this time she held up her palm to stop Dean. She swallowed twice to tamp down the words biting at the back of her throat looking for air. "You're the only one out there." It wasn't a question. Harley knew in his delusion, what he said was true. With effort, she kept her voice steady. "Lautaro and I work eighteen hour days while we're lucky if you show up for six. Tomorrow, don't bother showing up. You're no longer needed."

Harley spun on her heels, knowing she'd just made a huge mistake. *Another one*, her inner critic amended. She stalked back to the car, feeling the watchful eyes of the sheriff on her front and Dean on her back.

"I'll be talking to you later, Harley," Dean shouted as she retreated to her car. "We have to discuss compensation for my injuries."

"Then I suggest you get a sponge because our only assets are leaking onto the asphalt."

Chapter Two

By the time she cranked the engine, the sheriff had stopped traffic and waved her back into the steady flow returning to town.

"This is not happening," Harley informed the universe and anyone else that happened to be listening.

She practiced some breathing techniques Lautaro went on about in his zen Mexican-accented voice. *In through the* nariz. *Out with the* aire malo. She got to a count of three before her scream slapped against the interior of the Mercedes.

Not feeling better in the slightest, she focused her energy on getting through town without running anyone over accidentally. Harley made a quick detour to downtown Belle Terre, wanting to grab a coffee before hitting the long stretch of nothingness that made up Highway 1 after she crossed the river. Granny didn't believe in coffee. How the two of them were related meant the universe had a wicked sense of humor in Harley's mind. Coffee was life. Actually, coffee was life for those unlucky enough to be around

Harley whose day began when sunrise hadn't begun to tickle the horizon.

Harley slowed to a crawl on Front Street, hemmed in by one of the LCB Construction trucks in the front and a tailgating van full of pre-Mardi Gras revelers twirling beads from the windows. The river walk area was crowded for a Wednesday morning. Next week's Fat Tuesday celebration had people floating upriver looking for distraction and Belle Terre had craft beer and the best supply of crawfish and blue crab this side of heaven.

If Harley could get things together at Fortune's Brew, south Louisiana could boast one of the best small distilleries for moonshine - and only the second one owned by a woman - in the nation as well.

The truck turned off and disappeared behind the fence to the new AmeriMart outdoor mall coming to life at one end of the Main Street boardwalk. The tailgating van dropped back, the passengers hanging out a window to yell at others on the street. She zipped to the other end of the busy shopping area, squeezing her car into the last available spot across from The Book Nook.

The owner, Lara Caldwell, had opened a second business next door called Beans and Bubbles, a coffee house-slash-laundromat. Between the coffee, the state-of-the-art washers, and the book store, she had the market cornered on ways to kill time while the spin cycle did a number on your delicates.

Harley pocketed her keys as she took the two steps up to the boardwalk, the weight of seven generations of expectations dragging her feet. She sucked in a breath tinged with the bite of fresh brewed coffee laced with fabric softener. The tailgating van reappeared, squealing around the corner to draw Harley's attention. Around the side of the building she spotted a gold fender, the sun dancing on the custom paint job that faded from a fiery sunset at the base to a warm honey on the hood. Harley knew this car, and she remembered the sheriff saying Dean claimed a gold sports car had forced him off the road.

"Hope you have insurance," Harley muttered but she took a picture of the license plate, which was also custom: CSANDAU.

Curiosity as much as coffee pulled her through the doors etched with the business logo: an oversized mug of coffee with bubbly steam rising, the letters for Beans and Bubbles filling in the bubbles.

Her eyes adjusted slowly to the dim interior, the hum of washers and dryers in the background as a steady ripple of customers moved between the coffee counter and the book store.

"Hey Harley." Lara Caldwell breezed in from the book-store. Though barely four months preggers, the growing baby bump made it through the door first.

"Lara." Harley smiled but her attention was on the customers, looking for the owner of the golden chariot outside. He wasn't hard to find among the tourists and locals. Even when she'd met him out on the highway, he looked like neither. She gave him a once over. Then did it again because once wasn't enough.

He'd found the suit coat she'd suspected he owned, the color matching the grey slacks. It was tailored to look like he'd washed it on a hot water cycle, snug to his excellent build. She'd read that was a trend somewhere, though in her world the jeans and the untucked button down she wore was trendy enough. He'd at least tried to tone down the business-man's aura with the black V-neck tee bringing Harley's mind back to washboard abs.

Lara followed Harley's line of vision and joined her at the front of the store, an appreciative smile quirking one end of her mouth. "You look extra focused, Harley. Is there a problem or are you just admiring the view?"

Blushing, Harley tore her gaze away. "You're happily...happily, Lara," she teased, gesturing to Lara's midsection. "Why are you noticing the view?"

But Harley had to admit, the view was pretty nice. Six-foot plus of lean muscle packaged in a swimmer's body—broad shoulders tapering to a narrower waist and long legs—filled out the designer suit. Now that the sun wasn't in her eyes and the distraction of her ruined life perfuming the air, she could pay attention to other things. Purposefully, perfectly mussed hair the color of milk chocolate with a matching scruff darkened the sharply edged jaw and high slash of cheekbones. Everything about him screamed ego. Harley'd gotten dressed without turning on the lights, like she did most mornings. Thinking back, she couldn't remember if she'd combed her hair before putting on the ball cap.

"I am happily-happily," Lara said and nodded, her hand absently going to the aforementioned measure of happiness pushing against the red apron with a matching logo in white. "I'm not dead. You should definitely go for it though."

"Are you suggesting I ask him if he wants to see my Berber carpet?"

Rumor had it more than the new Berber carpet had been laid in the house where Lara first rekindled her relationship with her current significant other, Will.

She merely rolled her eyes and patted her protruding belly.

"Tell your cousin Piper I said thanks for the idea about the laundromat. It's doubled our business in the bookstore."

"I'll pass along the message."

A frantic looking man waved at Lara from the area of the washer and dryers and Lara started in that direction. "And are you sure I can't get you to come back to the coffee bar? You were the best barista we ever had."

"I've got my hands full out at the stillhouse. But Becky-Lyn is fully capable. She'll make a good assistant manager for you."

At the last minute, Lara stopped and turned. "Taking the first step is the only way you'll get what you really want."

Harley gave her a nod as Lara disappeared into the laundromat and wondered briefly what she would want if she wasn't wrapped up in trying to revive her dad's business. Even after fifteen years, it was still her dad's business, no matter what the lawyers said.

Her attention returned to Mr. Helpful. She moved slowly to stand behind the man just as his turn came at the counter.

"You're going to be my favorite new friend today, Julie." His tone, low and sultry still managed to be masculine but said he was used to being indulged when he used that voice.

Julie's eyes dipped down while Harley rolled hers, the young girl's shoulders rising slightly as the redness bloomed upward from beneath the collar of her white t-shirt. She absently looked to the name tag to make sure her name was Julie and the demi-god was talking to her. He'd won her over with one sentence.

"How can I help you today, sir?" The teen barista flashed an eager look, a black marker twined in her fingers as her hand hovered over the three stacks of cups. The bright red apron matched her cheeks and practically swallowed her thin frame.

The man angled his hands into the pockets of tailored

pants without disturbing the crisp line of the pleat, the sharp cuffs over shoes so shiny they reflected the grain of the hardwood floors. Miss Perla would be impressed. "I'd like a grande triple half-caf breve, half half-and-half, half soy, no foam latte, extra hot with a whip and double shot of caramel, upside down."

The smile wobbled on the teen's face. She snatched her hand back from the grande tower like it was an aggravated cottonmouth. "Uhhh...what?"

The look of calm on a face free of worry never fluctuated. He tilted his head down a hair to look over the rim of the sunglasses Harley recognized from earlier. She read the brand on the stem. Yep. Expensive. "Grande triple half-caf breve, half half-and-half, half soy, no foam latte, extra hot with a whip and a double shot of caramel, upside down."

"You want your coffee upside down?" The young girl looked to Harley for help. "Won't it spill?"

Mr. Helpful leaned toward Julie conspiratorially, his laugh easy and practiced. "Not if we do it right."

Gooseflesh pebbled down Harley's arms. She cleared her throat, drawing the attention of both customer and barista. "He just means he wants the espresso poured in last."

He rested his arm on the waist high counter and leaned his weight, then pushed the shades up to the crown of his head.

"Hello again." Amusement crinkled the corner of his eyes. Eyes which Harley realized now were not light brown but amber. Honest to god amber, like sunlight had been tanned to a warm gold then splashed with swirls of chocolate. "Must be my lucky day."

More flirting but Harley didn't take it to heart. Flirt seemed to be a steady state with this guy based on her two interactions with him. "Coincidence. If you want coffee in this town that doesn't taste like it was blended with diesel this is where you go."

He cocked his head to the side, his brows arching in disbelief. "This might qualify as a coincidence but my dad told me there was no such thing as a coincidence."

"And your dad would never lie to you?"

"Not when it involves women or whiskey."

The eyes never left hers, Harley noted reluctantly; didn't do the quick head-to-toe she was used to seeing from men who wanted to assess her place in their hierarchy of females: friend, fling, fleeting, or forever.

She thought of the gold car outside and her totaled truck being hauled to the old truck graveyard. "Then your dad was right this time. It's not a coincidence."

"Definitely my lucky day." He leaned a little closer, his posture relaxed. He scrubbed a hand over his ear. "Tell me you followed me from the highway or saw my car and stopped hoping to get to know me better."

While she hadn't felt small standing next to him out on the highway, Harley calculated the difference in their height and had to stop herself from stretching up to her tiptoes. "Something like that."

"Uhh, Harley, he wants his coffee extra hot," Julie interrupted, probably missing the death rays shooting from Harley's eyes to melt the golden-eyed outsider. "What does that even mean?" Julie's eyebrows were starting to draw together, creating a deepening ridge on a forehead still too young for wrinkles and worry. "Isn't all coffee hot? Unless it's iced and he didn't say he wanted it iced. Did you?" Julie deflated a little more. "I sort of lost track."

Harley moved closer to the counter, which put her too close

for comfort with Mr. Helpful. The woodsy scent of birch and something sweeter tickled her nose. She ignored the masculine scent even as she breathed deeply. "Heat the dairy to one-eighty. Lara keeps a thermometer near the machine if you're not comfortable doing it by touch." Harley pointed to a drawer.

Julie's blank look morphed into something more fearful, the whites of her eyes taking over her narrow face. "Lara!" Julie sprinted from the counter, the wake of her departure causing the cup tower to teeter.

Harley whistled slow and low, reaching over the counter just in time to halt the tumble of cups. "Holy cow, I think you broke the barista."

"I have Triple A," he shot back and winked, his head tilted at the absolute ideal angle to catch the single ray of sun filtering in through the blinds. The light played in the mahogany flecks of an amber iris. "I'm sure we can get her up and running again."

She had to shake her head to break the spell, enthralled by Mr. Helpful's eyes. "I'm sure you're good at jump-starting things."

"Only when invited." There was power behind the grin when he turned it on, the perfect amount of straight white teeth behind a crooked smile. "Otherwise I never touch a woman's battery."

The low pull in Harley's gut sent off warning bells in her head. *Danger, Harley Fortune. Danger.* He scrubbed a hand through his hair, every strand falling perfectly back into place. *Of course it did*, Harley admitted. He had to be an alien. Or supernatural. Or a supernatural alien.

Turning her attention to the counter, Harley smiled as another young barista took Julie's place.

"Hey, Harley," BeckyLyn Kenner lifted her chin in greeting, her body posture a little stiffer than the smile she forced. "You want your usual?"

"Hey Bex," Harley nodded back, pulling the brim of her ball cap a little lower, feeling the weight of the stare from the man pushed into her personal space by the rack of pre-packaged coffee at his back. "Please, but make it a tall today."

Mr. Helpful straightened, his broad shoulders now even with Harley's eyes. "I'll have —"

"Yours is coming," Bex interrupted without looking his way then returned to her station at the espresso machine.

He settled back to leaning on the counter, the relaxed posture putting him more at Harley's eye level. "You know your coffee."

The proximity was tempting, making her want to lean in closer, smell the cologne, check out the eyes. *He's like the Loch Ness Monster*, she consoled herself. Once it pops its head out you want to look closer, not sure if your eyes are playing tricks on you. "The doc checks my caffeine level whenever he does bloodwork."

"You can tell a lot about a person by the coffee they drink."

"I guess that makes you complicated and hard to understand." The words were out but she'd not meant to say them out loud. There was just something about the guy that made her want to take him down a notch or two. Or twenty. Get his clothes dirty. Muss his hair.

"No, I'm exactly what you see. I never try to be something I'm not."

But Harley saw the doubt behind the statement, if only for a second.

Bex appeared from nowhere and slid Harley's reason-for-living across the counter, breathing out, "Tall drip black," as she whirled in a single motion and disappeared back behind the counter.

"Plain black coffee for Harley." Mr. Helpful repeated, her name rolling off his tongue. "Unusual name. No nonsense coffee. Independent. Straight forward. Resistant to change. Probably hiding a secret love for..."

This time his eyes did roam her body but Harley could tell it was her clothes that drew the focus of his attention. What did he see? Ripped jeans. Wrinkled button down. Her dad's favorite ball cap. She spent eighteen-hour days trying to turn corn and barley into world-class hooch. She reached forward to snag her coffee, but he finished his thought.

"...a raspberry chocolate dream Frappuccino."

She hesitated, and his smile tilted to a knowing grin. She loved a raspberry chocolate dream Frappuccino. Had taught Bex and Lara both how to make hers. She just didn't indulge that often, cursing the genetics that had let her top out a hair over five foot three while her ass wanted to be six foot one.

The knowing look was back. "You like things a certain way. Your way. But you're very sweet about it so people don't mind."

His voice—rich, like him, smooth, also like him—coated her in warmth, made her want to snuggle in.

Harley mostly ignored the warmth and snuggling. He looked at her as if expecting peels of laughter, a feminine *oh-you're-so-funny* perhaps with a light slap on the arm. He even flexed his respectable bicep in preparation, Harley realized as he leaned forward so she didn't have to reach so far.

She knew how to rumple Mr. Helpful's air of perfection. "Would that Triple A be for the very expensive gold sports car outside?"

His eyes widened, a hint of panic dimming the sparkle.

Bingo, Harley chimed inwardly, triumphant.

"My car?" Coffee forgotten, he walked toward the front door, peering sideways through the front window. "Is there a problem?"

"Your car is fine. The driver from that accident this morning said a gold sports car forced him off the road. I'm wondering where your car was about earlier this morning."

The well arched brows—Harley wondered if they were plucked for that level of arc—knitted together over hooded eyes.

He pulled a cell phone from his pocket and swiped to wake up the screen. "It was with me." The voice came off as pleasant, the look more cautious as his fingers danced across the screen, reminding Harley a little too much of Dean's callous disregard earlier.

Her chuckle was forced, a huff of air trying for relaxed but a tension electrified the atmosphere. "You sure it didn't go off on its own? Maybe run that truck off the road out on Lake Opelousas Drive, then come back into town for a coffee order that should be illegal?"

The relaxed smile returned but didn't reach his eyes this time and he reached over to open the door for a woman toting an overstuffed hamper. She chirped 'Thanks" and shuffled toward the washers and dryers in the back. "My coffee order is the result of years of research and experimentation to get the perfect blend of hipster chic and tattooed badass."

Her curiosity reared its nosy self. Did he have any tattoos? Where? Of what?

He headed back to the coffee counter and Bex watched him approach under the brim of her red Beans and Bubbles cap. She didn't look pleased.

Harley wasn't either and followed on his shiny loafered heels. The uppity tourist wasn't taking her seriously and after the day she'd had, not to mention the news from her uncle about the pending family meeting, putting up with the runaround wasn't high on her list. "Then enjoy your coffee. You're going to pay for what you did. I have your license plate and I'm going to deliver it to the sheriff."

"Please do," he said, leaning his back against the counter on his elbows and crossing one ankle casually over the other. "I didn't run anyone off the road. I came upon the accident and stopped to help, called the sheriff. And if I caused it, I can afford to fix it. I don't need to run from my problems."

The relaxed posture was gone, however, replaced with something a little more determined, a little more dangerous. He wasn't used to being wrong. Harley would bet on it.

Bex delivered the man's coffee and Mr. Helpful pulled a leather wallet from his back pocket. He fished a twenty from a well-stocked line of fifties and turned enough to hand it to Bex. "Hers is on me."

Harley bristled. She couldn't be bought, and certainly not for the price of a large coffee. "Hers in on her own tab, please, Bex."

"Keep the change," he added brightly, nodding to Bex. Back to Harley, his smile less bright. "I take care of my responsibilities."

"I doubt you've been responsible for anything in your entire life. You have no idea what it's like to be left behind, having to clean up after the carelessness of others." She was projecting. Harley knew it. But the frustration of her day soured like over-heated milk in her stomach.

He pushed from the counter and grabbed his coffee, walking past Harley he added in a low rumble. "That's quite literally what I do for a living, Harley. I left a business card in the fishbowl. Look me up."

He didn't wait for an answer and disappeared beneath the jingling bell over the door, his stance relaxed again as if her accusation hadn't bothered him.

Harley fumed, her problems swirling in her head with hurricane force winds. The lost product. The contest. Money. Her family circling like vultures waiting on her to fail.

She sipped her coffee, nearly choking as the piping hot liquid burned her tongue.

"Perfect," she muttered and left the store to confront her life, certain the day couldn't get much worse.

Chapter Three

C hance Gold pulled the door to the sheriff's office closed behind him and stepped back onto the covered walkway along Main Street, satisfaction replacing the anger goading him after his confrontation at the coffee shop. It hadn't taken long to find the office and although the man himself wasn't in, the very efficient front desk clerk Connie quickly gathered his name and information.

When Chance offered a download of his GPS history to prove the timeline of his whereabouts since leaving the hotel in New Orleans before dawn, she'd provided an email address as well. The logger app let him track his mileage for billing purposes and today would not only earn him money, but apparently save him a ton as well. Once people discovered his identity—more accurately once they discovered his father's identity—they tended to see dollar signs.

It was why he'd started using an alias for his business, Diamond Spirits Consulting.

He'd learned early on that everything—and everyone— had a price. The currency and cost may change, but everything was for sale. For example, today he'd played good

Samaritan, not just once, when he stopped after seeing the loaded pickup truck skid into the ditch after the driver over corrected the drifting vehicle, but twice when he'd tried to make sure that Harley woman was not going to pass out on the side of the highway. It had cost him an hour of his time, not to mention a slice of his resolve to be the gentleman his father taught him to be, even when the alternative was tempting.

He stalked right to return to his car, eating up the boardwalk with long strides to burn off some of the frustration. That woman's assumption he was guilty pushed a few of his buttons. Like most people he didn't like being accused of something he didn't do. But it was her jab about being left behind that really irked him.

The insecurity needled him more.

A man darted out from the savings and loan as Chance rushed by the door, the two nearly clipping one another in their haste. Chance and the man circled like prize-fighters before recognition erased the tension on their faces.

"Mr. Gold." Everett Fortune drawled out the name more than necessary, punching his right arm forward for a handshake. "I wasn't expecting you in town for a few more days."

Chance accepted the man's hand, stiffening as Everett pumped his arm with more force than necessary. "Please, Mr. Fortune," he said, contained. "For business purposes I use CJ Diamond. Keeps my business interests separate from my family's and I prefer it that way."

The people who came to Chance for his consulting services hardly ever knew his real name. Working under the alias his entire career kept the connection to the Gold name as distant as possible. How Everett Fortune had learned his true identity was not yet clear to Chance but he'd find out eventually.

Everett winked conspiratorially and Chance winced inwardly. He thought back to the same gesture he'd offered Harley in the coffee shop, not to mention the flirting on the side of the highway. He normally liked that people saw him as charming. Today it made him feel slimy. No wonder she hated him even before accusing him of fleeing the scene of an accident.

"Of course, Mr. Diamond." Everett guided Chance to an out-of-the-way space of the boardwalk with a hand to his elbow. A stream of shoppers and construction workers passed by, their voices mixing with the low rumble of the train passing around the corner.

The noise settled into a steady hum and Everett jumped back into their conversation.

"As I said you're earlier than expected. I'm not sure they're, uh, ready out at the property for your arrival." The man pulled at the tailored cuff of his dress shirt nervously.

Working his jaw back and forth, Chance glanced to the steady traffic inching along Main Street, clearing his throat. What else did Everett Fortune want to hide? Chance didn't know if it was just the man's unease about the operation at Fortune's Brew, or if there was more going on. Unwavering instinct told Chance where to put his money, however. "That's why I'm here early. I find I get a better sense of the operation if you haven't had too much time to plan, put the lipstick on the pig as my dad would say. I can't offer sound advice if I don't know the scope of the issues."

"A very solid approach, planning ahead for all contingencies. You've obviously had good role models in your father and mother."

The words scraped along Chance's spine. And his pride. Did Chance's mother have something to do with Everett's insider knowledge of Chance's true identity? If Chance worked hard to keep himself separate from his father's name, a name well respected in the industry, he worked doubly hard to keep his connection to *that* woman a national secret. Even if she made it impossible with her choice of brand name: The Gold Standard.

Your father couldn't make his dreams come true, Chance. What makes you think he can help with yours.

How she made her dreams come true was not well known but Chance did not have the blinders most sons wore for their mothers. If he was being polite, she was an unrepentant industry spy and gold-digger. When he wasn't being so nice, the words would make a drunk Marine sound tame.

Chance's jaw clenched. "I didn't know you and my mother were acquainted."

Everett made a back and forth gesture with his head. "It's a small circle. Did Sondra mention she and I had a meeting recently where she floated the idea of a merger between our labels?" Everett's tone softened, his words edging out slower and slower.

Chance's attention snapped back to the conversation at the mention of his mother. Her label currently reigned supreme for micro-batch whiskey in the US, and was rapidly gaining traction in Europe.

Merger? Chase pushed the word around his brain. His mother likely wanted to acquire Fortune's Brew as part of her own distillery brand, if not crush it outright. Fifteen years ago, Fortune's Brew delivered Gold Standard's only defeat at the Crescent City World Spirits Competition and Sondra Gold Cassidy did not believe in second place. They likely would have continued to dominate the market had Elias and Vivianne Fortune not died on the way home that very afternoon.

"That's news to me, Mr. Fortune. My mother is not one to share so a merger doesn't sound like something she'd willingly do."

The fifty-something man squared his shoulders, tucked his chin against the finely ribbed neckline of the cashmere turtleneck, tugged at the hem of the skinny jacket, his frame too bulky for the narrow cut. Chance recognized the brands. He had a few himself.

Non-plussed at the correction, Everett let the gator-wide smile slide across his face. "Negotiation always starts some-place as I'm sure you're aware. A favorable report from you will surely improve our standing on the market when we sell."

Not *if* we sell; *when* we sell. Everett had no intention of making Fortune's Brew a winner. That soured things for Chance. He liked winning. He wasn't here to put a pretty bow on a bargain for his mother to snatch up.

"And you've hired me to evaluate your operation, not negotiate the sale. I'm not connected to my mother's company and," *more importantly*, Chance added silently, "she's not connected to mine."

Despite his efforts to remain separate, Chance knew he was correct about Everett's knowledge of his true identity when they'd signed the contract for his consulting services a few days ago. Usually, he asked better questions, ferreting out any details a client was trying to keep hidden. Hearing about his mother's interest in Fortune's Brew put a new twist on his arrival.

Chance thought of backing out right then. He'd worked very hard to maintain a respectable distance between Gold Standard Brewing and Diamond Spirits Consulting. It had taken him the last nine years to build a name on his own as a whiskey sommelier. While his dad was CEO of the number two label in the US, Isaac Gold was well respected in the industry. He didn't want his dad's reputation to open any doors for him; and Chance wanted help from his mother even less. He'd not needed her since she'd walked out when he was eight.

"Come to think about it, this is a pretty sizeable conflict of interest for me, Mr. Fortune. I don't think I'm the right person to work with you on this."

Everett's thick eyebrows bunched together. "You're being hasty, Mr. Diamond. I expect nothing from you except your expertise about our label." His lips parted in what Chance suspected passed for a reassuring smile. "You know the market and that is all I want; to know where Fortune's Brew sits on the food chain."

He considered his options. He'd already spent the last few days researching what he could find about Fortune's Brew's distillation process. Not that much existed. Not even Everett had the recipe apparently. He'd invested the time and he knew the business. Walking out now rankled his sense of pride in the job he did. He could stay impartial, even if Everett Fortune wanted him to do otherwise.

"Good enough. Just remember I'm not here to grease the wheels with what happens between you and my mother."

"I understand, Mr. Diamond." Relief flowed out of Everett Fortune. "I've not shared the details of the offer yet with my niece and ask that you keep it confidential for now as well."

Chance bristled at the deception but he was under obligation to Everett, not Charlotte Fortune. Of course, he was using an alias for business purposes so his high road was limited. Still, he wasn't pretending to be anything he wasn't. CJ Diamond knew whiskey and whiskey distillation. Everett was paying his fee, and Everett could divulge the details of their arrangement as he saw fit. Whatever his final report to Everett said, it would be based on his unbiased opinion of the brand's potential.

What Everett Fortune or Sondra Gold Cassidy did with that information was not his responsibility.

But it rankled his pride. He could make Fortune's Brew a top contender. He'd done it with other distilleries with less promise. Everett kept his gaze narrow, obviously seeing short term profit over long term growth and sustainability.

Chance continued down the walkway, his dress shoes making a hard *thump* against the wooden walkway in rhythm to the *thump* of his heart against his rib cage. Chance didn't like someone thinking they had the upper hand. That was his play and he did it well.

Everett followed at a clipped pace, arms clasped behind his back as in serious thought.

Eager to get on with his day, Chance tempered his disappointment. "What you decide to tell your niece is your concern, Mr. Fortune. The trust gives you the authority to have a third-party evaluation done prior to the assets being distributed to the beneficiaries. Your mother is still the sole trustee, correct?"

Everett stopped short, then rushed to catch up as Chance exited the first set of boardwalk buildings and crossed the street to the second set. The luscious aroma of apple pie floated out from the River City Cafe, luring in customers and making Chance's stomach grumble in protest as he passed without stopping.

Everett came even with Chance once again, grabbing his coat's cuff and stopping their forward motion. "I'm surprised you know that, Mr. Diamond."

Chance pulled his sleeve from Everett's grasp. "I requested a copy of the trust deed from your attorney, as stated in my contract. I have to know the legal restrictions and ramifications before I go into a situation such as yours. You and your sister only have voting authority to sell if," Chance lifted his chin, looking over Everett's shoulder, and repeated the document verbatim, "*the primary beneficiary, Charlotte Vivianne Fortune, doesn't have the business operating with the high likelihood of profit in the estimation of the trustee by the time she turns twenty-five.*"

The man fussed with lapels of his jacket, his expression sour. "I don't know that I like that you've pried into our business affairs as such, Mr. Diamond."

Chance went statue-still and narrowed his focus. "Then fire me, Mr. Fortune."

Chance played a mean game of chicken. Like everything else, he didn't lose. The ultimatum was a calculated risk. Chance was not just his name but what he liked to take. He'd not built a name for himself playing it safe. He'd never been wrong so far.

Everett hesitated but Chance read the decision when the pucker disappeared from the tight line of the man's mouth. "That's not what I meant."

Crossing the final length of the boardwalk, Chance retrieved his keys from his pocket, the familiar rush of adrenaline as he opened the car door and settled against the leather seat of the classic Corvette. True, his career was made through change and advancing techniques used for generations but behind that he held a great respect for the old ways. And he just loved his car. "I'm going to finish up my tour of the local eateries and bars. I'll be out to the distillery in a few hours, Mr. Fortune."

Everett hesitated, the telling pucker back.

"Have you even told her you've hired me?"

Everett studied Chance beneath hooded eyes. "She'll be informed today." Short, clipped words.

And likely would not be too pleased about his arrival, Chance added internally. His brain flashed back to the feisty coffee connoisseur that morning. He was on a roll for pissing off women today.

Why should Charlotte Fortune be any different?

"Lautaro Sanchez is our master distiller. You'll likely find him in the still house. There's an office toward the back. I'll let him know you're arriving today. Shall we say around six? They're usually wrapping up things around then."

"Thank you, Mr. Fortune, but please don't notify him." Chance knew he would anyway, but at least he'd done what he could. "I prefer to see the operation as real world as possible."

"Very well, Mr. Diamond."

Chance started the engine, the rumble of all that horsepower a soothing white noise and backed away from the building under the scrutiny of Everett Fortune. The man yanked his cell phone from a jacket pocket before Chance even made it down the street.

The lunch hour was just beginning and Chance wanted to make a quick circuit of some restaurants he'd tagged online. They all served alcohol and he wanted to understand the place Fortune's Brew held for the locals. He'd only found two restaurants in New Orleans that served the brand, and a half dozen more up the highway in Lafayette. Not strong market placement for a local brand that once took top honors at the Crescent City World Spirits Competition. He didn't know what kind of business-woman Charlotte Fortune professed to be, but he intended to find out.

Then tell her where she'd gone wrong.

Love and Miss Fortune is available now.

Find Love and Miss Fortune online.

About the Author

Maggie Preston is an award-winning author of contemporary romantic fiction. She fell in love with romance before she knew what it was, stealing paperback novels from her grandmother's closet when her mother wasn't looking.

She loves to travel and tells people that anything and everything they do could end up in her next novel, so if you recognize yourself in the pages of her books, remember you were warned.

Maggie currently balances her life between the right brain and left brain, quality consultant and technical writer by day, romance writer by night.

www.AuthorMaggiePreston.com

Follow Maggie on Social Media

Facebook:
www.facebook.com/MaggiePrestonAuthor

Twitter:
@maggie_preston

Instagram:
@authors_maggie_and_selena

Bookbub:
bookbub.com/profile/maggie-preston

Goodreads:
www.goodreads.com/goodreadscomauthormaggiepreston

Also by Maggie Preston

Hearts of Louisiana

Sex and Insensibility

Love and Miss Fortune

Hearts of Carolina Anthology

Two If by Sea

Back Home Again Anthology

Dance of the Butterflies